Gutusipe Daindi

Gutusipe Daindi

Steve Aitchsmith

The Book Guild Ltd

First published in Great Britain in 2022 by
The Book Guild Ltd
Unit E2 Airfield Business Park,
Harrison Road, Market Harborough,
Leicestershire. LE16 7UL
Tel: 0116 2792299
www.bookguild.co.uk
Email: info@bookguild.co.uk
Twitter: @bookguild

Typeset in 11pt Minion Pro

Printed on FSC accredited paper
Printed and bound in Great Britain by 4edge Limited

ISBN 978 1914471 728

British Library Cataloguing in Publication Data.
A catalogue record for this book is available from the British Library.

Chapter One

Beneath the infinite expanse of a spectacularly crisp starscape a small group huddled around a weakly flickering campfire, all wrapped by the intense darkness and cold of a moonless desert night. A gentle whistling breeze wafted across this eerie and remote land which would one day be known as Nevada.

Lieutenant Sebastian Ash, a deserter from the British Army, sat with his companion Katsitsienhawi, daughter of a subset of the Mohawk tribe from the north. Her's the branch of the Iroquois who had allied themselves with the British forces against the French and later the Americans, who were fundamentally English anyway.

On the other side of the fire sat Dakayivani and three other Shoshone warriors, a people sympathetic to the Mohawk with whom they had traded over long distance for as long as anybody could remember. Everybody in the meeting was heavily armed, a fact that spoke volumes about the times in which they lived but did not reflect the friendly nature of the conversation.

After a few hours of pleasant small talk the first dimly perceptible light of dawn slowly brightened to illuminate the land. The morning chill was slowly dissipating and Sebastian unbuttoned his green Royal Irish, regiment of foot, great coat. The Shoshone were beginning to shed the various furs they wore around themselves for warmth at night.

"I am about to disarm, the weight of weapons is uncomfortable to me and I have no need of them at this time," Sebastian said in his privileged-class English accent. He pulled the pistol from his belt and lay it on the ground. He did so slowly using two fingers, then he unhooked the green velvet-covered metal sword scabbard from his belt and placed that weapon on the floor with the firearm.

The Shoshone watched with apparent indifference but clearly remaining within easy reach of their own weapons. They appreciated his implied respect for their fast reactions and vigilance while also showing enough trust in them to disarm himself.

"I also feel the weight of presently unrequired weapons," said Dakayivani. Unexpectedly, he spoke with an east coast American accent and was clearly fluent in English. As he placed his knife, small axe and pistol on the floor he smiled at Sebastian. This friendly expression was all the more remarkable because Dakayivani had until that moment maintained the expressionless inscrutable features common to the native peoples. Sebastian returned the smile but it did not escape his notice that the other warriors remained armed.

"You speak very good English," observed Sebastian.

"I was educated in New York," replied the warrior.

"Is that common amongst your people?" enquired the Englishman.

Dakayivani laughed softly. "I was on a lone-trading trip to the Mohawk; I wanted to trade a hand-crafted bone and iron wood hoe for a beaver pelt or two. I was attacked in the woods and robbed by a couple of settlers. They stole my hoe and my weapons and they left me with a nasty head wound. I staggered blindly towards a homestead."

"I apologise; the Mohawk area should be civilised," exclaimed Sebastian.

Dakayivani scoffed gently. "That depends on how you define civilised. Luckily for me the old couple in the homestead decided not to shoot me but adopted me instead. I was only twelve and to these white people that made me a child. I'm not angry with them; they were decent people and took care of my wounds for me. When they took me to a school I realised that here I could come to understand the white man and his complicated and often duplicitous ways. I enjoyed it so much that I stayed for years and studied to a higher level. I only left when they tried to send me to university in England. I would have enjoyed the further education but that cold, that rain and wind, no no no." Both Dakayivani and Sebastian laughed.

"Did you not fear you may have become soft and gentle when you returned to your own people?" Sebastian sounded concerned.

"Really?" mocked Dakayivani. "A Shoshone amongst white boys? Trust me, I did plenty of fighting, especially when we all noticed girls, my word, but they were determined to stop me even looking at white girls." They both laughed again.

"That's why you speak with me?" asked Sebastian.

"No, I speak with you for two reasons. I have learned that many whites are decent is the first reason. It's not your fault you are from the people most able to dominate others. I suspect that if any other people had developed the means to subjugate less well-armed societies then they'd behave just as badly. We shall judge you by what you say and do, not by the people you come from."

Sebastian nodded his gratitude. "And the second reason?"

"Girls," laughed Dakayivani. "I couldn't get at the white girls so I took up with the Mohawk girls. I was young, you know what it's like. I have a child among the Mohawk and Katsitsienhawi here is a girl from the Mohawk – I'm naturally inclined to like her. I also notice that she's pregnant. Yours?"

Sebastian cast a stunned look at Katsitsienhawi.

She nodded. "I thought you had enough troubles at the moment. This one I could keep to myself and give you the good news when you would be able to appreciate it more or I could no longer disguise it. You have a full-time job just keeping us both alive at the moment."

3

Dakayivani spoke quietly in Shoshone to the other warriors. Two of them got up and wandered about twenty yards away where they started to play some kind of game with some bone or stone pieces that one of them produced from a pouch. The game involved throwing the pieces to the floor and apparently trying to achieve some kind of pattern, as far as Sebastian could tell. It involved a lot of laughter and pushing each other. The other warrior disarmed himself and lay down to doze.

"You trust me fully now?" asked Sebastian.

"I trust you not to be stupid enough to attack us," Dakayivani told him. "We'll see about full trust later; I can see that she trusts you and for now that's good enough – tell me your story; why are you here and what do you need?"

Sebastian explained about the war against the French in America and how it had grown into a revolt by the British settlers against the Crown. He referred to it as an English or British civil war fought on a distant continent and the French were just sticking their noses in.

"You don't strike me as a coward. Why have you fled this war?"

"I would have happily fought the French," Sebastian said. "They are my nation's constant enemy. The colonists I'm less happy to fight, they are my own people, but I would have done so."

"But you fled," persisted Dakayivani. "Why?"

"More than one reason. The Mohawk nations chose sides in this fight. Some groups sided with the French and some with us. They started to fight amongst themselves as if they were insane Europeans not really knowing why they fought, just settling old scores both real and imagined."

Dakayivani nodded. "Go on."

"I came to realise that this was not really a sensible war. Rich men on both sides were just protecting their own wealth by getting poor men to die for them. The rich Americans didn't want to pay tax on their goods, so they got the poor farmers to take up arms for them. The rich British wanted to tax and take tribute from the Americans so got their poor soldiers to seek to dominate the place."

"But this alone is not enough for you to abandon your people, I think," said Dakayivani.

Sebastian rubbed his face as Katsitsienhawi placed a hand on his shoulder. "No. I was ordered to take smallpox-infected blankets and deliver them to the Mohawk groups that were not on our side. I led the wagons carrying the blankets as if I were obeying but about ten miles into the woods we stopped to burn the load. Most of my soldiers turned a blind eye but one, a rough evil sergeant, tried to arrest me. There was a scuffle and I killed him."

"And the others?" asked Dakayivani.

"They looked to me. I told them to say that we'd been attacked, that the load was burned and the sergeant and I were killed. They agreed, except one who declared he'd been killed as well, ripped off his coat and ran away." Both men laughed. "I went to Katsitsienhawi's small group; I'd been friendly with them for years and with Katsitsienhawi herself for about a year. Her father had declared me his adopted son, so I knew I could trust them."

"The Mohawk are an honourable people," said Dakayivani.

"They told us to flee. They said the Shoshone could be trusted and we should seek refuge with them. It's a long way. The Mohawk escorted us for a few hundred miles but needed to return to their people; warriors need to be near their families as this war gets more and more terrible."

Dakayivani nodded. "Will it spread to our lands?"

Sebastian thought about this. "Maybe not this war but eventually the white man and his world will reach here. If the British win this war they will not spread west. In that case the Spanish or French will eventually come here. If the Americans win then they will spread west in time; they plan to hold the whole continent."

"Who will win?" asked Dakayivani.

"I don't know. The British are very powerful but this is a very expensive war for them to fight, so far from home, and they have many other lands to protect as well. The French are disrupting their cross-ocean supply lines and keeping several warships pinned down. They may decide that their forces are too far stretched and not commit further resources. The Americans are determined and tough and have French financing. Plus of course, in their minds they are defending their homeland; this always makes a man fight harder. Either side can win."

Dakayivani looked thoughtful for a while. He reached out his hand and the two men shook in the European manner. "You have something to ask of us," said Dakayivani.

"We ask for refuge. We ask to live with or alongside you. We will agree to all reasonable conditions."

"If we grant refuge it would oblige us to defend you against any troops the British might send to arrest you," said Dakayivani.

"I understand," said Sebastian wearily. "It's unlikely they'd send troops this far into the west but I understand that it is a concern for you. May we rest in your lands for a week before we move on?"

Dakayivani looked at him silently for a few seconds. "That would eventually mean the death of Katsitsienhawi and the child she carries. You will meet some other tribes that have no honour who will abuse and murder her."

"Then please let her stay; I will move on alone. My people don't know about her. Should they come here you can tell them that you drove me off. They will not seek to fight you so far from their support and reinforcements."

Dakayivani looked pleased. "You have honour, courage and good sense. We would fight for you; I declare you adopted son of the No'ipinKoi, sons of the Shoshone. We will give you land for your own use and only ask that No'ipinKoi and other Shoshone hunt and camp on your land at will."

Dakayivani called out in Shoshone. The sleeping warrior rose and the other two came back to the fire. The three warriors spoke briefly to Dakayivani and then all four stood and chanted in Shoshone. Then they all sat.

"I am overwhelmed," said Sebastian. "I here undertake to befriend all Shoshone of whatever group. I will work, support, assist and fight for the Shoshone whenever called on."

Katsitsienhawi hugged him.

Dakayivani spoke to his companions in Shoshone and then shook Sebastian's hand again. The other warriors copied him but seemed a little unfamiliar with the gesture. Then Dakayivani picked up his weapons and they all turned and walked away.

"Do you not have horses?" called Sebastian. "I could go find horses and show you how to use them."

Dakayivani laughed as he called back, "We have horses. The Shoshone boy you sent to find us said you were on foot so we left them over there in the foothills." He indicated foothills about five miles away. "We didn't want to alarm you by galloping up to you in the dark. I wish we had now; it's a long walk." Sebastian laughed as well. Dakayivani spoke to the other warriors in Shoshone and they too laughed as they waved back at Sebastian.

Sebastian and Katsitsienhawi struggled to build adequate shelter on their new lands. Although there appeared to be brush liberally scattered across the desert, they discovered it to be small thorny bushes. Verdant to the eye but with very little woody material. There were enough small animals, reptile and mammal, to provide sufficient food but nowhere near enough skins to cover a tepee even if they could find support poles, which they could not.

Amongst the items in his military pack, Sebastian had a small digging tool. Not much more than a thin folding spade but robust and effective. With it they were able to dig a small and shallow pit, sufficient to protect from the wind, and loosely covered it with Sebastian's army great coat and a blanket that Katsitsienhawi had with her. Here they lived for a week as they searched, unsuccessfully, for the resources with which they could build better accommodation.

Katsitsienhawi and Sebastian heard the laughter just a moment before they heard the hooves of two riders trotting towards their hole.

It was early morning and the sun was just beginning to warm the plain.

Two young Shoshone, a boy and girl, approached the residential hole. Sebastian emerged; he clipped on his sword but made no hostile gesture or move.

"I am Kettaa," said the boy. "This is Pamusikka," he added. They were both about sixteen, maybe a little older or younger. The boy looked physically powerful and the girl was strikingly pretty. She had a large knife strapped to one leg and Kettaa sported a small axe in his waistband.

"You speak English?" asked Sebastian.

"Yep, I am the son of Dakayivani. Not 'son' as you understand it. My father, the one who gave me seed to grow, was friend of Dakayivani and was killed in battle. Dakayivani adopted me and I now call him father as well."

Katsitsienhawi emerged from the hole and spoke in Shoshone. The girl nodded sweetly; she jumped from her horse and together they walked away to collect fuel for fire. Sebastian caught himself watching the girl as she walked and Kettaa laughed.

"I apologise," said Sebastian. "I live in a dirt hole like an unwashed troglodyte and maybe it caused me to lose both my manners and my common sense."

"It's not a problem," said Kettaa laughing again. "Among the Shoshone it is a compliment to admire another's mate. She's beautiful and you are just a man so I think we don't fight to the death on this occasion."

Katsitsienhawi and Pamusikka returned with some recently killed lizards and some wispy tinder wood. They lit a fire and started to roast breakfast.

Kettaa went to Katsitsienhawi, embraced her and kissed her on the mouth. She easily struggled free from him and stood looking a little bemused.

Pamusikka spoke quickly in Shoshone and slapped Kettaa lightly on the cheek. He replied in Shoshone laughing and Pamusikka giggled. Katsitsienhawi looked annoyed, walked over and punched Sebastian lightly in the chest. Sebastian fell to his knees pleadingly and reached up to Katsitsienhawi who laughed forgivingly at him. Pamusikka giggled some more, grinned at Sebastian then went to watch the food cook.

"We are all good now," said Kettaa. "We've complimented each other's mates, both got thumped for our troubles and still laughed at each other like friends. Let's enjoy our food."

Kettaa and Pamusikka stayed with them for the whole morning. They helped gather the plump cacti from which Sebastian and Katsitsienhawi squeezed water into sewed skins. They hunted small reptiles and mammals. They cleaned the shallow hole that Sebastian and Katsitsienhawi called home. They gathered the thin brush wood and helped to pile it. The two young Shoshone often seemed amused by what they were doing.

"Kettaa," said Sebastian as noon grew nigh, "why are you here? You are welcome and we like you; you are our friends, but why are you here this morning?"

Kettaa frowned. "My friend, you are making a real mess of living as Shoshone."

Sebastian laughed and nodded; Kettaa laughed with him and slapped his upper arm.

Kettaa suddenly stood still and looked off into the distance, his face returning to the usual native inscrutability. Sebastian followed his gaze and saw the dust cloud of galloping horses approaching. Four or five horses perhaps.

Katsitsienhawi and Pamusikka were about fifteen feet from the two men. In a single and swiftly flowing move, Katsitsienhawi produced and slashed with a steel knife. The razor sharp blade cut an ugly red gouge across Pamusikka's throat and neck, one end of which spurted hot arterial blood as the girl clutched her throat and sank to her knees.

Sebastian was a soldier with all of the instinctive and instantaneous reactions peculiar to that profession. He sidestepped the axe blow that Kettaa swung at his head. At the same time he drew his sword and shuffled a few steps from his adversary, the better to thrust into him.

The two warriors were sizing each other up, looking for weaknesses to exploit. It got no further than that as the knife thrown by Katsitsienhawi plunked into the side of Kettaa's head, cutting easily through bone and into his brain. He died instantly and crumpled to the floor.

Sebastian glanced towards Katsitsienhawi, Pamusikka now face down on the ground and unmoving in death.

"What?" said a confused-sounding Sebastian. "What? What just happened?"

"Liars," said Katsitsienhawi partly growling. "They are not Shoshone; they are Mohawk. Not my group, Canadian Mohawk, almost certainly French allies. They lie and my spirit guardians tell me they plan to hurt us."

Sebastian looked stunned. "Spirit guardians? You've never mentioned them before."

"Instinct, call it a sound hunch," she said sounding inappropriately happy.

"I hope so," Sebastian said. "I think that's Dakayivani riding towards us. I hope we haven't just murdered his adopted son and future daughter-in-law. I hope your spirit guardians haven't just got us killed."

As the riders drew closer it was clear that they were five. Sebastian replaced his sword in its scabbard and awaited their arrival.

Dakayivani was at the head of four warriors. As they came close a couple of them whooped as if in a war charge. Sebastian stood still but kept his hand near his sword.

Dakayivani jumped from his horse and walked up to Sebastian. The warriors remained mounted. Two of them behind Dakayivani and two trotted over to Katsitsienhawi.

"What?" demanded Dakayivani.

"I killed them, both of them," lied Sebastian.

"No you didn't; she did. I saw it, you idiot," Dakayivani corrected him.

"It must be my fault," said Sebastian. "I apologise and will accept your judgement if you allow Katsitsienhawi to live."

"And if I don't agree to that?" laughed Dakayivani.

"Then we fight and die here and now," said Sebastian as he began to draw his sword.

"Whoa stop," instructed Dakayivani. "What are you doing?" His face showed that he was not sure why Sebastian took this stance. He stepped back two paces. Sebastian noticed that one of the warriors put his hand to his axe.

"He was your son," said Sebastian. "We have killed him; I understand your anger."

"He is no son of mine," said Dakayivani.

"He said he was; he said you'd sent him," Sebastian explained.

Dakayivani waved to the warrior to unhand his axe. He spat on the young man's corpse. "You lying dog, you filthy French fucking spy." He looked Sebastian in the eye. "He is not my son. He was a spy sent by the French who feared you might be recruiting us. He also had a bounty paid to him by the British to kill you and me both. We were riding to warn you. You know, I was right about you. Courage and honour. You stood like a man for Shoshone to see. I'm impressed."

"I'm sorry," Sebastian moved his hand from his sword hilt. "Why do the British seek to kill you? Me yes, I understand that, but why you?"

"They have a bit of an issue over some guns I stole before I left New York. You know what they're like."

"You are very well informed for a Neolithic desert dweller hoping to be civilised by the white man," quipped Sebastian.

"Yes," said an amused Dakayivani. "My monosyllabic stone chipping spies in the colonies keep me informed." Both men laughed with relief and friendship.

Katsitsienhawi came to them; she hugged Sebastian and whispered with a slight laugh, "See, trust my spirits."

Dakayivani and Sebastian walked slowly to the hole of a home. Katsitsienhawi sat further away laughing and joking with two of the warriors. The other two warriors were busy looting the fallen spies.

"I suppose we'll have to bury them," said Sebastian.

Dakayivani laughed. "We already have the hole."

"Yes," agreed Sebastian. "We're struggling a bit to make a go of it. Katsitsienhawi's skills require decent wood and mine depend on a supply of servants and labour to do anything. I'm sure we'll die here due to our lack of any local survival knowledge."

"Sit here by the soon-to-be grave and I'll share some wisdom with you." Dakayivani spoke light-heartedly but it was clear to him that he needed to coach these incompetents or watch them fail.

Quite an instructive time it was, too. Sebastian showed clear wonder as the world of the Shoshone was described to him.

"Forget your European preconceptions," Dakayivani said to him more than once. "White man astonished red man not do things the same as him, what what old chum," he joked.

Shoshone means 'the people of the grass huts'. No'ipinKoi means 'top of the hill', so Dakayivani's hill-dwelling people became known as the No'ipinKoi Shoshone, a semi-autonomous branch of the Shoshone nation.

If significant wood was required, it could be obtained from forests about ten miles further along the hills. Dakayivani explained how these woodlands were planted by his people about five generations ago.

"We farm," he explained. "It doesn't look like your farming so you don't recognise it. The single species fields you so love, we are horrified by them. We think it better to mix plants and animals. The woodlands of which I speak, between the trees you'll find wheat, root veg, berry bushes and all kinds of herb. We hunt the animals that live there to provide our meat."

He also explained trading parties between Shoshone and Mohawk. Wood, furs, anything is traded and the two peoples are firm friends for the most part.

He went on to explain that the grass huts in which they live are made by interlacing the woody strands from the desert bushes, basically knitting them together. The hemispherical shape provides stability and the weave creates the strength that allows them to stand.

The desert was also a place for farming. The small bushes were carefully laid out to allow growth. The space between them filled with planted giant cacti, the pulp of which could provide water if you were unable to reach the sweet and pure water lakes at the foot of the hills.

Dakayivani laughed as he told Sebastian of how his people were amused at his survival attempts. "My brother offered to send his small daughter to help you."

Sebastian laughed as well – it was true. "I thought I might call this place Ash Hole," he said.

"We've already named it after you." Dakayivani laughed again. "*Gutusipe Daindi*, we have called it. It means Ash Confused." Both men laughed some more.

"That's fair – I'm lucky to have found good friends," commented Sebastian.

"We suspect that your descendants will become subsumed into the No'ipinKoi, but if you turn out to be a prolific childmaker and become your own group, we have already named such a group as *Nehwe* Shoshone. That means friends of the Shoshone so it links them both to you and the wider Shoshone nation."

"I'll do my best." Sebastian smiled. "I am so grateful."

"More than this, though," said Dakayivani looking a bit more serious, "we fear for the future. We fear the unstoppable expansion of the Europeans. We seek alliance, treaty and promise from your people. In spite of the fact that the American-based leaders of your people just tried to kill you, we hope to use you to both benefit your own first nation and us, your second nation."

Dakayivani took from his pack a leather document holder. From it he took an attractively calligraphic couple of sheets and handed the manuscript to Sebastian.

An agreement between His Majesty King George III (including and extending to his lawful heirs) and the No'ipinKoi Shoshone made this day called by the European calendar 20 September 1780.

For this purpose the Nehwe Shoshone, Nehwe No'ipinKoi Shoshone and the No'ipinKoi Shoshone are regarded as one people.

In this agreement the No'ipinKoi Shoshone are represented by their lawful chief and leader Dakayivani, known to the authorities in the British colony of New York by the adopted name of David Leadbeater and educated at the School of the Reformed Dutch Church of New York authorised by the High Church of England and therefore with the oversight of His Majesty King George III.

His Majesty King George III is represented by Lieutenant Sebastian Ash of His Majesty's Royal Irish Regiment of foot, loyal servant and subject of His Majesty. Having been wounded by natives acting for the bandit French, Lieutenant Sebastian Ash has been rescued by the No'ipinKoi Shoshone and, unable to return to his own people, has been adopted by Dakayivani.

Still loyal to his natural and God appointed King, Lieutenant Sebastian Ash claims the land described in this agreement for His Majesty and places it in alliance with the No'ipinKoi Shoshone in perpetuity.

The No'ipinKoi Shoshone hereby cede partial sovereignty of the land known to them as the flats, which by European reckoning would be the desert plain from the salt flats to the foothills in the west and noted by the buildings placed here by Sebastian Ash and named by him and Dakayivani as the territory and township of Gutusipe Daindi.

The No'ipinKoi Shoshone cede this land to nobody other than His Majesty King George III and his representative in this place, Sebastian Ash.

No'ipinKoi Shoshone retain rights as protectors of His Majesty's land and extend this agreement to the rightful heirs of both Sebastian Ash and His Majesty King George III, recognising that Sebastian Ash swears allegiance and fealty to His Majesty.

The Agreement:

1. *No'ipinKoi Shoshone shall not raid or war on Sebastian Ash and by extension consider themselves in treaty with His Majesty King George III.*
2. *His Majesty King George III shall not war on or seize lands of No'ipinKoi Shoshone and looks with friendly eyes on them and other Shoshone.*
3. *The produce of the soil of Gutusipe Daindi and the territory in which it stands benefit His Majesty except that Gutusipe Daindi and Nehwe No'ipinKoi Shoshone shall be granted joint benefit based on the importance and value of the produce. This clause includes crops, wildlife and anything else from this land.*
4. *If in the future No'ipinKoi Shoshone are forced to submit to bandits such as the French, Spanish or Americans, His Majesty shall send forces to free them.*
5. *No'ipinKoi Shoshone will adopt as enemies the enemies of His Majesty.*
6. *His Majesty will adopt as enemies the enemies of No'ipinKoi Shoshone.*
7. *The No'ipinKoi Shoshone declare loyalty to His Majesty within the parameters laid out in clause 8.*
8. *His Majesty recognises that No'ipinKoi Shoshone are a free people and possess the rights of self-determination and equality in the eyes of His Majesty. No'ipinKoi Shoshone may not be enslaved, abused or mistreated and nor may the property of No'ipinKoi Shoshone, as individuals or as a people, be seized or appropriated except as stipulated in this agreement.*

9. *This agreement sets out the principle of equality, respect and friendship between the No'ipinKoi Shoshone and His Majesty George III and his lawful heirs which exists from this day and lasts without limit for all time.*

Signed This Day 20 September AD 1780: Sebastian Ash and David Leadbeater aka Dakayivani.

"You should have been a lawyer," said Sebastian. "I assume you wrote this."

Dakayivani nodded. "Yes, my New York education was comprehensive and useful. Eventually I'd like to start a school among my own people; they'll take some convincing though. Please agree to sign this."

"Wounded by the French?" said Sebastian. "A little fib perhaps?"

Dakayivani laughed. "We laugh often, you know. A good sign of friendship. I think it will be many years before we need to deal directly with Europeans. By that time nobody will remember your little fight and flight in the middle of a confusing and crazy war. I could hardly write that the treacherous Sebastian Ash sticks his fingers up at the British army but still likes his king. I don't think that'd work."

"Yep, should have been a lawyer," said Sebastian. "Of course I will sign – it's a brilliant idea. Mark my words, though, you cannot trust the Europeans. Whichever country eventually comes to complicate your lives you will have to be on your guard."

"I know," said Dakayivani.

Sebastian reached into a small pouch on his belt and extracted a nugget of bright silver about half the size of a hen's egg. "I found this in my hole. It's all over the place. It's extremely rare to find this metal in its pure form; it's normally found as an ore and it's very valuable to the Europeans. Never let them see it until you are sure you are dealing with a country you can trust not to just use force and steal it all. I promise and warn you, they will send armies to take this."

"I know," repeated Dakayivani. "We call it *aishi-waahni*. That just means fox-coloured, really. We shall be fox sly with this metal and it will be a long long time before our children's children's children's children trade it to Europeans. Until then it sits safely in the land."

"I'll import wood and build much. I intend to cover as much of this land as I can and do my best to prevent any prospectors who might arrive," said Sebastian.

"Honour and courage, I said as much. I doubt it will be in our lifetimes. Now is the time for you to build and for us both to prepare our descendants for the difficult times ahead."

Chapter Two

Philip and Catherine Ash. Prosperous and unhealthily close siblings, dissolute and decadent. Plus, as usual, drunk and coked up. Driving at speed was not their best joint decision but it's hard to say just what good decisions this spoilt, privileged and narcissistic pair had ever made.

They together benefitted from a generous trust fund that allowed them to do just about anything they wanted. Being born into such privilege can create the best and worst of people. Philip and Catherine were not the best.

"Faster?" purred a lounging Catherine. About thirty, good-looking, slim, expensively garbed in a designer dress. She leaned towards Philip, the driver, her dyed blonde hair brushing his face. Unusually in those who change their hair colour she had ensured her eyebrows also adopted the same shade. Her left hand rested on his inner thigh inappropriately close to his genitals and she slowly stroked him.

"The car?" laughed Philip with one hand on the wheel and his other arm around her. A little over thirty, tired and almost washed out good looks beginning to hint at his long-term chemical abuse. His preppy casual clothing probably costing more than most normal people's monthly income.

She reached up to kiss him and he turned to her. He kissed her in return, his tongue venturing into an incestuous exploration of her mouth.

That will be why, on this wide, straight and full moon-lit northern interstate, he failed to see the three large cows sauntering aimlessly along the road. The small herd had probably wandered through some broken farm fence from their normal refuge. The unlit forest-lined road became an easy track to follow as the lunar light softly illuminated the course of their lazy bovine waddle.

The robust one-year-old Bentley smashed the first one into pieces, two tons of rich-guy car travelling at eighty miles an hour can make whole cow mincemeat in an instant. In spite of the large car's handmade stout construction it did not escape unscathed. As a spray of liquidised flesh, bone and muscle covered the windscreen, the front axle buckled and the engine smashed to the back of the engine compartment.

As Philip and Catherine looked up in dismay, the car, which was now sparking along on its fallen sump and broken axle, careered into cow number two.

This hulking beastie slid up the front bonnet and then through the windscreen. The heavily built animal made an unearthly but short screech as the offside roof support removed its head.

The two self-indulgent siblings made no sound as the muscular body squashed them into their seats, which broke backwards, and burst their chests, necks and heads.

The car itself spun into some nearby trees, slipping a bit on cattle blood and bodily fluids. The third cow viewed the carnage dispassionately, gave a loud bellow and continued on its purposeless amble.

* * *

It was two hours before a passing truck trundled across the scene. The driver pulled over, considered checking the car but then decided not to. The rear of the Bentley rested proud of the treeline. The front was clearly destroyed with blood, flesh and gore everywhere. The truck driver had enough bad memories from military service and general life, he didn't need to add to that when there was obviously nothing to be done. He dialled 911 from his cell phone.

Within twenty-five minutes police officers cordoned off the road. They threw flares about and set up spotlighting the car. Paramedic crews went to the car, shook their heads and walked away. After the police finished photographing everything, firefighters ripped the Bentley open so that the coroner could remove the human remains. Nobody knew what to do with the cow body. The head was found further up the road. In the end the remains of the steer were just left at the edge of the woods for scavengers to clean up.

Philip and Catherine were removed, although some parts of Philip ended up with Catherine and the other way round. Small bits of the cow ended up with both of them.

"Wow, I'm never having another burger," one officer said to his partner who laughed.

The saddest indictment of the Ash siblings' empty lives is that nobody really missed them. Nobody except their cocaine dealer, lawyer and accountant. Nobody wept for them. The trustees of their fund arranged for a spot at the court of probate in order to decide what happened to the money, after everybody had taken their 'expenses' and final professional fees were paid.

Philip and Catherine had an expensive funeral attended only by a well-paid minister and people who had a professional connection to the trust fund and didn't want to appear heartless. The mourners held a wake at the county's most expensive and lavish restaurant; it's what they would have wanted. At the end of the evening the accountants and lawyers divvied up the remaining champagne between them. The cocaine dealer popped in to pay his respects and say hello to a couple of his customers who were there.

A few court cases later, funded by the trust and employing as many lawyers as possible, the matter was settled.

Nobody now known to be alive was heir to the fortune. The money itself was invested across several states and was now likely to become either granted to individual states or relinquished to the federal government.

The 'never say die while there are still fees to be earned' lawyers dragged in a genealogist to look for distant relatives. An asset investigator was employed to trace any other money that might prolong this even further.

The results were both surprising and lucrative for those involved. There was just one surviving distant relative, apparently English and the great great great, however many 'greats', grandson of one of the children of the original Ash. It appeared that this child had returned to England. This meant more fees to engage lawyers and investigators in England and then agree matters with the English courts to ensure both legal systems were on the same page. Then came the simple matter of finding one Michael Key, the lucky sole survivor of this family line.

The problem was that most of the money was now gone. Nonetheless, the original investigations had thrown up an unexpected thing; apparently the Ash line owned a substantial amount of desert some miles north of Las Vegas in territory currently used by a local native tribe.

The lawyers used the last of the cash obtained from selling off investments and threw it at locating the current owner. The main firm involved had a contingency plan to manage dispute between the new owner, the state government and the feds. It wasn't certain that would happen but they hoped to advise and manipulate the Englishman when they found him.

The loss of ready cash to the Ash fund meant that the ornate and expensive grave in which Philip and Catherine reposed lost its maintenance contract. The spot slowly filled with invasive plant life and detritus, the pointlessness of their existence ultimately reflected in the vacuous conceit of their monument. In a final act of desecration, a passing stray dog pissed on the hand-sculptured Pentelic marble statuettes.

Chapter Three

South-west England at this time of year adopts colours of gold and brown as nature, exhausted by two seasons of creation, settles down to a winter slumber. The climate, wounded by generations of human enterprise, still manages a temperate half warmth to lullaby the resting environment. Indifferent to the recent human culling effect of the pandemic, the world of flora anticipates the following year's quest to prosper.

Sweaty and breathless, Mike Key took a rest. He sat on an old and unravelling wicker chair drawing on his vaping pipe and quaffing a can of scrumpy. His axe and bow saw were temporarily abandoned at his feet. The chair was a little small for his six feet four heavily built frame. The slight belly he never quite found time to exercise away caused him to lean back just a bit in order to breathe more easily.

Trees are tricky things to trim, especially when fallen. Cut a small branch thoughtlessly and the entire thing can roll unpredictably and crush you or break a limb. His resting time was spent observing how the large oak was laying, the direction of forces and interplay between the branches touching the floor. This field was quite a distance from any help and he didn't want to risk injury.

Mike was enjoying this old-fashioned harvesting of a felled tree. The farm on which he was working was owned by an old school friend. After the divorce he asked to park his camper on the edge of a field. The old friend agreed and put him to work for a small cash wage. Not that he needed the money, he had a few quid stashed away but he was finding this cash-in-hand casual work therapeutic.

He and his newly former wife never really recovered from their son's death. The stupidity of it, a drunk driver and a diesel spill combining to turn a small boy into pulp, just made it in some way worse. An event that propelled him into nihilistic numbness and rendered all plans and ambitions futile.

He'd given some thought to hunting down and killing the driver. Somehow he didn't feel rage towards the man. Even though Mike knew his own propensity for violence, he also knew that it required direction. The driver was an idiot, he behaved in an antisocial and dangerous manner, but that was not enough. Mike's dark impulses overwhelmed him only in the face of evil. The contemptible and stupid just made him despair at the ultimately inconsequential destiny integral to the human condition.

Five years ago this woman and this boy became his salvation. After the loss of their son the two tried to continue. It was never the same and it became clear to both of them that it would end.

Mike's previous life had a legacy of memories. Sometimes his nightmares and daydreams confused the bloodied burning souls of that life with his son's contorted lifelessness. He hadn't seen the mangled remains but could imagine it vividly; he tried not to. A tendency to anger, intrusive memories and an ill-defined shame made life difficult for Mike.

Meeting Mel and fathering John brought him back from his history. Together they were, if not the cure for his past, then at least his reconciliation with the world. The crash, he was unable to call it an accident, ended that period of his life. He still thought fondly of Mel but they drifted apart in melancholy loss of connection. They parted. Mike gave her his portion of the house and took to the road. As he approached middle age, well early fifties-ish, he saw his remaining life as just drifting slowly and sadly to its end in a few decades.

As he finished his cider a sixth sense told him to look behind him, old habits learned in dangerous places ingrained into him. As he did so he saw a marginally overweight balding man of about fifty-something walking towards him across the field. Mike just sat and waited for him to arrive.

He judged the man as having some life experience, the clue being his covertly wary but not unconfident eye movements as if assessing threats and risks. As he drew close Mike noticed the guy positioned himself just off-centre and stood with an unthreatening alertness disguised as a casual stance, feet a bit apart, hands casually held in front of him and just out of arm's length.

What we do in life reflects on our faces, except sociopaths who feel no emotional effect from their actions and therefore tend to have untroubled faces. Not this man, this man's eyes revealed something dark, unpleasant but hard to identify. He'd seen or done some bad stuff.

"Hello," said Mike.

"Michael Key?" The voice revealed he'd spent some part of his life in an official role, police maybe.

"Only if it's good news. Just walk away if it's bad."

"It's OK," said the man, clearly not easily frightened away. "My name is Justin Blake. I'm a private investigator and I have information for Michael Key that is very much to his benefit."

"What, rich Uncle Fred who I've never heard of has died and left me his stately home?" laughed Mike.

Blake smiled at that. "Not far from the truth. If you can show me evidence that you actually are Michael Key, then the American law firm I'm hired by have something very similar for you."

"Hmm," said Mike. "A foreign adventure might suit me just now. How did you find me?"

"I'm an investigator," Blake told him. "A good one, too. Your ex, who still likes you by the way, put me on your trail, and once I made it clear I had no trouble for you, your friends pointed the way for me."

"Take a seat and have a can. I need to finish off this dead tree and then I'll go with you to my van and prove who I am. Then you can tell me all about this thing to my benefit."

Justin Blake proved he had an impressive capacity for alcohol as he finished off Mike's cans while watching the tree get chopped down to manageable logs. He kindly left one for Mike to refresh himself with.

* * *

For Brits, America is both a familiar and a strange place. The space, wide roads and large, well-spaced buildings create a bit of a Brobdingnagian feel. However, the occupants are a little less respectful and virtuous than the fictional giants.

This is a land with a superficially similar culture and almost the same language. This coupled with the constant exposure from TV shows and films creates an easy and comfortable recognition.

At the same time regular examples of very foreign attributes invade this relaxed sense of easy assimilation. The prevalence of firearms, the casual possession of other weapons such as openly carried hunting knives, the strident and demanding religiosity and the curious mixture of false politeness and rudeness; 'have a nice day, arsehole'.

Mike's cab delivered him to the pavement outside the firm of Valtin and Adams Associates, Law and Lobbying. During the ride through Washington, Mike had been a little shocked to see some clearly deprived people in poorly maintained streets and housing.

Here, though, was the wealth and influence one might associate with the capital of the world power. The building had a wide, fogged glass front, gilded metal-framed doors and just dripped with the suggestion of money.

"Dunno if I'm rich enough to walk in there," said Mike as he opened the car door.

"Twenty-four dollars," replied the driver with a Pakistani accent that somehow managed a slight American twang. The cheapness of cab fares was just another foreign thing in this land of familiarity and contrast. A journey of this distance in London would have cost twice as much.

Mike gave him a twenty and a ten, waved his hand to show no change was expected and crossed the pavement to stand before the tall, impressive doors.

Mike approached the long, high reception desk.

"Yessar," said the olive-skinned, heavy-set, middle-aged woman behind it. Her voice had just a trace of her Latin origins, and if she lost weight, her face would be pretty. Nah, she was pretty, the fat thing was just Mike's own values being unfairly projected, and he knew it.

"Jan Adams," said Mike.

"Canya take a seat, sa," asked the lady, picking up a phone at the same time.

Mike didn't sit but stood a few feet away waiting. The receptionist spoke on the phone, the words indistinct to Mike, then smiled charmingly at him.

"Y' Australian?" she asked.

"No," responded Mike. "I'm English, probably some London in my voice."

People from southern England, the ones who don't have a plummy accent, get used to being mistaken for Australians in America. The Australian accent evolved from that of south-east England before the homeland accent morphed into a nasal estuary monotone. Same with America really. The basic US accent is closer to earlier English than English is. Many things that Brits call Americanisms, like the use of Z instead of S in many words, is in fact old English.

Jan Adams arrived through opaque double glass doors on the far side of the reception hall. She was about mid-forties, shoulder-length dyed blonde hair, dark almost black eyebrows, powdered pale skin and dark mascara eyelashes on almost bronze eyeshadowed lids. They flickered over brown eyes that hid, to any observer of people, a steely distrusting soul. She wore a grey business suit with a knee-length skirt too tight at the hem which caused her to walk in short quick steps.

Now that handshaking was back, the recent Covid pandemic mainly controlled and sort of past, they shook hands. There were still a few people masking up and hand gelling constantly but now a bit of time had passed, most people relegated it to the same precautions as flu; regular vaccination and normal hygiene precautions. It was still about but no longer at the forefront of their fears for most people.

Mike nodded at the receptionist, then Adams led him to a comfortable small meeting room where Mike showed her his passport, birth certificate and driving licence.

"You are the only living relative of Catherine and Philip Ash; they sadly died in a tragic car accident," announced Jan Adams.

"If you say so," offered Mike. "I'd never heard of them before this matter came up."

"Well," she continued, "I can confirm it. It has been before state courts here and confirmed through DNA taken from you by Mr Blake."

"Yep, I'm not denying it," said Mike. He remembered the sample Blake took. The man had preferred finger blood to mouth swab but Mike thought that he just liked to make people bleed.

"It's been shown beyond doubt to the courts here," explained Adams. "We also obtained agreement from the English courts although, strictly speaking, that wasn't necessary. The place we need to talk about was founded by Sebastian Ash, a deserter from British forces during the revolution. It was formalised, staked as they say, by a later descendant of his. That line is now extinct. You descend from a grandchild of Sebastian Ash who returned to England in the nineteenth century. You are the last surviving Ash, whatever your actual name."

"Wow," said Mike. "Just goes to show, he who fights and runs away lives to get rich another day."

"This is the position," continued Adams, "you inherit a significant portion of land in Nevada. There's nothing else left of the estate because the Ash siblings were profligate and always overhired professionals. The wealth built by the industry of successive generations is now gone. The Nevada land was discovered by state asset auditors and now falls to you."

Mike snorted. "Yep, it was rich old Uncle Fred after all." He explained to Adams that Uncle Fred didn't exist and it was just a personal joke.

She seemed unamused. "We have some documents to sign and you may if you wish hire this firm to seek removal from your land a large band of squatters who like to call it home."

"No, don't think so," said Mike. "I'll go see them and hear what they say. I'm not in the business of evicting people I've never met. How much land is it?"

It soon became clear that it was huge. About seventy miles by a hundred miles of Nevada desert about a hundred and fifty miles out of Las Vegas. The papers he signed referred to it as 'Ash Land' but described nothing else. He was given directions and land coordinates so that his possession could be identified.

Adams was obviously on a mission to win him over and after several failed attempts to persuade him to hire the firm to clear what she called 'squatters' she said, "OK, Mike, I hope I can call you Mike, we will hold ourselves ready for you when you've seen it. Come back to me, Mike." Her words almost whispered, "And I'll do anything you want."

Mike looked at her. Was she really offering herself for the business? Was he imagining that? "No no," he said. "I'll return if I need to but some business I can find in any dive bar." He hoped that was cryptic enough to deal with the cryptic offer she'd made. *Maybe I'm just tired*, he thought.

He'd found a small hotel on the outskirts of Vegas. The greyhound ride here was less comfortable and possibly longer than the flight to Washington. The room was clean and tidy and nothing like the loud, glossy, over-the-top glitziness normally associated with this town.

He'd ignored the casinos just a few miles away. The bus driver advised him to head for this suburb since the rest of Vegas was either full of rich suckers getting poor or poor suckers who will never get rich.

"Don't be a sucker," the friendly young black driver had told him. "Make Vegas a memory as soon as you can – it's a poisoned oasis." Then the young man drove off his route to deposit Mike there.

"You're a good guy; take care in life," Mike told him.

After a good meal Mike slept deeply for a few hours. He woke to pee, take some water and sit for a while drawing on his vaping pipe. Views of vaping were a bit odd in this country, one of those foreign things in a familiar land. It was frowned on by many people, often the same people who were perfectly happy with cigarette smoking. Apparently there were all sorts of varying state laws to restrict it. He had no idea where to buy more e-liquid but if push came to puff he could either stop or return to tobacco for a while. No problem, he was well stocked up anyway.

His second sleep was less resting. Dreams with which he was well acquainted intruded into his psyche. A small girl child burned through and peeling, her mother burned and battered in the corner. Which came first, the battering or the burning? Had her lower clothing burned away or was it torn off? Was the teenage boy shot in the corner burned before or after? And in the middle of the floor his son, John. Not burned but mangled and looking pleadingly to his inadequate father. Mike awoke and just lay there for a few more hours. He rose as the first hint of daylight glanced through the window.

His reflection in the bathroom mirror showed the tear tracks down his face. He showered and as he did so felt the usual early morning anger welling up. He needed to hit, smash, strike at the corpse of the world as he avenged himself on life itself. He punched the perspex shower screen a bit harder than intended and cracked it.

As he checked out, he informed the elderly male hotel owner that he'd accidently damaged the screen and asked for the cost of making it good.

"Accidently punched it, did you?" said the man. "That mark on your knuckle didn't get there by itself. You a vet?"

Mike didn't understand at first, then realised he meant veteran not veterinarian. "Yes and no. Sort of, kind of," said Mike.

"Forty bucks will do it and no harm done or offence taken. I did 'Nam myself. Whatever you did, thank you for it."

Mike paid him and thanked him.

"Whatever you got in your head, learn to live with it or it'll sure stop you living," advised the old man who patted his hand.

Mike nodded and touched the man's arm.

He went to a local car rental firm. There he met a young man who introduced himself as Pitcher. Is that a real name? Who calls their child 'Pitcher'?

After some discussion, Mike selected a good-quality four-wheel drive pick-up on an initial three month open contract. He wasn't sure what conditions he'd meet but did know that he'd be off road and might need to carry some equipment. This seemed the best vehicle. As long as he kept paying by direct debit the firm didn't care how long he kept it.

The discussion amused Mike. Pitcher was proof that people of his manner exist worldwide. Overconfident, undereducated but apparently unaware of it, not really interested in the wider world and completely oblivious to the failure of his attempts to dominate and control the transaction.

"What's this?" demanded Pitcher in his high-pitched nasally voice, almost a whine really.

"It's a driving licence," said Mike.

"Oh, I asked for a permit."

"Same thing," sighed Mike.

Pitcher looked at it for a while. "What's the circle of stars?"

"That's the EU flag," explained Mike. "I'm British."

"British same as EU, then?" asked a confused Pitcher.

"No, Britain's not in the EU anymore but the flag still turns up on some things. It's valid," said Mike, somewhat in disbelief that Pitcher hadn't seen one before.

An older man emerged from a side office and took over. He explained that Pitcher was new and not fully aware of foreign permits. The paperwork concluded; Mike went to the vehicle.

He threw his small bag onto the passenger seat and took from his pocket a small map and instructions given to him by Jan Adams.

It seemed he just needed to locate Interstate 95 and keep heading roughly north until he saw signs that would direct him to the Ash land.

He had driven some boring journeys in his time but this one set a new standard. A long, straight deserted road. Either side there stretched dull desert scrubland scattered with wispy short bushes and tall plump cacti. Hills and mountains in the distance just increased the sense of isolation.

He'd been driving for about three hours, most of it within the speed limit but with the occasional burst of speed just to relieve the monotony. He almost missed the wooden sign on a short post and braked hard, coming to a halt about fifty yards beyond it.

The gearbox squealed quietly as he reversed back to it. 'Ash Hole' declared the carved sign and an arrow pointed into the desert. He could see some not very recent tyre tracks leading away from the sign and into the void.

Ash Hole, maybe Ash Lands? If nothing is attempted, nothing can be achieved. Mike turned the pick-up off road and followed the tracks, keeping to below twenty. He had a four-pint bottle of water he'd bought at a gas station just outside Vegas. It would be enough to explore this route.

After about an hour he stopped the car. He got out and looked around him. The distant hills seemed no closer and the interstate was out of sight.

"I am alone in a desert," he said to himself. "I never thought I'd get this stupid."

"Not alone," a man's voice behind him said.

Mike was startled and jumped, half ducked to one side and reached to the back of his waistband for a weapon he didn't have. At home he often carried a small metal cosh on the back of his belt. He didn't think he was some insane nutter always tooled up but having something close to hand often eased his mind.

The man was about seven inches shorter than Mike and a bit stooped. Obviously native, he was dressed in khaki trousers, boots greyed with dust and a tatty camouflage shirt. His eyes were squinted against the sun which further screwed up his heavily lined face. Mike guessed the man was about seventy but physically fit. He carried a .22 rifle on his shoulder, the strap frayed old leather. A couple of dead lizards were in his hand, one of them clearly decapitated by a shot.

"Some kind of fool you are," growled the man, "talking to yourself in the middle of a desert and reaching for a weapon you don't have." He laughed.

Mike laughed as well. "I'm sorry, just habit. My name is Mike and I'm told I own somewhere called the Ash Lands and I'm just trying to find them. I saw a sign for Ash Hole and thought maybe that's it."

"Gimme a ride and I'll show you," said the man.

Mike agreed and they climbed into the pick-up. "Where did you come from? I didn't see you until you spoke," asked Mike.

"That was obvious," said the man, half laughing again. "Maybe I have special native super sneak up powers or maybe you're just not very observant. Take your pick."

"Probably the second," said Mike. "I didn't catch your name."

"I didn't give it but you can call me George if you like."

"I assume it's your name."

"Might be, can be for now," said the old man.

"Mysterious bugger, aren't you?" said a grinning Mike and they both laughed.

They drove in silence for the next forty minutes.

Chapter Four

"Hi, Mentos. The guy was here and will probably be on the lands soon. I don't see a problem, just go ahead as before. Should you encounter him, he'll be the only white man there, got a bit of Indian in him though. Don't do him any real harm, I need him for the land transfer." Jan Adams sat at her desk in her expensively furnished office.

"No problem," the voice of Mentos replied through the speaker. He had a not-quite-correct Latino accent, sounding as if it were attempting to disguise itself. "There's just one more dig to make and then we are gone. We'll probably be back in this country in a year or two. What if any tribal interference again?"

Jan Adams sighed. "Try to avoid anything extreme but if you must you must. We will shift the tribe using the law when you've done and we've pinned down the Englishman. He doesn't seem interested at the moment but eventually he'll move our way. He doesn't seem like an immovable object but we'll see. Do what you're going to do and when we've done our side I'll contact you about mining rights and a workforce. Blake is flying over to deal with the guy for me. He can make this an English thing; that distances us all," she said. What she meant was 'keeps me within the law, you don't matter'.

Mentos sat at his cheap desk in a tatty office at the back of an empty warehouse in a small Californian town. He placed the landline receiver back on its cradle and rubbed his face. Then he ran his fingers through his streaked blond hair.

At first glance Mentos looked a little like a fancy dress idea of a senior Latino gang member. From his features he was clearly a white man with a too liberally applied orange fake tan. His clothing was clean except for some stains around a checked neckerchief. His short blond hair was carefully styled but clearly not as thick as it had once been. He didn't look unfit but not very fit either. Physically he had the appearance of a man, about fifty, who worked out but then went straight to the fried chicken store after the gym. Fit and fat battling for control. In truth he was early sixties with a history that kept him fit and hard muscled. Since arriving in the States he'd struggled to maintain that as he tried within the boundaries of life in a soft and comfortable society.

A white man of about twenty-five entered the office. "How heavily equipped are we for this one?"

"Just handguns," replied Mentos.

"OK, Davey," answered the man and left.

"Mentos," Mentos called after him, "call me Mentos for fuck sake." He took a few mints from his pocket and stuck them in his mouth.

The young man walked back into the office. He swaggered exaggeratedly like the small-time pretend gangster that he was.

"Why?" he demanded. "Tell me that. Fucking Mentos not Davey, bullshit."

Mentos just stared at him, his eyes hard. The man stood there with his hands on his hips. The silence lasted.

"Anything else?" Mentos said quietly but with a slight animal growl.

"Nope, just making the point, you in charge but you not the top dog. I'll call you what I want, OK?"

Mentos stood and walked around the desk to face the young man. He opened his arms to embrace him and pulled him to his chest.

The young man screamed as Mentos bit off his ear. He tried to reach a small gun he had in the back of his belt. Mentos grabbed his wrist to prevent it, took the gun from him and spat the ear into his face.

"You fucking soft shit, I suck your blood; I turn you into my whore; I fucking own you," Mentos spoke almost lovingly in tone to the guy's face. He pulled a small knife from his side pocket and ran the sharp blade down the man's left cheek, sliced open from eye to chin. "You obey or you suffer. You are mine. Make me angry enough and you will never leave me. You want to work for me you act as well as my own men. Chetnik. You understand?"

The man mumbled assent. Mentos kicked him in the leg and he fell to the floor. A hard kick into the stomach ensured he stayed there. Mentos undid his fly and urinated on him.

Two young black men opened the sliding double doors of the warehouse. An eighteen-wheel truck followed by three vans drove in and cut their engines.

"We're loaded," called out the white driver of the truck. "Don't let the goods go off," he cackled.

Two young white men pushing a trolley loaded with water bottles and food packs joined the two black men. The rear doors of the truck were opened and the goodies thrown in. The shuffling of people inside as they grabbed the sustenance echoed in the empty building.

"Stay cool, people," called out one of the white men. "It's not in our interest to hurt any of you but if we have to do one we have to do you all, so stay cool and you'll be OK."

The men looking into the truck were not overtly threatening but both of them kept a hand on the guns they wore at their hips.

Mentos emerged from the office looking at the screen of his cell phone. "You two," he shouted, indicating two other young men, "go help the prick in my office; he's had an accident. Everybody else listen up."

The men at the big truck closed up the rear doors and wandered over. Everyone waited for Mentos to speak.

"I have just had a conversation with the boy being brought out at the moment." He indicated the bloodied and bent over man being helped towards a car. "I will tell you something. I am not here to war; I am here to make enough money to take my war back to my own land. If you cannot work with me, leave now. If you stay, my name for you to use is Mentos. That's it." Nobody moved. He smiled and applauded the guys standing around.

A large biker-looking greasy-haired man called out, "Don't give a shit who you are, you pay us we'll do it. Don't really care who you are. You say you're Mentos, you're Mentos."

Mentos smiled. "Mount up, soldiers. Long drive ahead. Two cars full of black guys back and front to distract the police. Let's go my people."

Chapter Five

"Stop here," instructed George.

Mike brought the pick-up to a halt. For the last few miles they'd been slowly climbing what felt like a range of hills. Then the incline grew steeper and they drove up a small hummock, a ridge, really, that flattened out further up.

"We're still in the middle of nowhere; the tracks I was following veer left so is that where I go?" he asked.

"Nope," said George. "That's where I'm going. You go that way for about half an hour." He indicated to the right as if it were a fork in the road.

"OK," replied Mike. "And how do I know when I'm on Ash Land?"

George smirked. "You've been on Ash Land since you left the road. It's not called that, though."

"What is it called?"

"Well, if you're an Ash you'll find out in time."

"Oh dear, still the mysterious bugger then."

Both men chuckled and George left the vehicle and walked to the left along the tyre tracks. He didn't thank Mike for the ride. Mike watched him for a little while. He thought the old guy had the gait of a much younger agile man. He gently pressed the accelerator and steered to the right.

After about five minutes he passed over the top of this ridge; the down slope was as gentle as the rise. In the distance he could see what looked like an old town. The buildings all looked wooden and to his mind it had the appearance of a dilapidated and abandoned film set.

The surrounding land as far as could be seen was still the same bare flat brush and cactus-studded desert. An offshoot of the ridge extended along the left side of the town and a few hundred yards from it, that part being less gentle than the track he was using. It rose at about sixty degrees to a rocky top.

He noticed the old tracks of several vehicles on the other side of the town leading either to or from it. In the distance were grey-streaked hills, maybe mountains but nothing else.

As he trundled towards the town, he could see substantial holes in the desert floor at various points. Most of them had extracted dirt piled up alongside in various states of erosion. They were not usually very far from his route and after a while he stopped the pick-up and went to inspect one of them.

It wasn't deep, probably about five or six feet and about fifteen feet square. He could see no obvious reason for it; there were no pipes, no cables, no water, nothing. He returned to his pick-up.

He reached the town, a neglected hamlet really, about fifteen minutes later. His first impression was just as he'd thought earlier, a falling down ghost town. A relic of the old west no longer of any importance if it ever was. The dry and splintering wooden buildings didn't look safe. He drove to what he guessed was the centre of this 'one main street and a couple of side turnings' of a town.

He left the vehicle and stood behind it looking around. The two buildings still in half decent condition added to the abandoned film set ambience. One of them had the word 'sheriff' painted across it and the other the word 'saloon'. Mike laughed to himself at the absurdity, the surreality of it.

As he did so he noticed somebody watching him from the upper storey of the saloon. They darted out of sight when he looked up. *One of the ghosts*, he thought.

"I'm unarmed and intend no harm," he called out. "I'm just here to see the place – a rich lady told me I own it."

The figure reappeared at the glassless window. He could see it was a woman, mid-twenties dressed in a spaghetti western poncho which just emphasised the odd and unreal situation in which he found himself.

"I'll come down to you," she called back, shaking her head to realign her shoulder-length black hair. "I'm not unarmed so don't do anything crazy."

A little while later she walked out of the saloon's entrance. About five ten, not very robustly built, wearing jeans and souvenir shop style cowboy boots. Mike could see that under her poncho she carried a short single barrel shotgun. Her facial features were clearly native American but with some European input. He thought her quite pretty but also noted that her glance was hard and clearly assessing him as a target. Her light ochre complexion a little sun darkened and her teeth as white and cared for as any wealthy city dweller.

"Some advice," she said, "around here don't ever tell anybody you're unarmed."

Mike laughed. "I stand corrected. My name is Mike Key; I'm told I've inherited this land from somebody I'd never heard of and I'm just here to look at it."

"What's your last name, Mikey?"

Mike laughed again. "Key. My last name is Key. My first name is Michael, Mike. Mike Key."

The woman laughed as well. "OK, my mistake. Do you work for Catherine and Philip?"

"No, I'm sorry to tell you that they were killed and apparently I'm the only living relative and some very expensive and probably untrustworthy lawyers persuaded a court to give it to me."

She looked at him for a few seconds. "Aw, they were a spoilt sleazy pair of rich brats but they left us alone so I'm sorry they died. What happened?"

"Car crash was what I was told," said Mike.

"Call me Wolf."

"OK, Wolf. Is that your actual name, then? That's cool."

"No," she said. "My actual name is *Pia'isa*. That's the Shoshone word for wolf but you whiteys get tongue tied on it so call me Wolf."

"You remind me of a man I met a little while ago. An old scraggy-faced mysterious bastard called George. Couldn't talk straight to him either," commented Mike.

"That man happens to be my grandad," snapped Wolf, "so don't badmouth him."

"You called me whitey, think I'll say what I like," responded Mike.

For the first time Wolf stepped down from the wooden deck in front of the saloon. She walked to Mike but stopped about eight feet from him. Mike noticed the short barrelled shotgun moved to point to the floor but in a way that made it easy to bring to use.

Wolf gave him a friendly smile. "OK, touchy Mike, we are close to the point where I find out if I can trust you. Can I trust you?"

"I don't know, will it cost me any money?" said Mike lightly.

Wolf suddenly brought her shotgun from under her poncho and threw it to Mike. He'd already started moving to one side as it rose but reverted to his first position and caught it.

"Not bad," said Wolf. "Now we find out."

Mike broke the gun open and saw that it was loaded. He closed it again and looked at her quizzically. "Is that really a good way to find out if you can trust somebody? You only need to be wrong once."

He threw the gun back to her and she caught it deftly.

"There's only salt in the shell; it was a minimal risk. You move well, better than you look like you would. I guess you're about twelve, maybe fifteen, years younger than Grandad George. You don't look as fast as you are and there are some dark things in your eyes. George would never have let you find me if he thought you were dangerous to me; it was never much of a risk." She unloaded the gun and stuck it under one arm.

Mike smiled broadly. "Ha, the mysterious old bastard looked fitter than me. He's a shrewd one, I'll give him that. You're pretty astute yourself, for somebody so young. Actually you're simply pretty, had to say it."

Wolf grinned. "Careful, I can reload the gun with some real buckshot. We go loaded for objectifying old gits round here. Don't talk trash about my grandad and I won't racially profile you, British devil. Coffee?"

"Er, yeah. Great," responded Mike and followed her into the saloon.

Mike had expected her to go to the stairs but instead she marched straight to the rear of the building and out through the back door. She walked at quite a pace and Mike had to increase his step rate to stay with her.

They emerged from the alley at the back of the saloon and she turned right into one of the few side streets. On she marched until they reached the last building, a small house looking as decrepit as the rest of the town. Up some porch steps and through the unlocked front door they went. Wolf bounded up the staircase and Mike sped up to keep up. At the top was a robust wooden door. She took a key from her pocket, unlocked it and they entered.

The large room looked like a squat. A mattress and rolled sleeping bag in one corner, a nearby table with jars and tins next to a camping stove on which rested a small kettle. Next to the table was a large plastic water container about half full. To one side of the table was an old wooden chest. Mike looked out of the window across the expanse of desert.

"The rest room is in there," Wolf said, nodding towards a door within the room. She lit the camping stove and made coffee.

Before they sat on the floor to drink she removed her poncho. Mike saw that in the small of her back was a holster holding a small calibre short barrelled revolver.

"You people sure love your guns," said Mike lightly.

"If you had salted me the five shot would have underlined your error," she said only half lightly, "and me and Gramps George are the only two of my people you've met." She sat facing him on the floor.

"I meant Americans."

Wolf sipped her hot coffee. "I'm not sure if I'm American but the federal authorities say I am. My people are the Nehwe Shoshone, sons of the No'ipinKoi Shoshone."

"Will I need to learn all the tribes if I own this land?"

Wolf almost sneered at him. "Nobody owns this land. The Shoshone are a loose confederation of clans that together make a tribe. The dominance of what you call western culture restricts us to this land but we see ourselves as its occupants and guardians. You may own it in the eyes of the federal law but you don't really own it, nobody does. Land is just land and people live on it. It can't be owned any more than sunlight or wind can be owned. Does that make sense to you?"

Mike felt a growing respect for this strong yet vulnerable-looking girl. "Yes," he said. "It does make sense and I even like the idea. I don't think it'd work in court, though, does 'restricted' mean you can't leave the land?"

"No," she replied. "It means that we can only live as Shoshone on this land. If we move from it we live as Americans, pay more taxes and salute the flag and all that. You have a lot of questions but I suppose curiosity is good."

Mike gulped his now cooling coffee. "Jan Adams, the rich lady I mentioned, said I own this land. I want to know about the people on it so I can decide what to do, if anything. If it's reserved for your people I don't really see what I can do, anyway."

Wolf thought for a moment. "Adams is a bitch first class and if she's involved she has plans she'll look to rope you into. Well, you could screw us over massively and seek federal authority to gain possession. You'd probably get it as well, we don't really charge whooping at the stage coaches anymore."

Mike grinned at her. "Maybe I could just spend some time here and come to some conclusion. If you lend me the shotgun I could kill my own food. I'll stay in one of the many buildings this place has."

"Can't stop you; it's not a bad idea and will give us all a chance to consider the new position." She took his now empty mug. "You can stay here tonight. I have a spare sleeping bag you can use. You can sleep in that corner over there; I'll cook us both some beans and sausage for tonight. Don't get any ideas about me during the night – I'd shoot your balls off."

Mike laughed. "I believe you, I really do. I try to be one of the good guys."

"I believe you," said Wolf. "I'm good at assessing people and I'm not often wrong."

"Well yeah," said Mike, "but like the gun throwing thing, you only need to be wrong once. Tonight isn't it."

"Like the gun thing, I have a response plan. You won't see it because I know you're a good guy. Mind you, I suspect that's a bit of a struggle for you at times."

Mike slept reasonably well. Wolf had put down some blankets with a sleeping bag on top. It was a bit small for him but did the job. Big men get used to functioning in a world where everything's made for tiny folk.

A few hours into his night he floated into half wakefulness and heard some barely audible tapping. He didn't move, just searched with his eyes and saw that Wolf was texting away on her phone. He went back to sleep.

The dreams were muted this night. Just a few broken bodies and some starving souls staring through barbed wire fences. One of the wretches was his son.

He woke gently. As he regained consciousness he saw that there was a cup of hot coffee at his side. The inevitable vague anger that always accompanied each new day was this morning consigned to his mental background. It was always worse when he was alone on waking; the presence of Wolf in some way placated that demon.

"Thanks," he called out to Wolf, who was standing at the window on the other side of the room watching something or other.

"You welcome," she replied. "Who's John?"

"Wow, direct, aren't you?"

"Have to be. Who's John?" she repeated.

"My son. Who were you texting last night?" Mike felt he had to show he was just as direct as she.

"A gang of car thieves who specialise in snatching rental pick-ups from falling apart deserted towns." She beamed mischievously.

"Go away, I'm surprised you even get a signal," said Mike.

"George. I was just chatting to my grandad. There's half a dozen masts around this land."

"Is he here yet?" he asked.

Wolf took a sip from a cup she held. "And why would he be here?"

At that point there was a hard rapping at the door. Mike laughed.

Wolf opened the door and in walked George.

"Come on, you," he commanded Mike.

"However did I end up here?" complained Mike. "Why didn't we take my pick-up? This old jalopy was new some time in the sixties. Mine has got radio, air con, sat nav and everything else we didn't know we needed until we had it." They were in an old rusty red/grey farm truck crossing the desert and apparently heading towards the interstate.

George, tightly gripping the thin steering wheel of a waggon made back when power steering was just a rumour, spoke with a throaty rattle, "There are things you need. Have you got money?"

"Are you mugging me?"

George coughed his throat clear. "You own Gutusipe Daindi, then there are things you need and some things you need to know."

"Where? Is that the real name of this place, not the Ash Lands?" Mike was happy to finally get some information.

George cleared his throat and coughed. "Your great great great whatever great-grandfather or somebody, was called Sebastian Ash. He called this land Ash Hole. The local tribe, my tribe, called it Gutusipe Daindi. That means Ash confused, we don't really know that story. They were and are the proper occupants of this place."

"I have so many questions," said Mike. "Just one for now. Why would a beautiful young girl like Wolf invite a slightly overweight old git like me to sleep in her room within hours of meeting me?"

"Fat, not overweight," corrected George. "You are fat."

"Piss off, slightly overweight."

George laughed. "We knew you were coming. I'd already assessed you as safe and Wolf wanted to keep an eye on you."

"But Wolf was surprised when I told her the previous owners, the Ash siblings, were dead."

"Yeah," said George. "She can lie some, just one of her abilities that have to be respected."

"Oh my." Mike was almost laughing. "I wish I'd met her thirty years ago."

"In which case she'd be six years away from being born so you'd have to pursue her mother. That'd be my daughter so I'd have to cut your dick off," George laughed.

Mike laughed as well. "I hope I meet you daughter."

George looked sad. "She's dead."

Mike looked at him for a few moments and saw the look of pain in his face. "I'm sorry, I really am. My son, too," he said and just touched George on the arm for a moment.

"Wolf said you dream of him," said George. "That's good, in dreams we sometimes meet those we've lost."

Mike smiled and looked ahead. "I talk in my sleep, I guess," he said. They reached the interstate and George bounced onto it and drove sedately on in silence.

Mike didn't notice the name of the small town that they eventually reached. The street was American wide and George pulled nose first in front of a wide, glass-fronted store. 'Guns Guns Guns. Ammo', declared the sign across the front.

"I suspect they sell guns here," mumbled Mike.

"You need weapons," George explained.

Mike looked at him. "No, I don't. Don't like guns. Don't want guns. End of."

George looked back at him. "I respect that; it's refreshing in this insane world but here, in this place, in this land, best have something. You don't need to walk around waving military level hardware like some redneck porky momma's boy but you should have something. This is a land of armed people. Small intellects carrying big guns, don't be the target." George laughed at his own joke.

"Guns don't kill people, fat thick fucks with guns kill people," said Mike. "OK, when in Rome and all that. Don't expect me to be happy about it though. Anyway, I'm not American and have only been here a few days so I don't think I can buy anything. I don't know Nevada firearm laws."

"There aren't any, really. Concealed weapons need a permit and fully automatic guns not allowed, that's about it. Even the local grocery store lets you in wearing a gun. Not allowed in official buildings though. You supply the money; I'll sign for the goods," explained George. "I think you've got the balls to be armed and still behave."

Mike chuckled. "Yeah, well I have to behave cos Wolf said she'd shoot 'em off if I didn't."

George laughed out loud. "That's my girl," he roared as he punched Mike lightly on the arm.

The gun store itself resembled an eclectic armoury with racked rifles and wall-displayed handguns. There was a large sign declaring

'Sorry, folks, the mean federal government have banned bump stocks. Buy an AR15 military grade instead'.

"What's a bump stock?" Mike asked George.

"It's a natty little device that fits on the stock and uses the recoil to turn a semi-auto rifle into a slow full auto. Nice eh?" George grinned and Mike just made a 'for fuck sake' grimace.

The store owner was a fat, jolly, friendly chap. His pudgy hands seemed a little sweaty as Mike was introduced.

"Call me Ranger," he said. "Anything you want I can get; any friend of Chief George is always welcome here."

Mike smiled and nodded. "George says I need a gun, dunno why. I'm English – we don't really do guns so something not too big I suppose."

Ranger brought a small Glock from under the counter and slapped it on the top. "Easy to use and good for kids, girls and Englishmen," he joked.

Mike looked at him and then at the Glock. He picked it up and proved it, ejected the mag and pulled the slide to check the breech. Then he stripped it down and placed the major components on the counter, just the grip with slide runner alongside the barrel and spring and slide body, then he deftly reassembled it. "Don't like semi, too many moving parts and too macho. Got a model ten?"

"Mac ten?" said Ranger in an amazed tone.

"No, Smith and Wesson. Two-inch barrel and twenty rounds please."

George was looking at him half amused and half astounded. Ranger opened his inventory book and leafed through it.

The store didn't stock many traditional revolvers and only had one model ten but with a four-inch barrel. Unlike the five round snub nose it was a full six shooter.

Mike took that with a holster fitted to a shoulder harness that allowed the gun to rest covered by the arm and hanging low down the rib cage. Small leather loops on the harness could hold additional bullets. He had to buy a box of fifty rounds because it was the minimum available. He also bought a three-inch blade push knife in a sheath designed to be worn on the back of the belt.

He undid his belt and fitted it on in the shop. It all cost him just over a thousand dollars and he paid Ranger, shook hands again and they left the store.

George suggested they grab a quick drink in a nearby bar. They put the revolver and ammo under the truck's seat, along with a couple of boxes of ammo that George had bought, and headed to the drinking hole.

The place was dark but not oppressively so and almost empty. A young couple sat talking quietly in a side booth and an older man sat at the bar drinking alone. The barman greeted George by name and poured him a beer. Mike also asked for a beer and they moved off to sit at a table not far from the door.

"Just say it," said a smiling Mike.

George said, "OK. Where'd you learn to strip a gun like that and why do you like the model ten and why do you wear a nasty little stabber at your back?"

"A long story," Mike responded. Mike spent a while explaining that in an earlier life he'd been a police officer in London. In the middle of his career he'd been seconded to an international police unit under the aegis of the United Nations. This team was to work alongside the UN military in Bosnia.

The brief was to identify and evidence war crimes and suspects. If it was possible to detain any criminal without major conflict then they were to do so, but the primary role was to prepare cases for presentation to The Hague.

He'd been trained by the military in weapons and personal self-defence. He was then armed with a model ten and he became comfortable with the firearm.

The concealed bladed weapon at his back became a habit. Although his preference was for impact weapons, he felt that if he needed a gun, he still wasn't convinced, he best back it up with a nastier fallback weapon than a simple basher.

George wanted Mike to go to a nearby phone shop and buy a mobile, cell phone in local parlance. Mike declined. He said he didn't need one here and didn't much like them anyway. He mainly didn't carry one even back in England.

"OK then, let's go back now," said George.

"Not before I grab a burger for the journey."

Chapter Six

They'd left the road and were rolling over the desert towards Gutusipe Daindi, a few miles from the fork in the tracks. The vehicle now smelled faintly of old cheese burgers which caused George to whinge about it every fifteen minutes or so.

Unlike the journey out, this time they chatted. George revealed that his Shoshone name was *Dai'gwahni*, which means Boss Chief; he was the effective head of this clan and also the chief of the tribal police in this area. He also mentioned that most members of his clan now had American names and the traditional Shoshone names were being lost.

Mike told him how John had died and how in his head he had mixed it up with some of the things he'd seen in Bosnia. "Lots of murder and ethnic cleansing, that's what they called it but in reality it was just toxic male dominance, tough guy narcissistic rage. We ended up chasing one specific band, a gang of opportunist criminals led by a psycho. We and the soldiers with us had a couple of firefights with them but their leader got away. I saw what he did and I'd kill him on sight even now if I thought I'd get away with it."

"The dreams?" asked George.

"Just dreams, nothing more. Memories that like to remind me

that David Milenkovic escaped and so I failed." Mike pronounced the name 'My Lonko Vitch'.

George brought the truck to a sharp halt which pitched them both forwards. "Say his name again."

Mike did so. "A wicked fucker and a waste of human skin. He killed; he raped; he dominated with his manly murder and cruelty. He also had political protection and was able to disappear."

George told him that his daughter had been called Sitsienhawi which was a shortened version of a Mohawk name. She'd been named after the joint founder of this clan and land, the other being Mike's ancestor, Sebastian. "We, you, are the Nehwe Shoshone, part of the No'ipinKoi Shoshone. Actually we're just about all that's left of the No'ipinKoi, everything considered."

"I'm sorry that you lost her," said Mike. "We both know that pain and just how unbearable it is."

George went quiet. He looked out of the side window for a while. When he turned back to Mike there was a previously unseen hardness in his eyes.

"I'm a friend. Talk if you need to. Start a fight if you need to. Let it out and it'll just be between you and me," Mike spoke gently.

"Sitsienhawi was raped." Tears welled up in George's eyes. "The result was Pia'isa. Wolf is the child of violent rape. Nonetheless she was loved by us all. When she was twelve the rapist returned to take her. Sitsienhawi defended the child and she was killed, strangled. It's not a quick thing, to strangle someone, you have to mean it. I tried to hunt him but he was off of this land and I couldn't get close. The scum's people return from time to time, well armed and part of his own small army. Me and Wolf plan to kill him next time he comes here in person. There's a young Shoshone called Greg, stupid fucking name for one of us, he wants to help but I don't think he's up to it. He's just got the hots for Wolf, that's all."

Mike said nothing. There is nothing that can be said to that. They just sat there for what seemed a long time, then he opened the door and got out. He took the revolver from under the seat, loaded it and placed it in the holster and then put on the harness. He got back in and sat silently.

"Would you like to meet the clan? It's your clan too," said George.

Mike nodded and George drove forward, the old truck belching smoke for a few seconds. As they reached the fork in the track, George veered to the left away from Gutusipe Daindi town and along the route he'd previously taken on foot. Along the way were a couple of the pits like those Mike had seen on his first journey.

"Let me show you something," said George as he brought the truck to a stop alongside one of them. They both got out of the vehicle and walked to the edge of a pit.

This one was about five feet deep. George put one hand to the edge and hopped deftly down. Mike followed him into the dry, dusty hole.

George kicked at the floor for a few seconds. When satisfied he'd found a good spot he produced a large Ka-Bar knife from inside his shirt and bent to dig. After a while he arose holding a silver chunk about the size of a golf ball.

"*Aishi-waahni*," declared George triumphantly. "Fox-colour metal, the land for about sixty miles around this spot is full of it. Chunks everywhere, some of them bigger than this." He handed it to Mike.

Mike looked at it for a moment. "Silver?" he asked.

"Yep," George replied. "Pure, unusual to find it in this form. There's probably tons and tons of it in total. I have no idea how deep it goes but I've been down the deepest pit at about twenty feet and it's still easy to find."

"You mine this?" was Mike's question.

"No, not on a commercial level." George gestured to show that Mike should keep the piece he'd just found. "We dig some up and sell it carefully and surreptitiously to jewellers in several towns. We make enough to fund most of what we need."

They clambered out of the pit and dusted themselves down. Mike coughed to clear his throat, went to the truck and drank from a plastic bottle. "Dusty down there," he said. "I saw a few of these pits on the way to the old town. Did your people dig them as well?"

"They're your people, too," George corrected him. "We all share blood from the first Ash or from the Shoshone already here. No, we didn't dig those pits. A small but dangerous little team come here every so often and steal some. I've made enquiries in my role of clan policeman and I suspect that your lawyer lady is involved with them. They are led by a man I want to kill. He raped and murdered my daughter. I want your help."

Mike looked at the floor for a while. Then he looked around him before finally looking at George. "Yeah, OK. I'm not as young as I was but I'm not helpless either. I'll do what I can to help detain him and them but I'm not really happy with murder, in spite of what I said earlier. I understand your position though."

"Not murder, I'm the tribal law here. I'm only allowed to police the clan but I can detain outsiders if they commit crimes here and if they resist I can use force. They will resist."

They got back into the truck. "You do need to lose a bit of weight, though," said George with a short laugh.

"I'm not fat," Mike laughed back. "A bit overweight, granted. Not fat."

"You've got small moobs, man," George laughed some more.

"Pectoral muscles, pecs, OK?" snapped Mike light-heartedly.

"Fat. Start exercising and eat fewer burgers."

Mike snorted, took out his vaping pipe and puffed on it as they drove on.

George explained that they were about twenty minutes away from the main clan settlement. As they reached the top of a ridge he pointed out a flat plain about thirty miles away. "That's where they tested the bombs, great big ones measured in megatons. Big old bang and mushroom cloud."

"Where did they move you to when they did it?" asked Mike.

George laughed ruefully. "They didn't. We're the defeated people or, more correctly, now they say the preserved indigenous people, the first nations. Just words. We're still the conquered people. Slowly they dispose of us with subtle assimilation and respectful words. They don't charge over and massacre us anymore. They just let us fade away. You'll see."

"Radioactivity?" Mike blurted with concern.

"Mostly gone now, very low level. Nothing for you to worry about." George moved the drive lever down to the lower gears as they descended a steep gradient.

They reached the settlement. It consisted of well-spaced mobile homes and campers, or RVs as George called them. Not much looked new and most vehicles and buildings had a patched-up make-do-and-mend appearance. Lots of grey bodywork filler patches.

There were a few people walking about. Some kids chasing each other about on bikes and a few dogs rushing around with a noisy random urgency. Many of the homes had satellite dishes and some had washing drying on lines.

Mike could see just one power line into the place – it snaked across the desert on poles and went underground at the edge of town. There was nothing that could be fairly called a road and George weaved around arbitrary fence lines, avoided bins and rubbish piles and seemed to just invent his route through this disorganised and curiously unruly but not chaotic township.

He stopped outside the only seemingly permanent structure, a large single-story wooden building on a square footprint of at least a hundred feet each side. The wood looked sound but too dry and was coated in peeling white paint.

"Come and meet Mama," said George.

Mike expected Mama to be older than she was. In reality she was round about his age but looked a little younger. She came to greet them when they entered the building and stepped into a sizeable front reception area devoid of furniture apart from an old, poor-condition wooden desk.

She was a little taller than George with sun-darkened skin and long plaited hair woven with multicoloured beads. Mike thought her handsome with a broad smile that spoke friendliness as it spread to her eyes and facial features. She hugged George and shook Mike's hand when he was introduced.

"How're things?" George asked.

"Just about manageable," said Mama, revealing a soft and confident voice. "Hospital almost full but getting better. Stores a bit depleted but not dangerously so. Armoury's a bit disorganised but everything's in good condition."

"I'm giving Mike here the tour. OK if we just wander about?" George asked her.

Mama scrutinised Mike then turned to George. "Don't go into any of the hospital rooms but as for everything else, well you're in charge, aren't you?"

"So the council says," said George.

Mama looked Mike up and down again. "Who is he, George?"

"He's an Ash, a real one. Law says he's the new owner. He's gonna help with the killer when he gets here."

Mama looked even harder at Mike. "He's got a demon or two, they're in his eyes. He's comfortable with his weapons. Don't think he'll start a crazy war but think he'll do his best to right things. Who you killed, Mike?"

"Don't, Mama," George started but she waved him quiet.

Mike throat coughed. "Are you the mystic or the doctor?" he smiled.

Her smile back was positively inviting. Mike thought it horny but sought to maintain his composure. She smiled wider as if reading his thoughts.

"Neither," she said. "No doctors here, can't afford any. I have medical training; I used to be a paramedic firefighter in the Las Vegas area and now I do this. Not mystic, just know people. I'm giving you a provisional vote of OK; don't be put off if we are a direct and no bull people. We just don't have room for BS and we've been crapped on often enough to assess threats quickly. Who you killed?"

Mike looked back at her considering whether to answer her or tell her to mind her own. "Don't really know," he eventually said. "Maybe nobody, maybe somebody. I've been in a couple of fire exchanges though most of the fighting was done by soldiers who were with us. I fired a few rounds in anger but have no idea if I hit anybody. It was a long time ago in a different world. I hope nobody died but if they did it was the right thing at the time. It's past and gone and just a memory now."

Mama went up to him and unexpectedly hugged him. "He's a good guy with bad bits," she said to George. She put one hand to Mike's cheek and then left.

George laughed at Mike. "Not very inscrutable, Mike. You're one privileged new boy, Mama's never wrong about people and if she takes an instant liking to you, well I haven't seen that very often. Let's dampen down the embarrassing sexual chemistry and show you round."

The walk through the corridors of the hospital section was quick. There was a ward with a sign 'COVID PPE OBLIGATORY'. This sign was crossed out and replaced with the word 'VULNERABLE' in thick red marker.

Opposite it was a ward with a sign that said 'LEGACY' and further down the corridor another marked 'CLINIC'. Mike could hear staff moving about but didn't see any.

He was shown the armoury, about twelve old M16 assault rifles apparently in good condition, a few shotguns of various types and several boxes of ammunition and spare rifle magazines.

George showed Mike the small police office, with one miniscule and not very robust-looking detention cell. Beyond that was a hall which took up most of the rest of the buildings.

"This is for tribal council and public meetings," explained George.

"I thought you were chief, or boss or local cop or whatever."

"Yeah, I am. It's not a strict hierarchical system. Decisions are through councils and collective views. My position earns me respect and a voice but I can't dictate."

"That's not a bad thing," Mike commented.

The last smallish part of the tour was a storeroom containing a substantial number of tinned goods and a few bottles of wine. Five or six shelves were empty.

"I have a few questions," said Mike.

"Later. You have dinner with Mama later, ask her. I'm off soon because I have some checks to make on the town and area, just everyday routine work," George told him.

"Hmm. I'm not sure I want to be forced into a schedule by others. Still, I like you all so OK then," Mike replied.

Mama lived in a large mobile home, or trailer in the local jargon, close to the rear of the main and only permanent building the settlement could boast. Mike learned that her real name was *Mambi* which means bobcat. He also learned that she was an exceptional cook.

"That was great, thank you," he said as he pushed the now empty bowl of stew further into the table. They sat under an awning outside Mama's home; the evening was hot and windless.

"Can I ask you a serious question and get a serious answer?" she asked him.

"I'll try," he told her. "On condition I can ask you a few as well."

Mama looked at him compassionately. "Who did you kill?"

"Wow, you are tenacious," he said. "You think I lied to you earlier?"

"No," she kind of purred. "I think you protected your mind; I think you don't want to think about it. George told me your history. Please tell me."

Mike looked down, looked across the table, looked at the sky. He rubbed his face with both hands and then looked directly at her.

"Bosnia. A couple of us were being transported by a military unit to another location to collate and collect evidence of various crimes. It was a burned house, dead children and a dead raped mother. It was the work of criminals pretending to be soldiers and we went after them. They ambushed us – you may not be aware but ambushing a dozen Royal Marines is often a miscalculation and the baddies were soon on the run. Me and the other police officer embedded in this unit, a French woman I think, went after a straggler each. I caught mine, a boy really, about eighteen. I had him on his knees and was making him turn out his pack. Amongst his stuff was a rag doll with blood stains on it and some frilly knickers. In one of his pockets was a Polaroid snap of a woman being raped. I plead temporary insanity. I was mid-twenties and idealistically immature. I really believed that violence could solve problems as long as the good guys won. I shot him in the back of his head and put another two into his heart area to ensure he was dead. I told nobody when I rejoined the group. The French cop said her man escaped but I noticed she had no ammunition left. I'm ashamed but I live with it. You are the only person who knows."

Mama nodded. She stood and collected the crockery. "I understand. Thank you for trusting me enough to tell me. I will never mention this to anyone, nor must you. The mistakes we make mould us as much as the things we get right. It will serve no purpose to dwell on it or redress it. It is done and is best left in the past. It was not the murder of an innocent."

"Thanks. I'm OK with it but wouldn't do it again. Now, where is that bugger George so I can get back to the old town?"

Mama smiled. "He's not here and won't be for a few days. Tonight you can sleep on a mattress in the hall and in the morning I'll show you how to get back to Gutusipe Daindi. Don't fire on any strange noises or movements in the night, you have only friends here."

She showed him to the hall, handed him a water bottle and pointed out the toilets. A sleeping bag had been set up on a foam sleeping mat. Before she left she hugged him again and gave him a small quick kiss on his cheek near the ear.

He spent a few moments awake after he bedded down. *Am I nuts?* he thought to himself. *Why the hell am I telling these things to strangers? What's wrong with me?* After that he slept well and his exhaustion worked to prevent any dreams, or any he remembered anyway. It was early light when he woke and unusually he felt no morning anger that needed to be quelled.

He dressed and washed his face and other waking ablutions. When he walked out of the building he saw that Mama sat at the outside table on which was a huge cooked breakfast.

"We call that a full English," he called as he walked to her grinning.

"We call it sausage, bacon, egg, beans and fried sliced potatoes," she called back good-humouredly. "I had Greg get me some proper tea; you're English and apparently you are all addicted. He'll be over later and you can meet him."

"George says he has the hots for Wolf," Mike told her.

"Yeah, he does. She's kind to him but he won't be getting inside those pantyhose," she laughed. Then she looked more serious. "Wolf has some daddy issues she's going to sort out. I'm hoping somebody, maybe a friend with issues of their own from violent mistakes, might find a way to persuade her not to take on that burden. I love Wolf; I don't want her to suffer forever just because of her bastard of a father. His people killed a boy with his feudal work practices, worked him to death then just left him in a pit." She spat on the floor. "He sends teams for the silver and pays us to dig some. He won't find any workers next visit. George and Wolf plan a family reunion."

"I'll see what I can do, if I can do anything," said Mike. "She's very strong-willed but I'll try to talk to her. You should have been an interrogator; I can't believe I told you things. I guess you've already tried talking down Wolf, yeah of course you have or you wouldn't be asking me. You did so well that I forgot to ask questions I've got."

"Fire away," she said.

"Poor humour," smiled Mike. "Why haven't George and Wolf hit him before now?"

"This time will be the first time he's been on this land in person since he murdered Sitsienhawi. He normally works through some rich lawyer, you know the type. She told George that Mentos, that's the bastard's adopted street name, was on his way here. His real name's David."

"I know the lawyer, she's not exactly on anybody's side and can't be trusted but I suspect she'll work with whoever can make money for her." Mike tucked into the full English with gusto.

Mama poured him a tea. "Other questions?"

"Before now, why work for him at all?"

Mama sighed. "We need the money and dealing with the lawyer lady at least kept open the possibility he might visit. The boy who died was worked by a foreman of his not him in person."

"What's wrong with your people, why the hospital and why is this community so subdued?" Mike looked straight at her but then slurped his tea which spoiled the earnest gravity he sought to give it.

Mama laughed at his failed macho moment.

"I mean it," Mike said through his food. "This place should be more vibrant than it is."

"Here's Greg," Mama informed him. Greg was about mid-twenties, roughly six feet tall, slim and muscular but soft-looking. The muscle of the gym rather than the hard sleekness of real strength. His eyes had a direct stare but appeared tantrum-prone rather than dangerous. He wore jeans, boots, a waistcoat on an otherwise bare torso and had a tatty bandana around his head. He wore a large knife sheathed on his belt.

"Why you armed?" demanded Greg.

"Greg, stop—" started Mama.

"It's OK," said Mike. "I recently bought my weapons. I can't just leave them lying around so at the moment I'm wearing them just to ensure that there are no accidents."

"You harm Pia'isa and we have a problem, OK?" Greg stared at him.

Threats, especially angry threats, are meaningless and are rarely issued by anybody liable to do something. Mike just nodded at him and Greg turned and walked away.

"I'm sorry," said Mama, touching his arm.

"It's OK. He doesn't mean it. He just wants to show his deep and abiding obsessive focus on Wolf." Mike smiled. "I'll let her know that her rescuing warrior had her back."

Mama laughed. "If Mentos arrives and it gets bad, try to keep him out of it if you can. He'll try, he's no coward but, well that is, he's bloody incompetent in that sort of thing. He's got the soul of a poet trapped in the body of a warrior and the experience of a ten-year-old. It'd be nice if he didn't get killed."

Mike nodded and mumbled, "OK."

"You need to walk back to town. It's about four miles along the ridge offshoot and then double back around it. George won't be back 'til later, he's off for hospital checks today. The town and this place are just separated by the line of hills here and it's not far."

"Why does he need medical checks? I need to know cos if things go bad I need to know his risks," asked Mike.

"Just standard checks for leukaemia, diabetes, age problems and other effects of genetic damage. We all have them," said Mama.

"H bomb?" asked Mike.

"And that," Mama replied a little cryptically. "They check us but if treatment is needed we have to pay. Nobody will insure us. We really need that silver."

"Radioactivity caused diabetes?" puzzled Mike.

"Not really. That's just poor diet, a predisposition anyway and limited gene pool. The government's not murdering us; they're just letting us fade away." She drew him a small route map and pointed out the direction. "Since you don't have a cell phone, if you disappear we'll look for your body next week." She kept a straight face for a few seconds and then laughed at him.

Mike also laughed. "I'll be OK. I'll take a bottle of water, if that's OK. Animals?"

"Bear, bobcats, mountain lion, rarely some wild horses, rattle snakes, scorpions and mice," Mama warned him. In response to his concerned look she continued, "Bear hardly ever come into the desert. The big cats will make off but try not to startle them if you see any; they don't hunt people cos we hunt them. The snakes are normally in rocks but also avoid us if they can, same the creepy crawlies. Funny thing is, the mice are the most dangerous. They can bite resting bodies and pass on a bacterial infection. I can't remember the last time anybody was injured by the other animals but we have about three or more people a year need antibiotics for mice bite."

Mike chuckled. "OK. Come look for my body in a few days."

"Already been looking at it," Mama looked at him cheekily. She hugged him and kissed him on the cheek again. "Here, take this dumb hat, sun and wind can burn you up out there." She handed him a tatty wide-brimmed straw hat.

Mike kissed her cheek as well this time. "You must like overweight guys," he joked and put the stupid hat on his head.

"Fat," said Mama, "and you look like some lost hick hillbilly in that hat."

"Not you as well. Not fat, just heavy. Not fat. And it's your fault the hat's daft."

They both smiled and laughed as he walked away.

Chapter Seven

Mentos drove one of the vans himself and on his own; he always liked to drive himself because it made him feel safer. He also preferred to be alone when working with this collection of unreliable criminals. He was only really content when teamed with his own men.

He led the convoy onto a farm just over the California-Arizona border. The lead and rear cars drove off, they'd only been paid to come this far to act as decoys if there were any police interest in the line of vehicles. There hadn't been so the men in the cars had made some easy cash.

He led the remaining vehicles about a mile along a dirt track where a tall overweight white man waited. The guy waved as they approached. He wore a large Stetson, bootlace bolo tie against a white shirt; a ridiculously large belt buckle with a horse's head shape held his blue jeans, and on his feet were large, overstylised patterned leather cowboy boots. He wore a silver, long-barrelled revolver on his right hip.

Mentos smiled at the absurd sight. He knew that in this country, this state, a particular breed of tough-talking, gun rights-professing, wealthy, dim idiot ruled. Part of him admired their determined monoculturalism. He'd met this man a couple of times and knew him as Cowboss Kes. He had no idea if that was his real name.

"Mentos, my friend, how the journey?" Cowboss Kes greeted him as he exited the van.

Mentos shook his hand. "Good, easy, hot."

Cowboss Kes gave a loud laugh. "Workforce?"

"It's good. Usual conditions. Usual fee. You arrange for their return to Mexico when done. Or whatever, they are your people to do with what you will."

His crew were unloading the eighteen-wheeler. About forty people in total, including children, whole families, emerged. The crew herded them into a nearby barn where other men from the convoy handed out food and water.

Mentos noticed a woman of about forty leading a girl of about sixteen. He called them over. He pulled the worried-looking girl to him and held his arm around her.

"Hello, Mother," he said to the woman. "Maybe we come to a deal. What might money and a ride to any part of the States be worth to you both?"

"Whoa there, partner," called Cowboss Kes in a loud, affable tone. "That's a recipe for trouble from the Man. The feds will react if we go too far. We need to be low key to keep their eyes closed."

Mentos laughed. He kissed the girl on the head and pushed her back to the woman. As they scuttled back to the group he turned to Cowboss Kes and said in a quiet and gentle voice, "Fuck this country and your soft shit ways. Women and booze?"

Cowboss Kes looked relieved. "Down at the lower field house. Whores and as much as you can drink. All part of the deal, I've put in a hot tub and a couple of billiard tables as well. Have fun. See you next time."

With that, Cowboss Kes walked away to brief his new workforce and explain the fieldwork he needed from them, the promise of food and shelter and an undertaking nobody would be harmed. He also explained that the work would pay off the debt they owed for being brought to the States and afterwards they'd be free to take their chances as illegal aliens. He'd have them taken and dropped off in a large town and then they were on their own.

Mentos led his crew to the house at the lower field, which was a huge, rambling two-storey stone house about a hundred or more years old.

Inside it was a roadhouse biker bar type of place. There were tables filled with food and alcohol, pool tables to play on and a small table in the corner for cannabis, cocaine and other pills that Mentos didn't even recognise. Cowboss Kes was obviously keen to please his labour suppliers.

In addition, there were the girls. All age ranges and styles from worn out street hooker to fresh, young but not so innocent.

"Take your pick, lads, rooms upstairs. No charge but gifts always welcome," declared an older, ragged, overly made-up hag who appeared to be the whore supervisor.

Mentos grabbed a beer, snatched a young, unwell-looking girl and retired to the upper floor.

He reappeared about forty-five minutes later. The crew was well on the way to overall stoned rowdiness by then.

"OK, guys, thanks for your work; I'm off – I'll phone if I need you again. Enjoy your money."

It elicited a few half-hearted farewells but mainly it was ignored. The hag came over to him.

"She's OK," he said to her. "Here's a grand, share it with her – she won't be working for a few days."

With that, he left the building and headed to the van. He drove the van to a barn about half a mile away where he changed to a large pick-up. He let it warm for a few minutes and then drove slowly away towards the track leading out of the farm.

The hag went to the room he had used. There she found the girl naked, weeping and curled on the bed. Her face was a little bruised with teeth marks on her cheek. Her clothes were torn and piled on the floor. A small trickle of blood ran down her inner legs. Deep scratch marks scarred her back and her eyes had the look of a frightened cat.

Chapter Eight

Mama Mambi's little map was impressively detailed for a few minutes' work. The settlement was one side of a short ridge of steep rocky hills, the town the other side. This range a little higher and set at a tangent to the one he'd driven up. A walk along the base of about three miles reached the end of it. Then by simply walking around the ridge effecting a one eighty, the old town was about two miles back along the other side of the topographic obstruction.

The map indicated outcrops, dead-end gullies and the location of a phone mast towards the end of the range. That explained the phone signals this far from a built-up area and created a landmark for anybody further out in the desert.

Mike followed the directions through the settlement, which was useful given the randomly placed, thrown down nature of the dwellings. He noticed several people, some watching TV or gaming on consoles. At least one young man was stretched out on a threadbare sofa drinking beer. He saw no sign of any industry but in one RV he saw a young girl of about sixteen clearly studying with a couple of open books and deeply attentive to the PC screen in front of her.

Skinny dogs and scruffy cats seemed to wander the place as if looking for something they couldn't remember. The only colours anywhere were the faded primary hues on the RVs and homes and the overall impression was grey indifference, punctuated by rusted silver touch-up paint on many vehicles. There was something missing but he couldn't quite place what.

As he left the settlement and began his stroll along the bare wilderness, he puffed contentedly on his vaping pipe. After about half a mile, he saw somebody waiting for him about another quarter mile further on. As he approached, he saw from the insolent way the person lounged against the rocks that it was Greg.

"Hello again, Greg," Mike called when he was within distance. "We don't have a problem, you know. I'm no threat to Wolf, you or your people."

Greg was dressed as before but now wore a dirty and greasy grey Stetson. "You say," he replied, "I'm here to make sure you don't get lost or steal anything."

Mike laughed. "What? Just what am I going to steal? Thought maybe I'd jack a couple of cacti just to impoverish you."

"Don't get smart," Greg instructed him.

Mike stopped as he reached him, discreetly checking him visually for weapons other than the knife and keeping a reactionary gap between them.

"If I was smart I wouldn't be walking around this God forsaken land and getting into a conflict that isn't really mine," he said. He kept his hands clasped to his front to indicate zero threat.

The boy brushed some desert dust from his trousers. "I'm not here to attack you. I don't mean to be your enemy so maybe if we walk together we can gauge each other better."

"I'm hoping to see this thing through without violence, Greg." Mike wiped his sweaty face as he spoke. "I can make it on my own but still happy to walk with you. I'm going to try to persuade you not to get involved in any hassle with Mentos."

Greg thought for a moment. "I know I'm not a tough guy and I know that evil bastard is. I'm not going to take him on. I'm hoping that you and Dai'gwahni, George, can. I just want to get Pia'isa out of it."

Mike went closer to him. "We're on the same page, lad," he said. "I suspect that Wolf might be the toughest of us all but she's got no idea what it does to your head if you do bad things, whatever the reason. I'm with you on getting her away."

As they walked on to the mast end of the ridge and swung around it towards the town, the conversation grew in civility and turned into simple small talk.

"Covid really knocked us down," said Greg at one point. "It took out so many of our old people and sick youngsters; it felt like the world was ending."

Maybe that was it, thought Mike. It was the old people and the not fully fit that were missing in the settlement. That pigging virus culled these people. They are mistreated by being ignored and provided with a lip service welfare. Still, Mike felt that wasn't all of it. The place was subdued, almost close to submission. It just didn't feel right. Mike had seen places like that in Bosnia; it was a subtle though palpable ground down feel.

Gutusipe Daindi old town hove within view. Almost a distant mirage, a shimmering disturbance closer than the horizon. In reality about a mile or a bit more.

"I need to just stop for a bit," said Greg.

"No problem." Mike offered his water bottle which was eagerly accepted.

"I didn't eat before we left, my mistake. I'll be OK in a minute." Greg sat on a large rock and guzzled.

Mike took the opportunity to puff some more and look around the desert. He could see some old vehicle tracks about five or six hundred yards out and heading towards town. He remembered seeing them from the ridge when he first drove here. He tried to follow them to the origin by eye but they just dissolved into the vast landscape.

Greg didn't really improve. He was shaking gently and his speech was a bit slurred. His eyes seemed a little unfocused but he was still fully conscious and lucid if a tad slow in conversation.

Mike retrieved his water bottle. "I think you've burnt out your sugar, matey," he said. "Can't say I'm entirely happy about this but do you have piggyback in this country?"

That was how Mike walked into town with Greg on his back, the boy's legs resting through Mike's arms. They pootled to the main street where Mike could see his pick-up parked where he left it.

As he sat Greg on the bonnet, called a hood around here, he heard Wolf's laughing voice from the upper floor of the saloon.

"Jesus, Mike, don't let him turn you into his horse. Thought you had more sense than that." She left the upper window and soon reappeared at the entrance doors.

"He's not quite well," Mike explained. "I think it's low sugar or something; he didn't eat before we walked. I thought your people lived as one with this land, really not impressed."

Wolf smiled at him. "Yeah, it is a sugar thing. He just needs to eat; I'll take him and feed him. Back in a while." With that, she pulled Greg from the hood and led him staggering unevenly back into the salon, out of the back and off towards her room.

"Hey," Mike called to her retreating form, "are you on watch or something, why you at the same window?"

"You know I am. You know why," she called back without breaking pace.

Mike ran his finger along the pick-up's bodywork and found it smeared with a thin layer of yellowish sandy dust. He unlocked the vehicle and climbed in, leaving the door open as he swigged at the water.

He heard the distant engine way out in the desert. A powerful yet not heavy soft roaring. At a guess it would take a few minutes to reach him if it was coming here. Mike tried the pick-up's engine and was gratified that it started easily. He drove it to the rear of the saloon then shut it down. He went into the building by the rear door and walked to the entrance to watch out from the shadows.

A couple of minutes later a large motorbike came slowly along the main street and stopped short of the saloon. The driver was looking at the tracks left by Mike's vehicle but didn't follow them. He was a middle-aged man, probably mixed race or tanned white. He was appropriately dressed for the bike and the heat with open-face helmet, eye-protecting glasses, thin gloves, boots with lightweight protective trousers and tartan shirt.

Mike watched him curiously. Maybe just a tourist biker taking a small off-road adventure into the ghost town. Maybe not. Mike saw the rider check the upper windows of the buildings and then the ground-floor windows.

That's interesting, thought Mike. Mostly, lookout-type observers will seek a higher elevation like an upstairs window. People don't normally look up and that helps conceal the watcher. People who check out the higher places have usually been trained to do so. This guy had some experience, he decided as he drew further back into the dark interior.

"Hello," the rider called out, the accent a curious cross between Eastern European and Italian. "I'm just having a look, I'm not doing anything. Sorry to bother you." The bike turned and sedately left the way it arrived. Mike heard it speed up as it left town.

"He's no innocent," said Wolf behind him.

Mike turned, stepped sideways in a partial crouch and his hand went to his push knife. All this in one quick smooth movement before he had control of himself again. "Holy shit," he complained. "Will your family please stop ambushing me; my heart can't take it."

Wolf laughed at him. "Greg's OK. He's stuffing his face with my famous desert lizard pie. He'll be along soon."

Mike returned her amused laugh. "No, that guy was no innocent. He had some experience as well from the way he looked and reacted. He was a recon of the town. Somebody's coming."

"Yep," said Wolf, suddenly looking serious. "Let me show you your home. Our guests will be a couple of days yet."

She led him out the front door of the saloon and down towards the sheriff's office. The entrance to this building had a thin wooden door with several small opaque glass panes, a couple of which were smashed.

Mike observed that the glass breaking was not recent since there was no debris on the floor and the exposed frame wood was weathered.

The place was really just a large room with a half partition onto the jail area which contained two open metal-bar cells side by side, both facing the main room area.

Wolf led him into the left most cell and clanged the cell gate closed behind them. The hinges did not squeak and moved easily and the door locked with an unmistakeable clunk.

"Was that smart?" asked Mike. "Are we trapped in here now?"

Wolf went to the cage door and pressed what looked like a small protruding screw on the inside of the locking mechanism. There was a sound like a spring releasing and the door opened just a few inches.

"No," she told him, pulling the door closed again. She said nothing more and Mike gathered she was a little offended by his suggestion she'd do something that stupid.

In the far corner, obscured by the toilet privacy screen, she showed him a heavy wooden steel-covered door the same brick colour as the walls. This she unlocked with a key that she then handed to him.

Behind the door was a narrow staircase winding back on itself to the upper floor. Wolf led the way and Mike found himself watching her backside as she walked ahead and a little above him as they ascended.

"Eyes down," she said without sounding annoyed.

"Sorry, just trying to not fall up a step," he said. "Anyway, you psychic? How'd you know I was off-message for a second?"

She laughed as they reached the top. "I know guys," she said. "I know you a bit as well."

The room was large and clean. It gave access to upper windows front and rear and had a small shower and toilet area through a wooden door at one end. There was one small table on which rested a camping stove and a few tins of sausage and beans alongside some cutlery and crockery. On the floor next to the table was a two gallon clear plastic bottle filled with water.

"This place and my place are the two secure spots in this town." Wolf opened a cupboard in the front wall and pulled out a thin mattress and a sleeping bag. "The heavy door downstairs has strong bolts you can close when you're in here, the lock's not very strong." She reached into her poncho and pulled out a small jar of coffee and a half bottle of whiskey that she put on the table. "No milk, I'm afraid. There is running water but it's very slow to fill the tank. Enough for a toilet flush and a couple of minutes' cold shower every twelve hours. Don't drink it – it comes through a very small pipe from an old rusty rain collector about half a mile away. It doesn't rain very often so might run out completely. Collect potable water from Mama or George."

"Potable?" smiled Mike. He was thinking that most people would have said 'drinkable'. "Stay for a drink?"

Wolf opened the whiskey, poured out two large drinks into mugs and sat on the floor. Mike sat down facing her.

"Where'd you go to school?" Mike asked.

"MIT, civil engineering," she said. "You don't have to look so openly surprised. George spent a lot of money sending me to an expensive private high school and then on to college. He hopes I'll turn the silver into a decent business for the people."

"Will you?"

"Well, in federal and state law it belongs to you, doesn't it?"

"Don't worry about me." Mike gulped some of the whiskey. "Don't get me wrong, I'm not Mr Altruism and I'd expect to make a few bob, I mean quid, er dollars, bucks, whatever. Point is I'm not greedy, there's more than enough for everyone if we can work out and deal with any obstacles to extracting it. And no, it doesn't exactly belong to me, this is your people's land really, I just hold the title and in good old Euro fashion I'll nick a share. Er, that's Anglo slang for steal. No, it's your silver, or your people's anyway."

Wolf grinned at him. "Still don't get it, do you? You are of the people; we all descend from the original Ash and his Mohawk mate Katsitsienhawi. Either that or the original No'ipinKoi Shoshone. It's just that you appear to be the only legitimate descendant in law. Bit of a cheek really, calling us all bastards."

"So I'm told, never heard of the guy before all this. As far as I'm concerned, you bastards can have most of it, I just want enough to keep me in dosh for the rest of my life. Oh, dosh, that's more Anglo slang for money."

"I know," said Wolf, finishing her own whiskey.

"Another thing—" Mike started but Wolf held up a hand to stop him.

"No." She looked stern. "No, Milenkovic will come here and me and George will kill him. I know Mama wants you to talk me out of it but I'm gonna kill dear old Dad cos I saw what he did to Mummy. He will die for that. If George hadn't appeared firing enough shots to fight a war he'd have taken me." Tears appeared in her eyes.

"It's a name I used earlier with George and he reacted to it. It means things to me as well. What the fuck? Is it the same fucking Serbian criminal I should have caught years ago?"

Wolf touched his leg and half laughed. "I guess so. Don't know really. We've heard rumours that he has his own small militia of Eastern Europeans, so maybe."

"Holy fuck." Mike sounded confused and a little crazy.

"Hey, language. Young girl present. Try to make sense will you please."

Mike looked at Wolf. "Have you ever killed anybody?" he asked.

"No," she said. "But that won't stop me."

"It might – a momentary hesitation with this guy, if it is *the* David Milenkovic, and you're gone. Besides, once you've done it you carry that person's soul with you forever. It is a massive burden. It does your head."

"I believe you," she said quietly. A small tear trickled down one cheek. "I still have to do it. He has to go and he has to pay, some of our people are dead because of him. Many disappeared. My mother abused and murdered. I have to and so does George."

"No," Mike sounded determined and commanding. "Just no. I'll do it, me or George. Promise me that you won't, please Wolf, promise me." Past horrors whirled through his mind and this time a tear seeped down Mike's face as well.

Wolf put a hand to his face and collected the tear on her thumb. She then put it to her tongue and tasted the intensity of his emotions. "I can't promise fully, but if you or George fail, then I'll do it. I can't promise not to but I will promise to wait until either of you two have had a chance first."

"Thank you," Mike reached out and touched her face. "Thank you." The purity of the moment tarnished a little as he felt an inappropriate stirring in his loins.

At that point they heard Greg calling out in the street. Wolf jumped up.

"I'll go get him; he can stay with me tonight. Can you take him back in the morning?" she said.

"Yes, no problem. Thank you again – I mean it," Mike told her.

"No, I thank you," she said as she headed for the staircase. "That's a seriously heavy offer you made; I don't take the importance of it lightly. Oh, and yeah, you are a dirty old man. No way, Jose." She laughed lightly as she sank down the stairs and out of sight.

Mike laughed as well. "Oh dear, sorry," he said almost inaudibly to nobody. "Couldn't help it. No way, I know, should learn to behave."

He heard Wolf talking to Greg in the street and then they both walked off. He poured out the last of the whiskey, a decent bourbon but not a patch on a Scottish single malt whisky, then went to look out of the rear windows.

He was startled by a phone ringing. On the table he found a cheap flip phone burner which he answered.

"Nearly forgot to tell you," said Wolf, "since you are too old and technophobe to get a cell phone we bought one for you. Set it to silent and keep it on you. You have enough credit on it to last. Greg says thanks." Then she hung up.

Mike was amused and impressed beyond words with this girl. He finished the whiskey, took a pee and retired to his sleeping bag and thin mattress. His last conscious thought was that he needed to get some new clothes; he'd end up stinking if he didn't clean up. He'd only intended to take a quick look at this place.

Chapter Nine

Mentos drove the large pick-up along a straight and deserted woodland-lined road. The drive across Arizona to Utah had been tiring but he only stopped to refuel or obtain water and snacks.

He had driven carefully without exceeding speed limits. Always stopping at stop lines even when the road was empty and regularly checked all rear lights were working correctly. He did nothing to attract the attention of even the most suspicious cop.

Now he slowed to almost a crawl; he knew he was close. His eyes searched the nearside woodland for a small gap. Then he saw it, just wide enough for the vehicle and marked by a roughly made cross of Lorraine on a short post rammed into the soil.

He swung a bit wide to get his line and then turned right onto the track. After another mile or so of slow driving he travelled around a gentle bend to confront a metal gate barrier about five-feet high. A pole just inside the gate held a camera clearly observing anybody approaching it.

He flashed the headlights a few times and waited but nothing happened. He stood in front of the pick-up and waved both arms at the camera but still nothing happened. He sounded the vehicle horn loud and long, then returned to waving. The gate rolled open to one side, the moving gear protesting and straining at the effort. He drove through and waited for the gate to shut. It did so with the same reluctant and clanky discontent with which it had opened.

He drove for about another half mile to a wide clearing containing one large, single-storey log building. In front of it stood nine white men, all in the fifty to sixty range and all strong-looking, most with short crew cuts and two with short but better styled hair.

As he left the pick-up, the men all stood to attention and saluted. He returned the salute and grinned. After a short period of handshakes and arm punching, one of the men, a large man with a grizzled face marked by a couple of scars, stepped up to him.

"Colonel Milenkovic, your troops welcome you back to forward base, America."

The others made a few meaningless military style grunts, their own version of a chest bump 'oo… rah' and other alpha strongman bonding gibberish.

Then, as one, they chanted loudly, "Chetnik, Chetnik, Chetnik," followed by a short verse of song in Serbian.

The preliminary fighting man group reinforcement over, they all retired to the cabin to drink and be generally comradely.

The following day Milenkovic examined all available vehicles, which apart from his pick-up consisted of two powerful motorcycles and a small, dark people carrier. He decided that was enough.

He retrieved from a safe a briefcase containing a large quantity of cash. He handed out bundles to four of the men and told them to take all of the vehicles and have them serviced, cleaned and fully fuelled.

With the others he spent the rest of the day searching the camp to locate and burn anything that might be useful to an enemy or investigator. The bonfire consisted of paperwork, small items of clothing and photographs of earlier victims of which an individual wished to keep a souvenir, mainly young girls in various stages of abuse.

The day after that Milenkovic briefed his troops. He explained that after this final mission to extract some wealth and recover his stolen daughter, they had a few final loose ends to clear up.

He intended to end Blake, another team would deal with Cowboss Kes and his family. That team could do what they wanted with Kes's family but there must be no evidence or survivors left behind. They didn't need to worry about the workers on the ranch; they'd all make off as soon as they could.

He then set out the plan of approach to the Ash Lands and how they would first seize control of the old town. He had a spy amongst the occupants who would help; he fully expected that snivelling traitor to die at the end. He outlined how they would extract silver, march on the inhabitants' camp to seize his daughter and then make off.

If the Englishman was present he was not to be killed if that could be avoided; it might be necessary for him to talk with Adams at some future point and she'd back off if the Brit was dead. Anybody else in the way would be killed immediately and nobody was to kill or fuck his daughter. That got a laugh.

Finally, after the loose ends were cleaned up, they would all regroup again at a point near New York and fly back to the blessed soil of home to train and plan further incursions into the enemy's homeland.

Chapter Ten

The early light of a desert false dawn woke Mike. He turned in his bag and just lay still, letting his dreams fade. They had not been very bad last night, just a few ravaged girls and twisted shattered old men. John had been fine, just sitting on a rock watching his dad rage at the crimes.

The anger this morning was minimal; he felt no real urge to strike out. His eyes welled up but no flowing tears. He decided that the long walk and small bonding with Wolf had exhausted him and allowed better sleep. Not least of all because he had to carry that lump Greg for over a mile. The thought of that made him smile as he arose.

He stripped off and used the small shower head in the bathroom. Cold and slow-flowing water was far from ideal but got him slightly cleaner. He washed his sweaty places and dressed back in his beginning-to-stink clothes. From the roof space above him he noted the sound of a small trickle of water, not much more than fast dripping, as it refilled the now empty tank.

He heard the door at the foot of the stairs open and realised he'd forgotten to lock it. Wolf and Greg climbed up just as he emerged from the bathroom buttoning his shirt.

"Morning stinky," Wolf mocked.

"Yeah, I reckon you're telepathic," he said.

"Morning friend," greeted Greg.

"That's better. Mates now, eh?" Mike filled a kettle and started to make everyone coffee.

While they drank, Wolf explained that she would stay in town to keep watch. She also reminded Mike to keep the downstairs door locked.

They all went down and walked to the pick-up. Greg climbed inside; before Mike got in Wolf hugged him.

"See you both later you dirty stinker," she said. "See you later, tiger," she said to Greg and then walked away towards her place.

Mike started the engine and allowed the vehicle to creep forwards to the main street, no acceleration just foot off the brake. He waited a few seconds just in case Wolf reappeared but then decided she was gone and pressed the gas pedal gently and started back on the route he had driven here.

"Do you mind if I ask a few things, Greg?" Mike asked.

"Not really, ask away." Greg just stared ahead.

Mike took out his vaping pipe and puffed. He made a mental note to charge it up on the pick-up's USB sockets later. "The population in the settlement, it doesn't seem right somehow. I know you lost a lot of old people but it still feels wrong; I don't know why."

Greg glanced at him. "Just poor, I guess. The old being so much reduced makes it look a little unbalanced maybe."

They'd reached the top of the driveable part of the ridge, not far from where the track forked. Mike stopped and got out. He was looking back to see if he could identify the motorcycle's route the other side of the town. He couldn't see anything so got back in and drove on.

As he approached the fork there was a young Shoshone in jeans, shirt and Stetson standing in the road. He looked military fit and held a .22 calibre Winchester, old west cowboy style rifle. He just stood there, rifle stock resting on his hip as Mike came to a halt.

"It's OK," said Greg. "Hey, Timmy, it's me."

Timmy squinted then raised a hand in greeting to Greg. He stood to one side and waved them past.

Mike did not immediately drive on. He looked around and saw that further up the hill to the side, kneeling on one leg beside a large rock, another young Shoshone with a scoped hunting rifle was watching them.

He pressed the gas gently. "What's that about?" he asked Greg.

"Nothing," said Greg. "We just assert ourselves from time to time. Just to make sure we're still in charge around our own land. Note I said *our* land."

Mike snorted. "Didn't we go through this? Never mind. Your land, Greg. Nobody is taking it off you."

They reached the fork; Mike turned down the other track and descended the ridge to the settlement. He parked in front of the wooden town building after negotiating the confusing route through the homesteads. Greg left the pick-up and walked off.

"See you later, Greg," Mike called after him.

Greg waved without looking back. "Yeah," he called.

Mike spoke gruffly to himself, "Looking forward to it, you moody bastard."

He decided to call on Mama Mambi and walked around the building to reach her mobile home. He saw that George's truck was outside. As he reached the door, it opened and George stepped out smiling at him.

"Good to see you, George. Are you OK?"

"Doctor says I'm still alive but I'm not convinced," the older man grumbled. "Thanks for asking, I'm good." He put his hand on Mike's shoulder as he walked past him then drove off in his truck with a parting friendly hoot on the horn.

Mike rapped on the door frame and Mama called from inside that he should come in. He wiped his boots on the exterior coconut mat and strolled in.

In the kitchen dining area sat two more armed young men, both in their late twenties. One had a long rifle leaning near him that appeared to be custom-built; there were bullets in a cross body belt that he wore. The other wore some kind of small stubby automatic machine pistol on a strap hanging from his shoulder.

Mike nodded at them and stood near the front door assessing them. Young master long rifle nodded back. Mr machine pistol just stared at him.

Mama came from the kitchen side with a cup of tea that she handed to Mike. "Meet Joe and Jimmy," she said to him. "They are about to go and guard the desert side of the ridge to prevent approach to the settlement. My spies tell me you already met Timmy and his cousin on the ridge road side."

The two men rose and long rifle walked past him with another nod and left. Machine pistol walked to pass Mike and as he did so put a hand on his shoulder. "Pleased to meet you, bro. Stay dangerous." He left before Mike could reply.

Mike sat at a small kitchen table and Mama sat with him. There were a few seconds of silence, then Mama put her hand on his arm. "Go on," she almost whispered.

Mike looked her in the eye. He felt they were nice eyes, reflecting both pain and joy, recording the woman's experience. "I need questions answered," he said. "I feel like I'm being pulled into a private war and I need to understand. It seems serious. I understand the things that happened with Wolf; I've spoken to her and I've promised to work with her. I still need to fully understand."

"Wolf called me," said Mama, her hand still on his arm. "She told me about your talk. I will answer any question you have as fully and truthfully as I can. She says you know David Milenkovic."

"Maybe, if it's the same man. If it is then the only way that you'll make him safe is by burying him." Mike drank from his tea. "I've always considered coincidence to be unlikely. That doesn't make it impossible and the universe has a way of putting you where you need to be."

Mama retrieved her hand. She sighed deeply. "When he and his men first visited here, a long time ago now, they explained that they were taking silver." She put a hand over her mouth and squeezed her eyes closed. After a few moments she continued, "Not full mining but enough to make a few people rich. His lawyer called us later and explained that Milenkovic was a hired agent of the Ash trust and the money was to replenish the fund. It's illegal to take precious metals without a federal permit so we understood the clandestine necessity."

Mike was taking in the home's décor. A little chintzy for his taste but still pleasant. "So, why the armed guards? I know his crime but why a war footing?"

Mama rubbed her face. She looked tired and sad. "That first time, when they left they took children, a lot of them. The four young guys you've met so far, and Greg, are about the only useful young warriors we've got left. They work in towns most of the time but return when we ask. Many of the girls and some of their mothers went, were taken, as well. I reckon we lost well over half of that generation."

"That's it," announced Mike. "I'd noticed that this place didn't seem balanced. That's what was wrong. Oh, shit. He took Wolf's mother as well?"

"No," Mama spoke in a hoarse, emotional voice. "He returned a few hours later and attacked her, raped her. Then he fled. The only time he returned after that was years after to take Wolf but Sitsienhawi died preventing that. George went after him but was unsuccessful."

"Greg stays in the settlement?"

"No," said Mama. "He works in Vegas casino land and visits often."

"He's diabetic, does the food thing if he doesn't eat?"

Mama looked hard at Mike. "Yeah but not too badly. He has it well under control. What's wrong?"

"Nothing, I hope," said Mike. "It's just that I felt he might be play acting a bit and he didn't tell me about the road guards when he could have. Possibly just an oversight, forget it. Tell me about the people who were taken – didn't the police, the FBI, get involved?"

Mama laughed scornfully. "This land is Shoshone land, they said. Nehwe Shoshone matters are for Nehwe Shoshone law to deal with, that's George and no other resources. Of course if George tries to act outside of this land then federal law prevents that and he can't act against non-Shoshone, and if he needs to do that then he has to call the FBI first, by which time it's too late." She hit the table lightly with her balled fist. "No, we're on our own. Feds don't give a fuck about us," she wept quietly. "We'll never find them. We slowly die of radiation-caused genetic mutations, limited gene pool, poor education and fucking indifference. Fucking kill him, Mike. Fucking kill him."

Mike stood and she rose to meet him. They hugged and Mike kissed her gently near her ear. "I'll do what I can," he whispered, "but I'm just me; I'm not the solution. I wish there was one. I can't promise to kill anybody but I will see if he can be stopped and brought to justice."

Mama rubbed her face and wiped her tears. "I know. I'm sorry, life's hard and we abide but sometimes it gets me down."

"Don't apologise," said Mike. "These are terrible things; it is normal of you. Have you considered some kind of campaign, I don't know, social media or something?"

"We talked about it and tried a few things but soon discovered that nobody cared. We couldn't even get the attention of non-natives. Lots of posts on cats with head bows and stupid jokes on media but don't bother trying to do anything serious. Most social media is filled with self-centred, short attention span fools. If it takes longer than one sentence to explain, everyone gets bored. We don't really bother with it now."

They sat again and Mama went on to further explain the settlement's problems. Jan Adams sent them money from the silver sales, a way to keep them quiet, but not nearly as much as was taken. Adams tried to stop them taking silver for themselves but was told no. This small remnant of a formally proud and powerful nation needed money for ongoing medical costs, educating any young they still had and buying food and other essentials.

The Nehwe Shoshone survived, just, but did not thrive. They could partially protect themselves but not fully. No help would come from outside but were they to act against the invaders then federal 'justice' would be visited upon the people.

"So you have all your available defenders deployed," Mike summarised. "It's not clear to me how four guys can keep it up for a long period and they couldn't really stop invaders anyway but can threaten enough carnage to deter any more slave taking."

"That's about it," Mama told him. "We'll take the sentries food and water and they can cover each other for toilets and food breaks. They can keep it up for a week or so and that should be enough for the thieves to come and go. They only go to the old town now. They'll be here in a day or so I think."

In order to settle themselves after this conversation they took a long stroll around the settlement. Mike was introduced to a few people, none of them likely to be useful in the coming troubles.

The place was small and he'd seen all of it within two hours. He and Mama talked about everything and nothing, the kind of meaningless superficial verbal hokum that friends make to disguise the fact that what they are really doing is staying close to reaffirm and strengthen the friendship.

Towards the end of this tourist stroll Mike said, "You, I mean we, all descend from a distant Ash and a native woman, correct?"

"Well," she replied, "sort of, more or less. It's true they started the idea of Nehwe, along with the No'ipinKoi, but the fact is that Shoshone are a diverse conglomerate of several ethnicities in native terms. Everyone in the world is related if you go back far enough. Plus, we've had other input genetically, not just us first-footers and you crazy Europeans. For example, I've got a bit of African as well, other people have goodness knows what."

Mike nodded. "I suppose that in a mobile world all genomes will mix. Should be interesting."

Mama Mambi gave a short laugh. "Not recently, long before easy travel. As slaves escaped the south, most tried to head north. Sometimes they couldn't and struck out into the bayou or fled west. Some of them were taken in by Gutusipe Daindi; it was known for its liberal and independent-minded nature. Most non-Nehwe came and went and many left behind a bit of DNA." She laughed.

Mike laughed as well. "So what happened to turn the place from that to this?"

"The good old United States of America, that is what happened." She pointed out a shortcut back to her place. "Before 1864, Gutusipe Daindi was on Shoshone land, actually it was under treaty to Britain but that's not relevant anymore. Fact is that Uncle Sam first shot at us, then made us comply with incursions and eventually subsumed us. Annexed, I suppose, but still the pretence that we are a respected independent people unless we try to act that way."

When they returned to the home, Mama Mambi made some more coffee.

"I'm going to end up caffeine addicted," said Mike.

"Most of the people are opiate addicted," Mama told him. "The result of opiate medicine over the years and now many of them have to obtain further medicine to deal with the harm caused by the first medicine. We have to pay for that, welcome to America and the fate of the Shoshone."

"Mama," Mike started but she raised a hand to stop him.

"Call me Mambi, please," she said. "Get used to calling me Mambi."

Mike said he would but didn't ask why; she seemed quite happy to be called Mama by everyone but he supposed she had her reasons.

"I've been sizing you up," she explained, which made Mike

chuckle. Mambi smiled. "I have a few clean shirts and jeans for you, some underwear as well. In the bathroom is some soap, shampoo and body spray." She laughed at him. "I like you, Mike, but man you stink."

She showed Mike the bathroom and told him to leave his old clothes for washing. Mike noticed a new toothbrush and paste by the sink and cleaned his teeth. He picked up a clearly recently bought disposable razor, still in its bubble pack, and shaving gel which he used to scrape his face clean of stubble slowly growing into a short, unkempt beard. Then he got into the large, luxurious shower, roomy and multi-jet with warm water and soft interior lighting. The shower closet was opaque glass with small fleur-de-lys decoration.

He was in the process of washing his hair for the third time, using the resulting heavy foam to clean his face and body, when the bathroom door opened. He saw the shape of Mambi cross the room and open the shower door. She had changed into a light green dressing gown and smelled faintly of mint.

She grinned at him and slowly removed the dressing gown to reveal she was naked. She happily allowed perusal of her body which belied her actual age. "The reason I want you to call me Mambi is because if you call me Mama in a moment of passion it might just kill the mood." She entered the shower and embraced him.

Mike giggled. "Yes ma'am, Mambi. I concur."

Once again it was the desert dawn that woke him. There was something about the light, some way the light played subtle games with colour and shade. Something an artist might identify but which to Mike was a mystery. Something about the light that forbade sleep and demanded a slow drift into consciousness.

He was alone in Mambi's king-size bed. The thin, sky blue sheets already rolled back against the growing heat of the day. He lay enjoying the rare sensation of a dreamless sleep and a contented awakening.

Mambi stuck her head around the door. "Breakfast when you get up. I'll give you a few minutes. Clean clothes on the dresser, gun and knife on top of them. Boots clean. Your old belt's with them all, didn't have another one."

Mike emerged fully dressed and armed into the kitchen area and sat in front of a cooked breakfast and morning tea.

Mambi kissed him quickly on the cheek. "Don't expect constant wifely like domestic bliss. You have to clean and cook for yourself in this world, wherever we go from here this easy service stops, my friend," she said, grinning.

Mike smiled at her. "Wouldn't expect anything else. Do we treat last night as one of those things, like a second date accident, or are we cool?"

"We're cool; you are acceptable for a fat bloke," she said, sounding amused and hitting him gently around the head.

"Not fat," he laughed. "I am not fat, just robust and heavily built. And you now using English slang?"

"Got infected with some dumb Limey talk," she said and they both chortled.

"Your four warriors," Mike continued, "what work do they do outside?"

She thought for a moment. "Full disclosure now. We, or at least I, will always answer you truthfully. They are funded by us to try to find the taken kids. They've been searching across the state and beyond for the last four years. They were all survivors of the theft. No luck yet. All four of them are tough hombres and loyal."

"I'm so sorry this happened, is happening. You should organise to tell the world," Mike said.

Mambi was about to reply when her phone buzzed then rang, her inappropriate ring tone was the theme from the film *The Last of the Mohicans*. Mambi checked the caller then put the phone to her ear and listened for a short while. "Damn, too soon," she said. "Stay where you are; George will be there soon. Mike is with me and I'll update him."

"What's happening?" Mike asked. From about five hundred

yards away Mike heard the unmistakeable sound of George starting the engine of his old banger.

"Milenkovic is in Gutusipe Daindi, that was Wolf," she said in a flat voice.

Mike put down his cup. He stood and kissed Mambi on the cheek, grabbed his key fob from a small table near the door and headed for his pick-up. He ran around the central building to where he parked; as he approached his ride George drove up.

"I'm taking the desert side of the ridge. I'll leave the truck with Joe and Jimmy, climb over the ridge and head for the town on foot from the side," said George.

"I'll drive straight in from the other side of the ridge," responded Mike.

"Not sure that's wise," cautioned George.

"Yeah, it'll be good," explained Mike. "Me, white man with white man privileges. They don't know me, even if it is *the* Milenkovic, he has never seen me. They will know that I'm the owner in law and that I'm in contact with that lawyer bitch. They will also know that if rich whitey disappears then people will come asking questions. I didn't say it's fair but it is the way it is. They won't just shoot me without a reason."

George nodded and drove away. Mike typed out a quick phone text before he left.

Chapter Eleven

Wolf watched the group from the side window of her safe room. They were up in the main street but she could just about see them near the saloon if she stood at the far side of the window.

They had a quasimilitary look to them. Like Aryan supremacists but without the petulantly aggressive tribalistic flamboyance of a frightened closeted gay look. This lot looked like they could actually conduct an operation, not just shoot up a few vulnerable people.

She'd watched them arrive in one small people carrier, a large pick-up and two motorcycles. In all she'd counted ten guys, all armed. Among them the unmistakeable figure of her father. It took her some effort not to rush out firing. She rested an old M16 rifle in the crook of her arm and waited.

The cell phone in her poncho pocket vibrated a text message alert. She opened the message and saw it was from Mike to her and George.

'Please please please nobody act until I've spoken to him. Give me a chance at a peaceful ending'.

She thought she heard some movement below her on the ground floor of the house. She listened for a while but heard nothing more. She wasn't happy with Mike's suggestion of a peaceful ending but she'd wait to see what happened.

Mike stopped at the post guarded by Timmy and his hill sniper. Timmy strongly advised him against his plan but agreed to hold the position and not endanger the settlement by leaving it unmanned to help in the town.

Shortly afterwards, Mike drove slowly along the main street towards the group gathered at the junction by the saloon. He recognised the crash helmet hanging on one of the parked motorcycles as the earlier recon.

He also noticed that the group quickly spread out as he approached. Not moving aggressively and not threateningly but unrushed, like a well-trained group minimising its exposure to ramming, sudden fire or explosion.

Mike stopped about thirty feet from them. In front of the large pick-up he saw a large man, Trump orange with sharp eyes that missed nothing, wearing combat fatigues and holding a Kalashnikov, AK47 casually across his folded arms. Mike also noted that the weapon's magazine had another taped to it upside down, military style. On his right upper leg was a pistol.

Of the other men, Mike noticed that two of them carried AR15 rifles and sidearms. Another dressed in part-combat clothing had two sidearms. The remaining six all wore handguns; they looked like Glocks. This bunch were dressed as if for manual work and one of them leaned on a long-handled shovel. There were other similar tools leaning against vehicles or on the floor.

As Mike left his vehicle, the man by the large pick-up stroked his thinning blond hair. Nobody else moved and there were no threatening gestures. Mike walked a few steps in front of his pick-up.

"Stay there," called the man in an Eastern European accent. "I will come to you." He placed the AK47 on his vehicle's bonnet/hood, then walked forwards and stood about ten feet in front of Mike.

"Milenkovic?" Mike asked, his voice monotone flat and controlled so as not to display anxiety, fear or aggression.

"Yes," replied Mentos. "Call me Mentos; I prefer it. You are well informed. Are you Key?" His voice was also flat and revealed nothing through accidental inflection or emphasis.

Mike nodded. "I am. I would like you and your guys to leave. I will talk to Jan Adams later to discuss the wealth this land holds. I want you all to go now before there is any problem that pushes us all into something we don't want."

"You got balls, Mike," said Mentos. "Me and my guys can handle any problems, don't worry. What you need to do is let us dig for about a day; we'll take some silver and then leave. You can still contact Adams later if you want. It's not in my interest for you to come to any harm. I need you to leave and come back tomorrow."

Mike looked at him while considering his reply. "We appear to have conflicting requirements," he eventually said. "I know what you've done here before; there are plenty of people who want to harm you. Please leave, I'll ensure Adams sends you money to cover what you don't get today."

Mentos laughed. "Yeah, man, balls. No, we don't leave. You leave or if you stay we keep you tied up. You know nothing about the things I've done, trust me. I've met hard Englishmen before – one of them killed my son, shot him down like he was a dog. One day I'll find him and kill him after I've killed his wife and children in front of him. You leave, eh?"

Shit, thought Mike. *This is the Milenkovic and I killed his fucking son; I didn't know that.*

Mentos noticed the mental hiccup that Mike suffered. Men like Mentos notice some very subtle things in their opponents. Men like him notice many things but commonly misinterpret them. In Mentos's self-obsessed universe of which he was the centre, he was seeing Mike move towards certain submission in the presence of a man greater than himself.

"We'll compromise," said Mike. "You send out your miners; I'll stay here. It's my town, after all. You don't tie me up. You do what you came for and I'll stay here to do what I came here for."

Mentos looked proud at this surrender. "OK. And just what is it you came here for?"

Don't be obvious, Mike told himself. He managed to stop himself from saying he'd come to deal with a vermin infestation. "I wanted to check the overall condition of the town, you know, rotted wood and leaky roofs. I'm thinking I might rebuild."

Mentos laughed again. "OK. You do that. You walk around poking wood and pushing walls; my guys will dig some silver. Two of them will stay here to watch you wasting your time. Give me your cell phone."

"Fuck off," said Mike. He knew men like this. He knew that a direct refusal like that meant Mentos either had to challenge him or let it go as a joke. Mike knew that Mentos had to feel in control even if that control was confined to allowing somebody to refuse him. He reasoned that with holes to dig, avengers to watch out for and his future hopes for this place, Mentos would most likely not seek to complicate the day if he could avoid it. He was right.

Mentos laughed again after a short pause, "Balls, man, balls. I like you. Man, you should work for me. OK, you keep your cell but don't use it. If you do my two soldiers watching you will destroy it." Mentos didn't look as if he liked him but Mike just nodded.

"Greg," Mentos called out. "Greg, you measly little fucker, come on out and help our friend here check his town. You might even learn something by being with a real man."

Greg walked out of the saloon. "Mentos, you said I could stay out of the way," he complained, sounding infantile.

"Shut the fuck up," snapped Mentos. He swirled his finger in the air and the six diggers clambered into the people carrier. He pointed at one of his soldiers, Mr two guns on the hips, and indicated he get into the carrier, which he did in the front passenger seat.

Mentos retrieved his AK47 and indicated to the two men with AR15s that they should come to him. Simple military signage, he pointed to them and then to the top of his own head, with finger pointing down onto it. They went to him and he spoke to them in an Eastern European language. Not a language that Mike knew but one with a sound and rhythm familiar to him.

"Key," he called out. "We go to dig, back in six hours or so. These two angels will look after you and that miserable poof. Just do your checking. Don't misbehave – I promise they can and will deal with you if they need to. Don't make me have to explain that to Adams." With that he slid into the carrier's driving seat and set off back out into the desert. The two guards just stood watching Mike and Greg.

"What the fuck, Greg. Just what the fuck. What are you doing?" Mike said a little angrily.

Greg stepped back from him. "I'm protecting Pia'isa." Greg sounded a bit whiney like a child heading into a tantrum. He was about to say more but Mike pushed him backwards then walked up to him and pulled him in close.

"Don't fucking mention her name," he whispered into Greg's ear. "They hear about her they might start looking for her, understand?"

Greg pulled himself free. "I've done a deal with Mentos. I let him take silver; I warn him about any traps laid by George or anybody else; I let him talk to Pia'isa; and then he leaves with no trouble."

The right hook that Mike threw was fast and untelegraphed. It smashed into Greg's jaw just to the side of the point of his chin. As Greg's legs buckled and Mike pushed him to the floor, the two guards laughed.

Mike knelt down to him, his face close, and spoke with a quiet growl. "You fucking idiot. They will kill you both and probably me. Who the fuck do you think you are? You don't give away the silver and you don't decide what Wolf will or won't do. Stay near me and do as I tell you or I will fucking kill you; don't answer me, just nod."

Greg nodded. Mike pulled him to his feet.

"Hey, Anthony Joshua," called one of the guards, "get on with what you're doing. Remember, no phone. Don't reach for your revolver; we will put you down before you can draw it. And you, punching bag, don't take your knife out and stay near the Englishman, probably best just out of arm's reach." Both guards laughed again.

"Come with me," said Mike and pulled him towards the saloon. Greg was testing the joints of his jaw for damage and Mike was rubbing the knuckles of his right hand. "I'm sorry for that but please believe me, we are in serious danger. It's not like the movies; there is no spectacular Kung Fu take down on these guys. They have the upper hand and they will hang onto it."

Mike led a disingenuous survey of the town, starting with the saloon but avoiding the sheriff's office. He stamp tested stairs and floorboards, poked and pulled at wood here and there, made a visual inspection of joists and joints as if he knew what he was doing. He even hung out of windows pretending to check frames or eaves. Greg followed him but said nothing.

* * *

Mentos and his crew travelled about nine miles into the desert. His people had told him that this area had richer pickings than the previous holes closer to the old ghost town. They were approaching two holes already dug side by side.

"This is it, Davey," the passenger said.

"Mentos," said Milenkovic without anger. "Call me Mentos; forget my real name. I'm the colonel at the camp but outside, at the moment, I'm Mentos." The passenger just laughed.

They all disembarked and Mentos grabbed some soil. He laughed as he pulled a tiny silver pellet from it and told his crew to dig at this spot. A couple of the workers took large water bottles and the others took several large plastic buckets from the carrier which they set down ready to receive the silver. Mentos and the passenger retired to the shady side of the vehicle.

"What about that Englishman?" asked the passenger.

"Adams wants him. She says she can use him as the front to get the legal right to mine here. We supply the workforce and get a percentage. I'll probably kill that shit Greg, I fucking hate traitors, but the English guy, well at least he's got guts. If Adams can control him, we'll work with him. If not, we might have to kill him later. Hey, you could become him, steal his identity, that'll be funny. When we're done here today I get my girl and we go."

They both settled down for a long day of watching the others work.

* * *

After about three hours of fake building surveying, Mike was growing tired of the ongoing deception. Sulky Greg stayed with him and the two guards never let them out of sight. Only one of them ever spoke and Mike presumed that was to avoid accidently conflicting instructions – they were well trained. The little group had just exited the furthest building in town, a small house at the far end of the main street buildings on the desert's edge.

"Oi, tossers. I'm done," Mike called back to the guards. "What now? Without you two babysitters I'd just leave now."

"Back to the cars and wait," said the apparent leader, the only one who had so far spoken.

Greg walked rapidly away from Mike towards the guards who both raised their weapons. They ordered him to stop which he did about halfway between them and Mike.

"Mentos will want to talk to Pia'isa," said Greg. "I know where she is."

"Oh for fuck sake," Mike called out. "Greg, you shit, come back here and shut your mouth. I told you she's in Vegas, stop being an annoying idiot."

Greg spun very quickly to face him and then things happened fast. The guard who so far had remained mute fired his weapon and put two rounds into Greg's back. It was probably just a reaction to Greg's fast turn; the guy was anticipating action and small things can trigger it. Greg walked a couple of drunken steps forwards and then just crashed face down in the dirt.

Mike sprinted into the nearest house, out the back and quickly along the row of buildings before darting back into another one. He found what appeared to be the darkest corner, drew his revolver and waited to recapture his breath and for his heart to slow. He heard another shot and said to himself, "You fucking idiot, Greg." *How do I explain this to Mambi?* he thought.

"Come on out to us, English Mike," came the voice of the guard from the street. "We won't shoot you; you have to trust us."

Don't think I do, Mike thought, *why are you calling from the street and why keep saying 'us'? You lying little shitster, the other guy's checking the houses from the back, isn't he?* As if in confirmation, the other guy came noisily through the back door.

"Mike, don't fire. Greg startled us, the damn fool. We're not gunning for you," he called not too loudly but enough for anybody in this building to hear. This the previously silent guard, the killer.

Mike sunk into the deep darkness of his corner. The guard walked across the building to the front, waved at the man in the street then turned to return to the rear door.

"Stand easy, soldier," Mike said quietly and softly. "We can come to a peaceful conclusion if we're all sensible."

The guard stopped. His AR15 was hanging at his side. He made no attempt to bring it up and kept his hands visible at waist height. "We should have taken your gun," he said lightly with almost a soft chortle.

"Yep," Mike replied. "A dumb rookie mistake. I think you know the drill, on your knees, hands on head, fingers interlocked."

The man complied. Mike emerged from the shadows and walked to him, he made sure the man saw the gun and then walked behind him. Mike lightly tapped one of his ankles with his foot. Showing that he did indeed know the drill, the man crossed his ankles behind him.

"Thank you," whispered Mike. He placed his foot on the upturned uppermost sole and removed the AR15 from the captured guard's shoulder strap and slid it a few yards away. He then took the man's pistol, a Glock, and slid that to the rifle. He then searched him for other weapons but didn't find any. He did take the man's cell phone.

"It will go wrong this way, Mike," the captured guard said. "Come outside with me. Thanks for the professional approach."

"No more speaking," Mike told him. "Go face down, arms out crucifix style."

The man did as he was told and Mike went to the confiscated weapons and sat down facing his prone opponent. He reckoned he had a few minutes before the guard outside realised there was a problem.

"English Mike, please save us all this nonsense, just come out to us," the outside guard called again.

Mike grinned at the face down guard who grinned back. Mike recognised that as nothing more than a captive placating those detaining him.

Mike placed his revolver on the floor, pointing towards his prisoner. He moved his hand, then placed it back again to show he could easily grab it long before the man could regain his feet or launch an assault.

Mike had a slight problem with the AR15. All guns are fundamentally the same with similar functions and actions. The problem was that he was unfamiliar with the AR15 and didn't really want to use a weapon he had to fumble about with to find buttons, switches or other operating parts. He just didn't have the time to familiarise himself with this weapon.

To that end he removed the magazine, after he found the release button, and pulled the slide to eject the round in the breech. He pulled at the floorboards near him and one came up; he dropped the magazine through it and heard it thud to dirt a few feet down. He thought about trying to bugger up the firing mechanism but didn't know the gun well enough to do it quickly so just abandoned the thing on the floor. Finally, he turned off the seized cell phone and slid it away into the dark corner.

The Glock he did know. He checked the magazine and found it had nine rounds in it. He pulled the slide to load a round only to note that one already in the chamber jumped out so the pull was unnecessary. That's about all that is required with this model; it has three safeties but they unlock on an intended pull as a small trigger safety, which will only disengage with a deliberately curled finger, automatically releasing the other two on the pin and hammer. A very simple to use yet sophisticated weapon. He replaced his revolver into its holster and now held the Glock. He stood up.

"Hey, Mike. Yahoo, Mike. C'mon." That was George's voice.

"Up you get, matey," Mike instructed the captive. "I saw you murder a man. If you run, if you attack me or my friend, if you come too close, if you even look at me strangely, I will empty this Glock into you."

The man rose and nodded to Mike who indicated he should walk out of the front door.

As they walked out, the prisoner leading, they saw the other guard standing in the middle of the street, his hands on his head and his rifle at his feet. Behind him stood George, pointing a sawn-off shotgun at his back.

Hi, Mike," said the old man. "Mike, step five times to your left and cover this guy. He still has his handgun and the rifle is not made safe."

Mike thought it a strange order but followed it. As he stepped, he raised the Glock to cover his new target and then moved closer to him.

At the same time, George moved from behind and pointed his sawn-off at Mike's prisoner. George walked up to the man, showing no sign of anger or any other emotion. He put the sawn-off to the man's face and fired. His head went back as the buckshot made a relatively small entry hole, then it jerked forwards as the back of his head exploded and the mush inside it sprayed away. The man just crumpled down.

"Shit, George," exclaimed Mike.

George turned to Mike and the other Guard. "I am the law here; the federal authorities don't really care what I do as long as nobody important comes to any harm. In this context, important means American citizens and doesn't apply to Serbian war lords looking to fuck up my people. You hearing me, shithead?"

The surviving, currently surviving, man nodded and looked pleadingly to Mike.

Mike kept his eyes on the Serb but spoke to George. "I don't want to kill him unless I have to. I need somewhere to put him while we wait for the others. Somewhere secure enough to keep him out of the game."

George nodded. "I have just the place. I watched what was happening here then went out to see what the others were up to, took a long time. I saw the other guy kill Greg just as I sneaked back into town so I put him down, even if Greg did turn out to be a dipshit working with Milenkovic. I have no reason to kill the other one, well not yet anyway. Don't worry, nervous-looking failed mercenary, I'm not some psycho putting people like you out of their misery. I'm not to be trifled with either, remember what you saw me do and don't make the same mistake as him."

* * *

Milenkovic strolled around the hole, now about fifteen feet square and approaching four feet deep. He looked gratifyingly at the collection buckets which were nearly full. The diggers were messy, with dry dust adhering to their sweat and crusting their clothing. It didn't help that the rubbish heap from the dig was powdery and blowing a small dust storm in the gentle wind.

"Hey," he called over to the passenger lounging on the shade side of the carrier, "bring the rest of the water; these guys are parched."

"Thanks, Colonel," one of them said.

After the water arrived the two of them strolled back to the vehicle.

"What after?" asked the passenger. "Straight to the Indian camp, grab your girl and go?"

"No," replied Milenkovic. "The guys clean up, we rest up in the ghost town for a night. Tomorrow early we go in from the desert side of the ridge. The traitor told us that they have two guys on either side and that's it. We take out the guards that side, a couple of our guys then go off and deal with the two on the other side. The rest of us head into the camping site, kill the old man and Greg, I still fucking hate traitors even when they work for me, we get the girl and then we're away."

"I hope it's that simple," the passenger ventured.

"They're just the fucking dying dregs of their tribe. They're fucked. The Yanks would be in here like a shot if they knew about the silver. As it is they're just gonna let the lot die of anything and fade away. In the meantime we take what we can, fuck 'em up a bit more and go enjoy our hard-earned wealth." Milenkovic spat on the dry earth.

The passenger gave a lazy salute with his right hand. "Yes, sir. We should be done soon, I reckon we've dug about twelve grand's worth."

Milenkovic smiled and nodded. "More like thirty."

Back on the main street, the surviving guard had been fully disarmed and George led them all to the town side of the ridge, a walk of about four hundred yards. He had the AR15 on his back, the strap across his chest and the new captive's Glock in his belt.

At the ridge he told Mike to watch the man, then he went to a bush at the base of the slope and pulled it aside. There was a small opening about four feet square behind it. George crawled through it, then called outside for Mike to send the prisoner in.

The other side of the opening was a person-sized tunnel, a small person that is, curving away into the ridge. It was lit by a string of battery-operated white Christmas tree lights pegged along it. George led the way and Mike pushed the guard ahead of him after reminding him not to take his hands from his head.

They walked for about two hundred yards when they came to a door that looked like a segmented concertina-style bus door. George opened it and as they all entered, Mike realised it was indeed a bus. A buried and fairly old school-type bus, the seats removed and with some boxed supplies near the door and at the other end a large concrete block with a thick metal eye bolt on top.

"You are just full of surprises," said Mike.

"Yeah, mysterious old bastard, eh?" George replied and they both laughed.

"Is the girl in Vegas, then?" asked the captive.

"Shut up," Mike told him. "If you survive this, if we do, I'll take you to the casino where she works as a bouncer." This time the guard laughed.

George went to the boxes. He brought out a long, sturdy chain and a bag of padlocks. He chained up the guard, around his waist, under his groin, up round his shoulders, around his neck and then to the bolt embedded in the block. He used padlocks to tie the chain together at strategic points and then to the bolt. Each lock came with a key that George placed into his pocket as he locked each one.

"If you get killed, I'll slowly die in here," the guard complained.

"Yep," said George cheerfully. "Best hope we don't get killed then."

"You won't take down Colonel Davey," the guard warned.

"I'm putting an explosive charge on the outside of the door," George told him. "It will go off if the door is opened. We will come back to get you."

Once they were outside and the door closed, Mike said, "Explosive charge?"

"Yeah, fitting it now," George responded, scratching and tapping lightly at the door frame but fitting nothing.

Mike just grinned and started back along the tunnel. George followed just behind him.

"A bus?" Mike said incredulously.

"Yeah," George explained. "We dug it into there many years ago as at least some shelter in the event of more nuclear tests. Too late of course but better than nothing if we needed it. Turned out we didn't and I've used it since as a little hide out of my own and a small store."

As they reached the end, George turned off the small lights and replaced the bush.

Chapter Twelve

As they drove through the desert, Milenkovic told his passenger to phone the guards in town. The diggers sat dusty and grubby chatting contentedly in the back; they passed a bottle of Jack Daniels among themselves. After a couple of moments the passenger told him that there was no reply.

Soon they approached the town and Greg's prostrate body became visible. Milenkovic stopped the carrier about one hundred yards from the start of town, Greg's body being about twenty yards further in.

Milenkovic tapped the passenger's arm. "You on point to me. You guys in the back, three on each flank, loose spacing."

They all debussed smoothly and moved towards the town. Milenkovic toted his AK47 with easy familiarity. The passenger had a large revolver in each hand and the diggers all held Glocks.

As they drew closer it was clear that the body was face down with wounds to the back of the torso and the head. There was a large patch of rusty, brown-soaked dirt around his head with lumps of flesh and the accompanying smells of blood and violent death. Milenkovic and his men knew well the smell of violent death, a smell that those who have never encountered it don't even know exists. Those who have will never forget it.

Milenkovic grabbed the corpse by the shoulder and pulled it over. "Fucking Greg," he said.

"And there," one of the diggers said.

As Milenkovic turned he saw the other body about forty yards further in. It was one of his men, loosely curled in a kneeling position and a wide spray of grey/brown/red/white mess fanning out on the floor behind it.

His eyes took on a cold, hard menace. "Everyone be on alert; move forward in two group stages; drop and cover for the next group," he said.

That's how they moved – three ran forward about thirty feet, went down and covered everything they could as the next three moved up. Milenkovic and the passenger moved steadily with them, carefully watching the buildings high and low.

They eventually reached the saloon. Milenkovic noted that all of the vehicles were still present. He indicated to his men to take the saloon; they moved into it in the style of an armed forced entry. They searched it, found nobody, and Milenkovic declared it their temporary base and set sentries.

"My girl's in town," he said to the passenger. "She's got a panic room in the dirt road at the side of this place; I'll explain where. You take one other guy and go get her. I don't want her harmed – kill whoever's with her. I'm gonna think how we can locate that fucking Englishman and kill him. I might use my dearest daughter as bait or I might go get that old fucker and make him need rescue from torture."

Wolf had heard the earlier shots but could see nothing from her window as it all occurred on the other side of town near to the desert side. She'd thought about investigating but was prevented first by her reluctance to go blind into a fire fight and second by her promise to Mike.

The gentle rap at her door made her jump but it was in a rhythm previously agreed as a code: rap a rap rap a rap rap rap, short pause then rap a rap rap. She went to the door.

"Who's afraid of the big bad wolf," she said to the door but standing to the side of it.

"It's your Pia'isa delivery," said Mambi from the other side. Wolf opened the door; Mambi entered and hugged her. Mambi was armed with a wood and metal crossbow with a small collection of quarrels hanging on her belt.

"I heard shots," Wolf said.

"Yeah, one bad guy down; George took him. We lost somebody as well." Mambi took her hands.

"Mike? Please not Timmy. Not Mike either. Who?"

Mambi looked into her eyes. "First you have to know that Greg was working for Milenkovic."

Wolf looked stunned but then nodded. "I suppose if the idiot thought he might in some way connect with me through the evil bastard, or even save me, I don't know. Who killed Greg? Was it Mike or George? I hope not."

Mambi stroked her face and hair. "No, it was one of the invaders. George finished the murdering slime. I knew he planned to sneak into town from the ridge. I planned to follow him here but he went out into the desert first so I tracked him. I saw him watching the silver digging and then followed him back. He's getting old; ten years ago he would have spotted me."

"Is Mike with him?"

Mambi smiled. "Yes. I watched from hiding trying to see if I could help without making things worse. You need to know that Mike is pretty capable in this kind of thing, in a sort of don't want to do it way."

Wolf grinned. "I think we already knew that, didn't we?"

That's when they heard the stairs creak. Wolf pulled the slide on her M16 and retreated to a far corner. Mambi pulled and loaded her crossbow and took the other far corner, both staying low and covering the door.

The door swung open but nobody entered. "Girly, pretty girly," called the passenger. "Daddy says come on in now. Nobody will hurt you. If I have to carry you, you'll get a little spanking."

Wolf shot him through the wall. Armour piercing rounds on full automatic for a second or so. He was dead before he fell which he did in a floppy kind of way as the rounds severed his spine, ripped open his rib cage from behind, shredded his lungs, heart and spleen and created in him what the old Vikings would have called a blood angel.

The digger he'd brought with him burst through the door and was felled by Mambi's bolt as it embedded itself into his throat. He writhed and gurgled for a few seconds before thrashing about a bit, falling before trying to rise and then kneeling and dying with a kind of bad-tempered spasm.

"We need a plan," said Wolf.

"We need to move," advised Mambi. "They must have followed me – I'm sorry. I'm certain that they only saw me at the last moment as I came in here."

Wolf nodded. "Mike said that killing somebody hurts your soul. I don't feel anything."

"Give it time, right now you're in battle. Later when you think about it, we can talk then." Mambi blew her a kiss. "Mike says a lot of things when he's hot under the collar."

Using the telepathy that Mike suspected and her own natural intuition, Wolf gave a huge smile. "You two, you didn't? Yeah, you did," she laughed. "Good, I'm happy you did. God knows he needed it and you did too, you dodgy temptress."

Mambi laughed. "The frailties of guys can wait for better times. Right now we're warriors, OK?"

"Lead on, Mama boss, let's clean up this town."

Milenkovic strained to listen as the popcorn sound of not far distant automatic fire was heard.

"Not one of our guns," said one of the diggers. "Not sure of the gun but not AR15 or Glock."

"M16," Milenkovic informed him. "Just fucking great, they've got an arsenal. I think maybe we're going to fall back and return with some bigger fucking canons."

He stormed out of the saloon, pulling the slide on his AK47 as he went. As his men covered him as best they could, he opened fire full automatic on Mike's pick-up. The full magazine seemed to last a long time. Tyres popped; glass shattered; large silver-rimmed puncture holes appeared with a metallic smack on the bodywork.

The vehicle didn't explode as he'd hoped but petrol and oil poured out of it onto the dirt. He replaced the mag by turning it upside down to insert the one taped to it. He swirled his finger in the air and his men ran over to his large pick-up, leapt in the back and covered the buildings with their handguns.

"I reckon you've lost your deposit on that," whispered George. He and Mike watched this display of rage from the darkness of a not yet rebuilt abandoned shop about forty yards away.

"We can't let them leave – if they return heavily armed we won't stand a chance," Mike hiss whispered at George. "I need to know what the other shooting was as well."

"Don't worry about that." George patted his arm. "That was Wolf's M16. She'll be fine; the loser would have been whoever was in front of it. Here they come."

The large pick-up was being driven by Milenkovic. No great speed, just a sensible and steady roll towards the desert.

As they reached the shop that hid George and Mike, George grabbed the seized AR15, knelt and loosed fully automatic fire into the vehicle. At least two of the men in the back were hit, one in the head and the other a couple of times in the side. As George sprayed along the pick-up it swerved away and crashed into the wooden building opposite the hide.

Milenkovic leapt out of the driver's side and unleashed a deadly hail at the old shop. This stopped abruptly as George returned fire and Milenkovic darted into the buildings.

Mike emptied the Glock at the remaining men in the back of it. He hit one in the arm who toppled out the other side and fell from sight. The other two leapt out and ran at full pace back towards the motorbikes. Mike saw George sprint off towards the buildings into which the warlord had fled.

As Mike pursued the two runners he realised that both of them still held their guns. They ran clumsily in work clothing and boots so he kept pace with them. At one point he threw the now useless Glock at them but hit nobody.

As they reached the junction by the saloon Wolf stepped out and zapped away with her assault rifle. She kept the fire low and one of the men was hit in the legs. As he fell the other swerved to avoid the splattering and in doing so dropped his Glock.

When Wolf realised that Mike was running behind them she swung the weapon away and so the man still running passed her unharmed. As he reached the bikes he jumped on one, fired the engine and roared away towards the ridge road, the rear wheel kicking up dirt.

Mike cursed himself for not removing the bikes' ignition keys earlier. He reached the other bike, fired it up and chased after the escaping man kicking up another shower of dry dirt. It'd been a few years since Mike was on a motorbike but they say that you never forget. That revealed itself to be a truism and he very soon found it easy to manage the powerful machine.

The fleeing baddie had some genuine dirt biking mojo. He slid it about on the incline, managing to flip a few rocks Mike's way. He easily wheelied over small humps and even jumped a couple. The speed he maintained was greater than Mike could manage and slowly he drew ahead and away. They raced up the ridge road and were approaching the fork in the track.

A single shot cracked out. It tore a chunk out of the fugitive's upper right arm and he turned the bike over, rolled a few times and lay groaning.

As Mike reached the fallen man, he saw that Timmy had appeared and was standing over him. The hill sniper was looking very pleased with himself, grinning down at Mike.

"How did you know?" asked Mike.

"Wolf sent a telepathic message. Said two ugly white men heading this way." Timmy laughed at Mike's confusion. "You idiot, cell phone of course. Old guy forget tech? She phoned, said don't shoot the fat one."

"Oh for fuck sake, not you as—" Mike started but Timmy held up a palm to stop him.

"I'm sorry, dude," he said, still laughing. "Wolf told me to say that; she said it winds you up. Hey, if she's roasting you then she likes you. Live with it."

"Look after that twat," Mike instructed and turned his mount back towards the town.

He'd driven to within sight of the town when he remembered Timmy's taunt, 'old guy forget tech?'. He stopped the bike and called Wolf on the burner.

"Hi fatty," she answered far too cheerfully for the circumstances. "Spoke to Mambi, hope you embarrassed."

He chuckled. "Too old to be embarrassed. You sound chirpy – what's the situation?"

"All good. George has Dad, won't let me kill him yet. All invaders disarmed and those still alive are captured. We're letting them give each other first aid. Mambi has gone to retrieve the one you and George put in the bus. Don't worry, she knows what she's doing and he'll be walking back in chains and with a weapon on him; she'll be fine."

"Mambi? What the hell? Oh, never mind. I just didn't expect her to be there. As long as you're all OK." Mike tried not to sound like the protective strongman.

Wolf snorted down the phone. "Honestly, Mike, she's fine. We'll discuss what's happening when you get back, after I've settled a family issue."

"OK. We'll talk when I get back. Don't do anything until I'm back, please. See you soon." Mike toed the bike into gear and opened the throttle, a little faster now because he had to talk Wolf out of murder.

As he reached the town and trundled towards the saloon, he could see two prisoners sitting back to back. Wolf stood guard watching them from a few yards away with her M16 in her folded arms. These two guys were bandaged, one on his arm and the other on his legs and both looked in pain.

Another, Milenkovic, sat on the floor a bit further away with George keeping his sawn-off on him. There was no sign of Mambi or the bus prisoner.

Mike came to a halt about twenty feet from them. This time he removed the motorbike's ignition key and pocketed it. He walked over to Wolf and hugged her. After checking she was OK, he walked over to George.

"Two Englishmen to kill now," snarled Milenkovic.

"That's big talk for a beaten man on the floor with a gun pointed at him. Besides, it's only one." Mike immediately regretted saying that. Never volunteer information to the other side, not even if it's cryptic. How long before the bastard processed that and realised that Mike had killed his son. A man who has lived his kind of life must be used to the synchronicity, the common coincidences that permeate each route through this world. If and when he does work it out, he will be an even more dangerous man than he has been so far.

George nodded at Mike. "Mambi shouldn't be long. She texted a little while ago to say the prisoner is retrieved and walking back."

What happened next was as unexpected as it was impressive as a physical feat.

From a sitting position, Milenkovic gained his feet in one bound and with an instant roundhouse kick caught George square in the face. As George's head snapped back and he flopped backwards clearly unconscious, the sawn-off fired, spitting up dirt but hitting nobody.

Mike half drew his revolver but Milenkovic was on him in one leap. He threw a straight-handed thrust at Mike's throat but it missed as Mike half bent and stepped to his right so the blow hit his shoulder. It did dislodge the revolver which fell to the floor. With his left hand Mike pushed his assailant away. At the same time he reached to the back of his belt with his right and drew the push knife.

Milenkovic was back at him almost instantly and Mike thrust his fist held knife into the point where the man's under jaw met his throat. At the same time Mike saw in his peripheral vision a streak in the air. A split second later a crossbow bolt thwacked into the left side of Milenkovic's head.

It was not the first time Mike had seen the light of sentient presence become extinct in a man's eyes. Milenkovic had started to gurgle from the wound inflicted by the knife. That became a single bubbly spray of blood that dappled Mike's face and the leader of this attacking force toppled backwards like a felled tree; he jerked a little and then lay still. Mike heard a groan from the sitting prisoners, now with Wolf's rifle pointing at them. He looked to his right and saw Mambi, the crossbow still at her shoulder and the chained captive sitting at her feet.

Mike retrieved his gun and nodded at Wolf who rushed over to George. She took out her phone and made a call.

Mambi put her chained detainee with the other two prisoners and then went to Mike. She took a tissue from her pocket and started to clean his blood-spotted face.

"It was necessary, you sad-faced good guy," she said. Once she'd made a clean spot she kissed him.

"Go help Wolf," he suggested. "I'll guard these three."

As the two women tended to the injured old man, Mike glared at the nervous-looking prisoners.

From the distance, the roar of a flat out motorbike could be heard. Mike steeled himself for more violence but it soon became clear that Timmy, his sniper on the pillion, was rushing down to them.

This was clearly a day for remarkable acts of physical prowess. The bike didn't even seem to slow and the two young men were off it and running. The bike travelled for a while and then crashed into some buildings.

Timmy went straight to George and the sniper joined Mike. Mike noted that Timmy and Wolf shared a lover's kiss when he arrived at the scene; it pleased him that she had somebody.

"I don't know, must be Ash blood or something. You are definitely Shoshone, my friend," said the sniper. Mike just nodded to acknowledge the compliment.

Mambi joined them. "Timmy was a marine for five years. He's a trained medic; George is in good hands. I think he'll be OK but I need him back to the hospital as soon as we can."

"Where's the bastard I left with you two?" Mike asked the sniper.

"Joe and Jimmy have him. They're taking him to some of the older men in camp. Then they'll pick up a larger truck and head here. The older men can handle this lot. Actually they might be a little too keen to handle them," the sniper laughed.

George was regaining awareness but was still groggy and complaining that his neck hurt. It went without saying that his obviously broken nose hurt as well. His eye sockets were already beginning to yellow up around the lower orbit and a trickle of blood seeped from his mouth.

Mambi put her arm around Mike. "Don't let Wolf go back to her room; she killed one of these fools there and she will feel that later." Mike just nodded his agreement.

About fifteen minutes later Joe and Jimmy arrived in a large open-backed truck. All prisoners and the wounded George were placed in it. Mambi climbed in the back and all of the young men climbed aboard.

"Hey, Key man," called Jimmy, "we're all sorry we weren't down here, didn't expect this level of fight. With a bit of luck these sorry-looking dipshits will start on the way back and we'll leave them scattered along the road to feed the dogs. Respects man." Mike just waved back.

Wolf and Mike watched the truck leave. Wolf looked as tired and inwardly sad as Mike felt.

"Mambi says—" Mike began to say.

"I know." Wolf put her arm through his and hugged it. "I'll go to your place but you need to go and get something from my room and bring it over." Mike tried to give her the key to enter his safe room but she said she had a spare. After she explained what he needed to do she patted his arm and walked towards the sheriff's office.

As Mike ascended the stairs to Wolf's room he drew his revolver. He was still hyped from the fight and besides, he'd seen dead men suddenly become combatants again in the past.

At the top near the door he saw the man that Wolf had shot; the holes through the wall were shining beams of dust-filled light. Some flies had settled on the huge wounds. *Wow*, he thought, *that is battlefield dead. Ugly.*

At the door he saw the other man crumpled with his legs under him and a crossbow bolt sticking out of his throat and rear neck. Mike whistled and shook his head.

He searched both bodies but found nothing useful. He took their cell phones and left each cadaver with the few dollars in cash that each of them had. "Pay the ferryman," he said to nobody.

As instructed, he went to the wooden chest by the table and opened it. He found an old green heavy great coat, well made and with an insignia badge on the collar that he recognised as Royal Irish. There was also a sword, a flintlock pistol and a pile of documents in a leather binder. He bundled the paperwork in the coat, held the old weapons in his hands and headed back.

On the return journey he visited the now stiffening corpse of David Milenkovic. Putting down his burden he searched the body and took the cell phone. He placed it in a different pocket to the others, then picked up the goods and continued to the sheriff's office.

As he entered the room, Wolf had just finished making the coffee. This time he remembered to bolt the heavy entrance door before he came up; he'd had enough surprises for one day. He put the coat and other things on the floor and took the mug he was offered.

"I could use more whiskey," she said as they sat facing each other either side of the bundle and weapons.

"I know," he told her. "It's not a good idea, though. Booze can be a poor coping strategy. How do you feel?"

She told him she was good but he wasn't convinced. He decided to delay this conversation and turned his attention to the goods. He opened the coat to display the pile of documents inside.

Wolf looked at him gratefully for not pursuing the 'how are you' line. "This is the property of Sebastian Ash; his companion Katsitsienhawi doesn't appear to have left us anything. The weapons are his, they and the coat are over two hundred years old," she said.

"They are in good condition, probably the dry air. We can leave it for now if you need to sleep or something," Mike offered.

Wolf smiled at him. "Nah, just listen. The documents may be important. They are hand-drawn maps of the area, the location of something called 'Ash Hole' which we think is just an early attempt at shelter. There's a copy of the Nevada constitution, the US government order annexing the state and an agreement, signed by Ash and the then tribal senior Dakayivani, part ceding the territory to George III."

Mike laughed. "I bet we could cause some trouble with this lot. Seriously, we might be able to kick up such a fuss that Nehwe obtain authority to extract minerals."

He took out the mobile phones he'd looted. He gave her two but kept Milenkovic's. "It's getting late, let's just crash now and continue in the morning. We'll have to clear up outside as well."

She nodded. "Timmy and the gang will be back for that. We'll talk over what to do next, go see Mambi in the morning and decide what to do with the prisoners."

"OK," said Mike. "If you need me in the night, don't suffer in silence – wake me."

Wolf laughed. "You wish. No, no, it's OK, I know what you really mean. Point me to the corner I'm sleeping in."

Mike woke early. There had been no bad dreams in the usual sense. He'd been walking along a beach with John, simply strolling. Just before he woke he'd seen Milenkovic floating in the sea about thirty feet out. He felt the mildest anger but only because he'd seen Milenkovic, no real rage. It was just getting light, the normal insistent desert morning light. He didn't want to disturb Wolf so just lay there for a couple of hours.

"Morning," called Wolf from the sleeping bag in the corner. While she used the bathroom Mike made the coffee and warmed up some beans in a pan.

As they sat he put the pan between them with two spoons. He grabbed a mouthful and then took out Milenkovic's phone. Surprisingly it was unlocked with about thirty per cent power. He scrolled through the contacts until he found the one he wanted.

"I guess it's about nine on the east coast," he told Wolf. "I'm going to make a call. I'll put it on speaker." Then he tapped the contact he was interested in. It rang for a few seconds before it was answered.

"Good morning, darling," said Jan Adams.

Mike put his fingers to his lips to stop Wolf from responding. He waited for the silence to provoke further response.

"Hello, David." No response. "Hello, Milenkovic, how did it go?" she continued.

"Not that well," Mike replied. "You know who I am."

There was a short pause from Adams. "Mr Key, Mike. Are you with David, where is he?"

"Gone," said Mike. "I know your sort; I think you'll only be in as deep as you can be and still ensure there remains a legal way out for you."

"I don't know what you mean," she said. There was a very quiet but audible click on the line. "You said David Milenkovic is gone. What do you mean by gone?"

"Just gone. Gone to somewhere else I guess. Left his phone with me. I know you just started recording. I'll see you in a day or two, depends on how long it takes me to get to Washington." Mike ended the call and then turned off the phone so that it couldn't be traced. Who knows what other contacts she has?

As Mike and Wolf left the sheriff's office they heard chanting from across town, from where Greg fell.

"What's that?" he asked.

Wolf mumbled something in Shoshone. "That's the boys. They're collecting Greg first. He hasn't earned the chant for fallen warriors but that's a weaker version of it. Basically it's just a traditional thing. Originally to tell a departing spirit that it was still Shoshone. I guess they just want to say that they don't hate Greg even though they're less than impressed by him."

They had left the old weapons and the great coat in Mike's room. Mike carried the document case and they walked over to the motorbike. Mike put the ignition key in it so that anybody who needed to could start it. Then they walked down the alleys behind the main street buildings and out of town on the desert side, towards the people carrier.

"You were right – the keys are in it," Wolf called over to him as she clambered in the driver's side.

Mike quickly searched the vehicle. "Five buckets of silver, one Glock mag, a pile of shovels and some part-eaten sandwiches with an empty bottle of Jack Daniels," he informed her. Then he put the documents on one of the back seats and climbed into the passenger seat.

As they drove back through town they found Joe and Jimmy pulling Milenkovic over to the other pile of bodies. They informed Wolf that Timmy and the sniper, who was apparently called Hunter, had taken Greg back in a truck and would return to help with the clean-up and cremation which would be in the desert. They agreed to collect all possessions and phones from the dead.

Once back in the settlement they learned that Mambi was struggling to make George behave for a couple of days.

As they entered the hospital wing of the main building, only building if you exclude the sea of tents and trailers, they met with Mambi who hugged them both. George was in a bed and waved to them.

"Tell medicine woman here that I need to get up," said George. His voice sounded strong but his face looked as it should for an old man who recently got thumped in a serious fight.

"I need to go to Washington," Mike informed them. "I'll take some of the silver that the invaders left us. I was hoping Mambi might come with me."

"I need to be here to look after this awkward old *davê muzup*," she said staring at George. Wolf laughed.

"That's a desert plant," George explained. "It's shaped like a penis. She just called me a prick. I'm the chief around here, back me up Mike."

Mike laughed as well. "I'm not getting in the middle of this fight; I know my limits."

"Help me manage him today and in the morning Timmy can take you and Wolf to the airport, if that's OK?" said Mambi.

"That's OK," Mike told her. "I need to visit the car rental firm to try and explain why they won't be getting their pick-up back. It's not a major problem; I'm in a position to buy it from them if insurance won't cover it. I think maybe George has to make calls to try and square what happened here. Can he do that at least? You can matron him and make sure he doesn't overdo it."

Mambi nodded and George grunted. At that point Timmy walked in. He went to George and hugged him and then hugged Mambi. He gave Wolf an eagerly returned passionate kiss and then walked over to Mike.

"Thanks, bro," was all he said and extended his hand, which Mike shook. Then he and Wolf left.

"You take one of the hospital beds for tonight," Mambi told him. "You can help me with George if I need it. Just rest for now and I'll fetch you both some food."

"I need to talk to the prisoners," Mike told her.

Mambi's reply was unequivocal. "No, you rest. Elders in the council will talk to the prisoners. You've done enough. They are well enough guarded."

"Well, that's you and me both beaten by the woman," laughed George.

Chapter Thirteen

Mike sat at a desk in the comfortable hotel room. He and Wolf landed in Washington early and had been shopping all day. Before they left the lands he'd beaten some silver into rough ingots and today he touted them around a few jewellers. Eventually he'd found one honest enough to offer a decent price but dodgy enough not to ask too many questions.

"I'm off to buy some clothes and things, see you back at the hotel," Wolf had told him after he gave her half of the cash.

"Only use cash, not plastic," he'd warned her. She just rolled her eyes and sashayed off. *Jeez*, Mike thought, *now it's like I'm her dad.* Then he did some further shopping for bits and pieces.

He placed a new Nokia burner on the desk. With a pot of tippex he drew a circle on it. He dotted in two eyes and then a small open half circle on top of it to look like horns. "This," he told himself, "is the long spoon with which I shall sup with the devil. I therefore name it the devil phone."

When he'd blown his artwork dry he punched Adam's number into contacts and left it to charge. Then he settled back to enjoy the huge pastrami on rye he'd bought in a deli that he found by accident.

He was just stuffing the second half of it into his mouth when the lock on the door clonked to unlocked and in walked Wolf.

She wore a body-hugging red T-shirt with a white jacket, red jeans and ankle-length pink boots. "No wonder you're fat," she said.

Mike laughed. "Well fed and robust. You're looking very girly. Decided to accept the role of pretty girl being meekly decorative, have you?"

She grinned and flipped him the finger as she disappeared into the bathroom. She explained that his room was closer to the hotel entrance and she needed to go urgently.

Mike had learned years ago that vaping did not set off hotel room alarms, never mind the signs that hoteliers put up. It's just water vapour and has no effect. Feeling safe in that knowledge, he vaped as he made drinks using the room pod machine.

As they sat at the desk drinking she asked about the plan for the day.

"I think that's about it for today. We rest up now and then go to see Adams in the morning. I suggest we eat in the hotel restaurant this evening."

Wolf nodded. "New phone, I see."

Mike showed it to her. "This is the devil phone. We only use it to contact Adams, nobody else. If we need to flee it can be dumped. All contact with Mambi or George will be on either the phone you gave me or your phone. Don't use the hotel phones."

She laughed softly. "All cloak-and-dagger, you are."

Mike returned the laugh. "I'm probably taking too many precautions but trust me, it's better than not taking enough." He looked more serious. "Listen, Wolf, about a month ago I was just a divorced, slightly screwed up middle-aged man. I had a fairly pointless future that I intended to use as best I could. Now suddenly in a short period I've made friends, friends I love, and I belong somewhere. Things have changed fast for me and I'm glad. I'm surprised how quickly some things happened but that's how it is sometimes. It's weird how I got here just ahead of Milenkovic, a monster from both our pasts. I'm not really into fate but wow, sometimes, you know?"

Wolf laughed and touched his arm. "We were all surprised at Mambi moving that fast but she knows what she's doing. Regrets?"

"No, definitely not. I didn't expect to get into a war or kill anybody. I have a slight anxiety about legal consequences but not regrets. I can live with what I did, for me in some way it was clearing up loose ends from the past. What about you?"

She looked thoughtful. "No, no not really. The guy outside the room, he was going to kill Mambi and take me. I suppose it helps that I didn't see it as it happened – it was through the wall. I tried not to look when we left. It was a military weapon I used, one that Timmy had made sure would work on full auto and take some powerful rounds. I know it made a mess but Timmy says it's better to make someone a mess than they do it to you."

"Timmy is right," he told her. "Promise me that if it haunts you you'll talk to somebody. I think Mambi is your best bet but that's for you to decide. Please promise me that if you need to, you will talk to somebody you trust."

She smiled. "I promise. I'm a bit shocked that I'm OK with it as much as I am. If I get the panicky flashbacks later I will talk to somebody."

They agreed to meet up at the restaurant in a few hours and Wolf got up to leave. She got as far as the door then walked back to Mike. She hugged him then returned to the door.

"We all love you as well, fatso," she said as she left.

Mike checked the time, not five yet, then called Jan Adams on the devil phone. "It's me," was all he said when she answered.

"I've had some ideas for a good way forward," she replied after a short pause.

"I will be with you tomorrow afternoon." He then hung up and turned off the phone. The rule of thumb for this part of the game is to limit information you give the potential enemy and when you have to give some make it as inexact as possible. He fully intended to be with Adams first thing in the morning.

Next morning Wolf and Mike took a cab to a street about two blocks from the offices of Valtin and Adams Associates, Law and Lobbying.

They briefly touched hands and then walked in separate directions. This was another of Mike's precautions. They'd planned that they would approach the upmarket-looking entrance from opposite directions at the same time. The idea being that they would both be in a position to see if anybody was following behind the other.

It was just after nine in the morning when they swept through the doors together. The entrance hall had changed. There was no identifiable receptionist, the approach boasted an airport-style security arch and three large men in police uniforms. Two were older men, one white the other black. The final man was of mixed African European ethnicity and about twenty-five years younger. They all looked a tiny bit startled by the swift yet unrushed way the two breezed into the obvious protection zone.

Mike felt some satisfaction; it meant he clearly had Adams rattled. "Jan Adams," was all he said.

Two of the guards stayed further back beyond the arch. The large older black cop – the kind of heavy, almost fat, build that hides real physical strength – came towards him and Wolf.

"Are you guys police or private security?" asked Mike.

"Both," the man replied. "My name is Jackson. We are capitol police employed by this firm when we're not working for the capitol. We remain police officers with relevant powers but perform a security role for this firm at this time."

"Is that even legal?"

As the man assured him that it was lawful, Mike just noted it as one more of those strange and unfamiliar things in a familiar land.

"What's your name?" the man asked him. When he was informed, he went to a table near the arch and picked up a phone.

The younger man was staring at the pretty girl. Wolf spent her time smiling back invitingly at him. Mike grinned and thought, *damn you are one dangerous young lady.*

"Ms Adams is not expecting you yet, sir," said Jackson, still on the phone.

"Please tell her it's now or never. If we walk out we will find another firm to act for us." Polite words given deserve a polite response. Nevertheless, Mike had to make it clear that she would see them now or not at all.

After speaking on the phone again, Jackson beckoned them over. "Ms Adams will see you. I apologise but we must search you before you enter. This is a request in our security role and not a police order."

Mike acknowledged for them both. He was asked to stay where he was and Wolf was asked to walk through the arch after putting all metal objects in a tray. It came as no surprise to Mike when the alarm went off.

All of the men put their hands to their pistol grips. Jackson said, "This is for our and your safety. We make no threats towards you but from here on in please either do as we ask or leave. If we find illegal items on you, we will take police action. The girl will be searched first. I am sorry that we have no women present to do this so need your spoken explicit consent. It is being recorded."

"I only consent if that pretty young man searches me," said Wolf. The two older cops laughed and Mike smiled.

He briefly searched her torso and legs, then stood back having found nothing. "Nothing," he declared.

"You didn't check my inner thighs or small of my back," Wolf said with a false breathlessness. The young man looked a little flustered.

Jackson laughed again. "She's messing with you, Rex. Stand back. Miss, I'm sorry, and I do appreciate why it's funny, but I have to have whatever set off the alarm."

Wolf laughed cordially and reached into her ankle-length boot to withdraw a kubaton, a small metal rod used in martial arts. She held it in two fingers to show it was safe and put it in the tray.

The older white cop took it. "You can get this back when you leave. Please walk the arch again."

She did so without activating it. Jackson then searched her properly this time. He used the backs of his hands and made sure that nothing he did could be misinterpreted. He was so efficient that at the end Wolf thanked him for his consideration when touching her.

He now looked at Mike. "Bud?" was all he said.

"Rear of my belt," said Mike, raising his hands to his head.

"Please don't move," Jackson told him as he moved towards him. From the rear of Mike's belt he took a small stun gun shaped like a little torch. He checked the device and smiled when he found the torch bit even worked. "You'll get it back when you leave," he intoned.

Mike submitted to a bit of further searching and then walked through the arch without activating it. Jackson expressed surprise at the amount of cash Mike had on him but gave him a look that said he understood about lawyers and their need for financial feeding.

"Gentlemen," Mike spoke to them all, "thank you for a professional and competent greeting." He turned to Rex. "I'm sorry about her, she's next to impossible to control."

"I don't doubt that," said Jackson with a wide grin.

Jan Adams sat upright behind her desk. She wore a new-looking cream suit and smiled with her mouth. Her eyes remained steely and almost predatory and were not affected by her false smile. She indicated two chairs on the opposite side of the desk which Mike and Wolf went to and sat in.

"It's nice to see you again, Mike," she started.

Wolf answered, "I have e-mailed you some documents; you may need time to read them. We can wait here."

Adams gave her the bitch face. "I am only interested in dealing with Mr Key. You have no legal position in this and if you interject I will have my boys remove you."

"They better be as tough as you hope they are, then," Wolf replied belligerently.

Mike raised hands to stop them both. "Wolf is my representative. Any member of her group, known as Nehwe, speaks for me unless I say otherwise. Don't try to strong-arm Wolf; it will end badly. Don't try to trick me; it will end in a massive loss of business. What is your connection to Milenkovic?"

At that point the door opened and in walked Justin Blake, the man Mike last spoke to in an English field some weeks ago but seemed like years ago. Mike stood to face him.

Blake held up his hands in a placatory gesture. "Hello, Mike," he said. "I've spoken to a few of my contacts in official positions back home. Some of them know you and I've informed Jan that I can assist in working with you but any plans for anything other than legal action against you will have to happen without me." He took a chair from the other side of the room and sat at one end of the desk.

"It'll help if we can all be frank," Mike told them. "You know we don't have any recording equipment; we were searched."

"OK," said Adams. "So that you know that I'm not recording either, I will say this. The original plan was for Mr Blake to persuade you by any means to sign some land rights to us. Events have indicated that you may not be inclined to permit anything approaching intimidation and Mr Blake informs me that you have previously worked in an official capacity for the UK government and may be able to call on them for assistance or official contacts here."

Wolf snorted. Blake looked at her with an evil eye before quickly returning to a more normal gaze towards Mike. The fleeting display of something very nasty did not escape Wolf or Mike.

"I have a way forward that will benefit us all if you will sign a contract as our client," Adams advised.

"I ever see you on our lands you may not be leaving," Wolf said straight to Blake.

"I ever see you alone we can discuss that," Blake replied, staring at her as if he were acquiring a target.

"Stop," insisted Mike. "Mr Blake, you have no place in this. I thank you for your work and your aversion to, er, another less consensual route. I would consider it a courtesy were you to now remove yourself from this meeting and not return."

Blake stood, nodded to Mike. Shook hands with Adams and ignored Wolf. He then left the room.

"He'll be well paid," Adams said. "I made a mistake with him."

"I asked about your connection to Milenkovic," Mike reminded her.

"He was just an agent employed by us to realise some value from the Ash Lands to replenish a dwindling fund." She ran her hand across her mouth.

"Yeah, OK," Mike replied. "Bollocks. He's gone, who knows where? If you want me as a client then you act in my interests, our interests, in the interests of Nehwe, we need to be clear on that."

Adams slumped a little. "It is clear. We leave the past where it belongs and move on. Did you know that the FBI are on the Ash Lands?"

"No I didn't," Mike told her. "Doesn't matter. The head guy there is a friend of mine and will let me know." It occurred to Mike that Adams thought he meant the head of the FBI whereas he actually meant George. *That's OK*, he thought, *a little misinformation can't hurt in this situation.*

In life we fear from others what we ourselves would do, often at the expense of reality. It is good to know the fears of others because it can warn you of what they might try to do and also conceal your own real moves. Adams was a power groupie and therefore feared others might possess better contacts. The thought almost made him laugh.

"I know that David Milenkovic died in that ghost town," she declared. "The FBI don't seem to be doing much about it. I hold a lot of his money in an account set aside for contractor benefits. We will deal with his probate if we can find relatives."

"I'm the stinking pig's daughter. Give it to me," Wolf demanded.

Adams fell back into professional mode. "It's not quite that simple and will take a year or more to deal with but I will note what you say; I can't guarantee anything. It's a couple of hundred thousand dollars."

"Small potatoes against the money available on the lands," said Mike.

"I spent last night reading the documents that the young lady sent me," Adams informed them.

"My name is Wolf."

"Yes, the papers that Wolf sent me. They are very interesting and I believe we can achieve a substantial amount with them. In conjunction with other documents I think we can make a reasonable case that will benefit you greatly."

"What other documents?" asked Mike.

Adams grinned. "Oh, small things like the US constitution, Magna Carta, international treaties, Nevada's constitution and the presidential order of territorial recognition that preceded it. I've spoken to lawyers in London and they are reasonably confident that they can do some things there that will support what we might do here. It won't be cheap, though. It attracts significant costs."

Mike thought for a moment. "I think that the Ash Lands can produce enough to cover almost anything. I can meet initial costs."

Adams handed him a document that he read. It was nothing more than a standard client contract and set out fees and other costs. Mike handed it to Wolf who also read it.

"I won't hand over any land rights. I expect you to act only for me on this matter. If I learn that you have in any way acted against me after today I will in the first instance seek to have you struck off, whatever you call it here. Disbarment?" Mike said to her.

Adams nodded at him. "In the second instance?"

Mike gave a short laugh. "Let's not go there. We have a short but unfortunate history. Your previous questionable plans for the lands are dead. Whatever your plans were with Milenkovic no longer apply because he is dead, as you said. You never visit the lands; I can't guarantee your safety if you do. You deal directly with me or Wolf and I refer to the Nehwe council, it's that way or no way."

Adams nodded. She called an assistant to come in to act as witness. Mike raised his eyebrows to Wolf who just stared at her lap for a few seconds. She then nodded at Mike and told him she was going to chat with the cops before she walked out of the meeting room.

Mike signed the contract and then so did Adams. Mike photographed the signed document on his phone and they also gave him a second copy that they both signed again.

"Remember you act for me, nobody else. The sad fact is that you are probably the best lawyer to deal with this, all the background knowledge and involvement," Mike told her.

She asked for a five thousand dollar initial payment. Mike paid her in cash, which caused her to give one of her unclear and unsavoury inviting smiles. The rest would be paid through money raised from the silver.

"I've already got a court date for the morning to get you initial mineral and mining rights. I'll let you know." She seemed very happy.

Mike left and found Wolf in conversation with the young cop, Rex. She seemed so sweet and almost coquettish that he felt more laughter threatening to burst out.

"Oh, man, remember when you were that easily captured by a pretty girl," Jackson sidled up and whispered to Mike. The man offered his hand and Mike shook it.

"Come on, sweet thing," Mike called to her. "Don't want to be late for your acting lessons."

Jackson and the white cop laughed. Wolf touched the young cop's arm and went to Mike.

"Just making some contacts in case we need them," she said to him once they were outside.

Mike just pursed his lips and shook his head. He waved down a passing cab and asked to be taken to the hotel.

"I'm going out for dinner this evening, with Rex," Wolf told him in his hotel room.

"No," was his sharp reply.

The proper Wolf glared at him, the one with the M16 and gutsy character strength. "Sorry, would you like to rephrase that attempt to control me?"

Mike raised his hands in surrender. "I'm sorry, didn't mean to sound like your guardian. We don't really know him and he was working for Adams – I don't fully trust him."

"Nor do I," she said. "Mike, we need contacts and I can maybe get information from him. I'm committed to Timmy in case you hadn't noticed. I'm gonna pump him for information but that'll be the only pumping involved. Besides, he is actually a nice guy."

Mike laughed. "Do you know, I've been in some crap situations since I got here but it's been a long time since I laughed so much. Can we compromise, I'll follow you like some nutcase stalker?"

Wolf laughed this time. "You won't need to, just sit at the bar. We will be eating in the restaurant here. Mike, I'm glad you used the word guardian and not dad. You know how great my shit rapist murdering dad was. Since I lost my wonderful mother, George and Mambi have been the best parents I could ask for. In just a couple of weeks you're coming a close second to that. Thank you. We have a table booked for seven." With that she left the room.

At six-thirty Mike took up position at the bar attached to the foyer, with a clear view of the restaurant but not clearly in view himself. He paid the barman a hundred dollars to set up a fake vodka optic from which to serve him water. If he wanted a real drink he'd order bourbon or beer but most of the time he'd drink water at vodka prices.

He saw Rex arrive dressed in an immaculate three-piece suit that looked tailor-made for his slim but muscular frame. He spent ten minutes trying not to look anxious until Wolf arrived. She looked fantastic in some more stylish clothing, a dress, she'd bought. Mike finished his beer and ordered a double vodka.

"You want water or ice with that?" asked the barman facetiously which almost made Mike laugh.

He called George on what he now referred to as the Wolf phone because she had given it to him. It was a cryptic conversation on his part because he was worried about any eavesdroppers. Even so, George was able to tell him that the FBI had been on the lands and had now left with the bodies and the prisoners. They'd made Timmy and the gang disinter the dead, excluding Greg, and were unimpressed that they'd burnt them.

Other than that, George assured him that things were OK. The invaders were not American; they were known criminals illegally in the country and everything had happened on reserved native land, notwithstanding the non-native ownership, and the federal authorities couldn't care less. For them, George was exercising his authority as local law and not infringing the rights of any US citizen. Nehwe would have to pay for proper disposal of the bodies.

The call ended. "This is a fucking strange land," he said to the barman.

"Dunno what you're talking about, buddy," the young man told him. "Still, you are right, it is fucking strange."

A couple of hours later Wolf and Rex emerged from the restaurant. They seemed happy together and Wolf walked to the entrance door with him. As they stood outside, Mike repositioned to the foyer to continue watching.

The two chatted for a while, then Wolf kissed Rex on the cheek and re-entered the hotel. Rex walked away looking laughably wistful. She blew Mike a kiss as she passed him.

As Mike started back to his room the barman beckoned him over.

"We finished with the fake vodka now?" he asked.

Mike thanked him and told him it could go now.

"That was cool, my man," the barman told him. "It's good to care and it's good to protect. If you'll accept some advice, be careful not to overprotect and accidently stifle her."

Mike liked that, the young man knew nothing of the real situation but meant well. Mike thanked him again and gave him a twenty dollar tip. Then he walked quickly to the elevator/lift for his room because he was bursting for a pee.

As he entered his room, a crashing blow to the jaw caused his legs to buckle. Before he could react, another blow to his temple caused his head to smash into the wall and he lost consciousness.

He came around in a while, he didn't know how long. His wrists were tied with thick plastic quick cuffs and his arms were around the toilet base. He noticed he had urinated in his trousers and surmised that his ambusher had dragged him into the bathroom.

"Hey, shithead, I'm awake you sucker punching arsehole." There was no reply and he could hear no movement in the room. His head was swimming and buzzy; he decided he was concussed.

He tried twisting his wrists against the plastic ties but they started to cut into his skin. He was overwhelmed by cold deep anger and the adrenaline that accompanies it. With grunts and snarls he pulled the toilet bowl from its cemented base, tore it from the waste pipe and smashed it against the wall so that it broke, then furiously threw it to the floor.

He grabbed a sharp piece of the toilet bowl debris, then rushed out into the room but discovered it was empty. He returned to the bathroom where he worked the blade out of a disposable razor. With a lot of effort he twisted his wrists, cutting them on the ties as he did so, and worked the small blade against the plastic until it was cut through.

The hotel supplied a couple of face flannels/washcloths each day. He used these to bind his bleeding wrists then dashed out of the room armed with a chunk of broken ceramic. Wolf's room was one floor above his on the fourth floor. Ignoring the lift/elevator, he ran up the stairs and emerged breathing heavily and looking like a lunatic in a rage.

Just as Wolf had a key card for his room, he had one for hers. He was trying to find it as he approached but saw that her door was open.

He just charged inside in full atavistic fight mode. He recognised Justine Blake who was face down on the floor, his hands cuffed to the rear. Standing over him with a pistol held close to the front of his torso stood Rex, the naive and allegedly nice police officer.

With his bloody wrist bindings, piss-soiled trousers, bruised face and wide-eyed rage, Mike knew he must be a disturbing sight. Rex obviously thought so as he raised his weapon to cover the incoming apparition. He heard Wolf calling out for Rex not to shoot. Then he heard a pop behind him.

As he turned, he saw Jackson, who was pointing a yellow taser at him. The electrodes reached him at the same time and he went into an electrically induced spasm, fell to the floor and lost consciousness again.

He woke this time in a hospital bed in a private room. A cannula in his left arm attached to a tube that ran to a bag of liquid suspended from a pole next to him. An uncomfortable catheter ran from his bladder to a half full bag attached to the bed. Wolf was sitting alongside the bed, Jackson sat over by the wall and Rex was just entering with three coffees.

"Oh," said Rex. "I should have got an extra one."

Wolf put her hand on Mike's arm. "Don't rush to do anything. The doctors made you sleep for three days. Everything is good. Your concussed head and bashed about body needed rest."

"Hi, buddy," said Jackson. "Hope you're good; Rex here is my son. I'm sorry I zapped you but man, you should have seen yourself. Remind me to run if you ever get that pissed with me."

Mike smiled at him. "Your son. Give thanks for every day you're with him."

Jackson smiled back. "I do, I do. He was sniffing after your girl, sorry miss, a bit crude. Glad he was, he went back to her room, cos he's too dumb to know when he got blown out, and she was being attacked. That bastard Blake, he works for Adams but she fired him after you left."

"You OK?" Mike asked Wolf. She nodded.

Jackson chuckled. "Rex says she was giving as good as she got. One thing I will say for Rex, he can handle himself. Put the arsehole down in one, well done boy."

Rex chuckled. "Dad, she was gonna win. I was rescuing the guy."

"The guy's ex-British army," Jackson informed him. "I thought they could fight better than that."

"Takes more than one army to put her down," Mike replied to general soft laughter. "Besides, it's only Americans who think that tough means never losing."

Jackson grinned at him. "Yeah, well it's only Brits who think tough means getting hit a lot." Both men gave a friendly laugh.

The story was simple. Blake was angry at getting fired and losing some kind of private deal he had with Milenkovic. He blamed Mike for both and had a general misogynistic fury against Wolf for being young, pretty, capable and independent but most of all for answering him back.

He learned where they were staying from contacts in the secret services and then lay in wait for Mike. After that, he went to Wolf's room; when he'd finished with her he would return and kill Mike to prevent him from searching for his assailant. It seemed that the reason he didn't kill first go was that he wanted Mike to know what he'd done. Maybe like showing him Wolf's bloodied underwear or something equally sicko.

His plan to intimidate her into surrender and then humiliating compliance with a hard punch to the face badly backfired. She not only avoided the blow but was in the process of giving him a good old-fashioned kicking when the lovelorn Rex appeared, immediately switched into cop type and restrained him. He called his father for backup who arrived just after Mike and reacted to what he saw, which was mad Mike out for revenge.

"Thanks, mate," Mike said to him. "We owe you. Can't help you with her but I consider I owe you."

Wolf got up and hugged Rex. "We've talked. He knows about Timmy. We're cool. We're friends. Oh, I visited Adams, wanted to remind her who she was sided with now."

"And?" Mike enquired.

"You have a land owner's mineral and precious metals extraction permit. We can dig the silver and sell openly. Timmy and the guys are going to stay on the lands now; our wealth needs protecting. Also, Adams is content now that she knows she can screw a load more fees out of all this. She'll contact you about the upcoming legal moves, but they are mega. You're maybe gonna make history and you definitely gonna make the papers."

Jackson applauded. "When you're rich and running a multinational, maybe you think about hiring me and Rex if you can forgive me for tasing you. What's a few thousand volts between friends?"

Chapter Fourteen

Since Mike and Wolf's return, life on the territory of Gutusipe Daindi had fallen into a routine. Mike lived permanently with Mambi; Wolf lived with Timmy.

Joe and Jimmy lived together; they'd called a full council meeting to declare that they were gay and committed to each other. They seemed a little put out when their grand revelation was greeted with indifference. George told them that everybody had known they were gay for a long time and nobody cared. They were both told off by Mambi for not uncloseting sooner.

Hunter brought in a girl he lived with outside the lands. She was of mixed race, African and Indian, of South African origin. In spite of post-apartheid SA her parents felt she might be subjected to diverse forms of racism and fled to the States. She had one small boy from a previous relationship. Hunter was fine with that and George had the council declare the boy adopted son of Nehwe sons of the No'ipinKoi Shoshone.

George carried on as normal and organised extraction and sale of silver. Mike created a Nehwe bank account in Carson to hold the accumulating wealth. Everything settled into a valid and functional developing community.

General security was becoming more complicated so after liaising with the council, Mike called Jackson. He and Rex agreed to come work on the lands as deputies to George and protection for the people and the silver. They were both disenchanted with capitol police work. Since the storming of the capitol in 2021 and the subsequent inaction by politicians, they'd decided they felt unsafe and unappreciated. There was just the two of them. Jackson's wife, Rex's mother, had died during Covid. They saw this as a new start.

One of the Vegas casinos made an offer to collect and pay for the silver at ninety-five per cent value. They'd take on the hassle of passing it to market. After discussion, the council accepted the offer; it saved the Nehwe from that part of the operation and also saved them the associated cost. Timmy and his small band of warriors did the digging, never deep and always refilling. The two ex-cops chased off any trespassers. Mambi kept the books and the council supervised.

Mike negotiated with the council to arrange for timber shipments and to allow some construction workers to come onto the lands. He intended to rebuild Gutusipe Daindi and persuade the rest of the people to move into it. The council regularly reminded him that he was failing to take some wealth for himself. He told them he'd get around to it, maybe, and in the meantime had a few tens of thousands sent to his former wife so that she could at least live comfortably.

Adams, with Mike's permission, went for broke with the legal matters. In total it took over a year to make representation to the US Supreme Court, the UK Supreme Court and finally the United Nations.

In each pinnacle of judicial deliberation the arguments remained the same. Adams' team and an opposing legal team in each jurisdiction happily argued, employed sophistry and procrastinated for their rapidly escalating fees.

It went something like this:

There is no doubt that the agreement between Dakayivani and Sebastian Ash was made in 1780, while the war between Britain and the rebellious American colonies was raging.

The question therefore becomes twofold: one, were the signatories legitimately entitled to enter into the agreement and two, is the agreement valid in law?

The opposition argued, no. Dakayivani is a vague historical figure in a small undeveloped stone-age tribe and Sebastian Ash had no authority to make an agreement on behalf of his nation.

Adams' team expressed shock at the disrespect towards the ancient No'ipinKoi Shoshone and stated that Dakayivani was a known and recognised chief while Ash, like all British officers at that time, was absolutely entitled to enter into a Crown agreement.

The opposition then presented the simple point that since the United States achieved independence from Britain, with a unilateral declaration in 1776, the agreement cannot be valid since only the US was legally able to cede territory to another country or internal group.

In response Adams' team launched into one of those complicated and sophisticated diatribes beloved by lawyers. The type of arguments that requires concentration and some hasty notes even to follow.

The agreement was made, as we have seen, in 1780. The Declaration of Independence was made in 1776 but referred only to the original thirteen English colonies and signed by representatives from each.

It had no legal force, being merely a declaration, until the Treaty of Paris in 1783 ended hostilities. The US then operated under the Articles of Confederation, written in 1781 and given legitimacy by the Paris treaty. The Articles were later replaced by the US Constitution written in 1787 and passed into law in 1789 through the processes set out in the Articles. Still at this time the law related only to the thirteen states, formally the colonies.

In 1845 a newspaperman, John O'Sullivan, sold more papers by inventing the concept of US Manifest Destiny. The result was a rush for the west coast. The discovery of substantial mineral wealth on that coast led to a greater rush and the need to legally recognise some land in-between.

In 1850 the original United States decided that the land of Utah became a protectorate, a territory, of the US. It didn't become a state until 1896 because that would have brought a legal spotlight onto the treatment of native peoples there. The US Holocaust Memorial Museum encyclopaedia has likened it to the Nazi expansion for Lebensraum.

Nonetheless, the Americanisation of the land continued. Then the civil war erupted. In 1861, with a need to gain more senators and more land, the US declared Nevada a US territory allied to Utah. Nevada itself was incorporated as a state in 1864, long before Utah, and the pesky native peoples either moved on, got killed or were confined to worthless areas.

The people now known as the Nehwe No'ipinKoi Shoshone live on land now owned by Michael Key, the same land that the No'ipinKoi Shoshone and Ash allied to Britain.

The simple and clear fact is that the United States had no legal authority to annex the land now known as Gutusipe Daindi. The Nevada Constitution refers to 'with the agreement of those living there', this agreement was never obtained from Gutusipe Daindi. The original agreement was made earlier than, and therefore on this land superior to, the legitimate legal powers of the US. Legal authority, proper legal authority, cannot be used to arbitrarily annex territory claimed and occupied by people with a legitimate claim who do not agree to surrender it.

Were we to accept otherwise then such claims of US ownership may be extended to, say, Canada or the British West Indies and even to India or Australasia.

The purpose of the American war was to free a specific land and people from British control. It did not extend beyond that land. Historical sources suggest that the revolutionaries considered an attack on British Canada. They concluded that such an act was outside their remit. This implies that the colonies did not consider their rebellion to extend beyond the east coast states.

The only possible conclusion is that Gutusipe Daindi is an independent nation landlocked within the United States and under treaty to the United Kingdom. The peoples of this small nation retain autonomy and legitimate jurisdiction over these lands. Nothing subsequent to the agreement between the Nehwe No'ipinKoi Shoshone and the Crown can negate that alliance without agreement and it was in no way changed by the development of US legitimacy.

Both Supreme Courts and the UN committee immediately responded with stunned silence. The audacity, the implications, the sheer chutzpah. Each august body adjourned to consider the position. Politicians on each side of the Atlantic sat up and watched. The Nehwe held a huge barbeque and rumour, possibly malicious, had it that the French had a bit of a snigger.

As is often the way, the need for careful legal review and a couple of expensive holiday breaks delayed the decisions. When it came a couple of months later each Supreme Court declared one dissenting member and the UN was unanimous. It was widely reported that the fact the dissenting members each side of the pond were cousins was irrelevant. They insisted that they had not consulted and the disclosure of a joint weekend break on a Caribbean island owned by a US congressman was just a family matter.

Each judicial body returned its decision in quiet and sombre carefulness:

The US Supreme Court:
The legitimacy of the 1780 agreement rests on whether it was lawful at the time to make such an agreement. Clearly it was so the agreement started life legitimately and outside other jurisdiction.

The question is now whether the United States could legitimately dissolve such an agreement at a later date. Such a thing can only occur in two ways, either by further agreement or through the proper occupation by force during conflict lawful under International Law.

No agreement was ever reached and the United States did not annex the land during the conflict with Britain and cannot do so lawfully after the 1783 Treaty of Paris.

Therefore, the land of Gutusipe Daindi retains autonomy, independence from the US. The land retains alliance with the UK. It is for governments and not the court to decide the future of the land. This means that in addition to the US and UK governments, the council of the Nehwe No'ipinKoi Shoshone is recognised in law as a national government and may liaise with the other two.

The US has no lawful power to profit from the extraction of precious metals or other minerals.

The UK Supreme Court:
This court's decision was almost identical to that of their US counterpart. However, it made the additional observation that the 1780 agreement requires the UK government to provide assistance and protection to Gutusipe Daindi and is free to negotiate a share of the mineral and precious metal wealth.

The United Nations:
The UN accepted the same arguments as both Supreme Courts. It remained silent on the question of protection by the UK but did refer such a matter to the Security Council. It issued a requirement that either nation taking anything similar to military or law enforcement action must refer to the UN first. Finally, the UN declared that it recognised Gutusipe Daindi as an autonomous nation and admitted it to the UN.

The US and UK governments immediately arranged high-level talks between them with the UN.

The Nehwe held another huge barbecue during which Rex got a bit drunk and ended up sleeping with a Nehwe girl named Joanne. Nobody minded; it was clearly consensual and everybody liked Rex and Jackson. Joanne advised Mama Mambi, who checked with her, that she'd been sober and fully aware of what she was doing.

Adams sat back and studied her now huge bank balance with intense satisfaction.

Rumour has it, still possibly malicious, that the French openly laughed.

Chapter Fifteen

Rex was very pleased with the large and powerful armoured Humvee that had been bought for him and Jackson to use. It was his dad's day to chill in the sun with some beers and just mess with friends he'd made in this place.

Jackson's friends mainly consisted of council members, men of about his age. Most of them suffered various health problems but were still able to drink and talk drivel with pals. A few of the older women joined in as well. Many of them exhibited an underlying sadness, he thought.

Rex just followed his usual habit for the day. He drove into town to see how it was coming along. He stopped outside the new building in place of the old sheriff's office. It now sported the sign 'Town Manager and Law' – it had become known as 'Mike and George's Office'.

"Hey, Rex," Mike called from the scaffold on the side of the building slowly replacing the saloon. "Who's controller today, I forgot to look?"

"Mambi again," Rex informed him. "She just loves that radio and power."

George emerged from his office. He went over and talked with Rex. Mike joined them and they all enjoyed a soft drink and chat.

Then Rex climbed back into his chariot and drove out of the other side of town.

As usual he was heading for several spots throughout the desert. At each point he climbed on top of the Humvee and observed around with a pair of binoculars.

He didn't see much. At one point he could make out Timmy and his crew, the Warriors as they were now always known, busy extracting some silver from a distant hole. They liked the gang-sounding title, it kind of formalised what most people had started calling them anyway and they felt it reflected their status.

Rex drove along the desert side base of the ridge extension, through the settlement and onto the track that leads to the highway. This was his next observation point.

As he stood on the Humvee and looked through the binoculars, he could see a thin dust cloud far off towards the highway.

He watched as the cloud continued in his direction until he could see it was a car. Not just any old car, even at this distance he could tell it was a Bentley, the transport of rich people, powerful people and rock stars.

He watched as it approached. His assessment was that it was a bog-standard motor, if such a term can be used towards such a car. He meant that it did not seem armoured, adapted for off road or otherwise intended for anything other than a nice ride.

When he judged it was close enough he climbed down from the roof and took one of the AR15s from a rack in the Humvee. Timmy was an expert with almost any gun and kept them all functional and fully automatic. He always said that in the event of any official interest he could quickly return them all to semi-auto.

When the car was climbing towards the fork in the tracks it flashed its headlights. Rex took this as a signal that the occupants acknowledged his presence. He angled himself so that the Humvee afforded some protection but did not adopt an aggressive stance. He had informed Mambi by radio and she said she'd send some people.

He'd told her it was OK at the moment. He just held the AR15 across his body.

The Bentley stopped in front of the Humvee. He could see four people in it, including the driver. The front passenger was an older white man, grey-haired and well dressed. In the back were a white man of about forty, dressed in casual tough clothing of the kind used for extreme hiking, and a white woman of about thirty, similarly dressed.

The front passenger got out of the car. "Good morning," he said in a carefully spoken managing-class English accent.

"Good morning," Rex replied. "Sir, you are accidently trespassing. If you have no business here please leave. Do not allow anybody else to leave your admittedly beautiful car. I will not assault you but I can and will defend myself and I have reinforcements on the way."

The man in the back of the car applauded and the woman said loudly, "Good man. That's our lad." She had a Scots accent.

At that point a pick-up approached from the direction of town. This replacement for the mortally wounded old rental vehicle was driven by Mike, and George was passenger.

They pulled up by the Humvee and got out. Mike was wearing his revolver and George had a shotgun. They spoke quickly with Rex and then went to the grey-haired man. Rex stayed where he was and the two rear Bentley passengers nodded approval in unison.

"I'm Mike Key; this is Chief George Nehwe, sheriff and manager of Gutusipe Daindi," Mike said to him.

The man smiled and offered his hand. "My name is Duncan Mulgrave. I represent the British embassy in the US," he informed them.

George laughed. "The British are coming, then."

Mulgrave gave a friendly smile. "To whom should I address myself?"

"Both of us," said Mike. "We are very keen to avoid any conflict in light of the court decisions."

"Oh, so are we," Mulgrave told them. "London has decided that we should send representatives to stay here as part of our obligation under the 1780 treaty agreement. Jon and Fi here are to do that. They are from a specialist military group and answer to me. I guarantee they will cause no trouble and are here merely as a token presence."

Mike thought for a moment. "No weapons," he said. "We undertake not to harm them; they can stay if the council approve it, they will, and George has no objections." George nodded his assent.

"I see. They each have a small personal weapon but nothing of military grade, will that be alright?" Mulgrave asked.

Mike looked at George, who nodded again. "OK but nothing automatic or heavy calibre. I suppose in this country we are all forced into arming ourselves. That right to carry arms thing is a real bummer." Everybody laughed. Mike continued, "Who are they, SAS SBS?"

Mulgrave shook his head. "No. Not special forces. Special grey ops if you like. Military but a bit off the grid, downmarket Bond, kind of clean and smiley or down and dirty, whatever's needed. Not a group you'd send to war but individuals you'd send to do an off-tangent job."

Mike nodded. "Their job here is?"

"Just a token presence," Mulgrave assured him. "If we were invading the States we'd send at least fifteen more people." He and Mike laughed at a particularly unserious British joke. George smiled but didn't really get it.

Mulgrave offered to take the special soldiers to the town. George declined that and indicated they should climb in the pick-up.

"That's good," Mulgrave said. "The Americans know we're here. They may send some people as well. If we weren't so comfortable in dealing with each other, well, this has the potential to go disastrously wrong. Just a presence until the politicos sort themselves out."

Jon and Fi grabbed a large bag each and jumped into the back of the pick-up. Mulgrave left with his driver.

"Decent guard job, careful and alert, well done, son," Jon said to Rex in a London accent as he passed him.

Once in Gutusipe Daindi town, Mike searched the two large bags. It was mainly ration packs, water, clothing and personal survival gear. They both had phones that they were allowed to keep. When asked to show their weapons they each produced a Glock and a Royal Marines-style dagger. They were also allowed to keep them except that Mike only permitted ten rounds in each handgun; other ammunition was confiscated with apologies.

A few places had been rebuilt so far and Mike offered them a small flat each. They said they preferred to share, no offence but safety and security and all that.

"None taken," Mike told them. "Makes sense."

They were given a flat in the side street opposite the Manager's Office and told that they could go anywhere. If they had any problems with anybody they should ask for Mike or George to be contacted. After a warning about water use they went off to their new home for however long that may be.

Mike told them to write up a shopping order for things like tea, coffee, snacks, whatever. They should hand it to George and it would get sorted, courtesy of Gutusipe Daindi. Daily meals would be supplied and they would be considered to be guests.

As Fi passed Mike she smiled at him. "Just so you know, everybody in both governments know that you killed Milenkovic. Nobody minds. Fucking good job, mate."

Two days later Mike was again working on renewing a building. He directed the visiting builders and carpenters as well as doing a little himself.

He was on the roof of a house in one of the side roads when he heard the frantic hooting of a car horn. Looking into the desert he saw the Humvee racing towards town, throwing up a rear cloud of dust. He slid down the ladder to ground level and rushed up to the main street.

George joined him just as the big vehicle came to a halt by both of them. Rex and Jackson jumped out.

"I think the Man's coming," said Jackson, pointing to the distant sky. The group were joined by Jon and Fi who were both now wearing desert camo combat jackets with Union Flag patches.

"I think Uncle Sam is about to announce his intention to dispute the court's opinion," advised Jon.

As they watched, the approach from the air became clearer. Three military grey Chinooks escorted by eight sleek black Apache helicopter gunships swooped towards them. The stars and stripes was clearly displayed on each machine.

Jon laughed and handed a one hundred dollar bill to Fi. She laughed, took out her phone and tapped it until it played The Ride of the Valkyries.

"I love the smell of testosterone in the morning," she exclaimed.

Jon responded to Mike's enquiring look. "I reckoned they'd come by road, all *7th Cavalry* and brash John Wayne," he said. "She reckoned they'd go flat out for an *Apocalypse Now* dick boast and fly in to make an impression. She won."

"Think we're going to be overpowered by force?" Mike asked.

Jon shook his head. "Don't think so. We're just seeing a reminder of who is the biggest, toughest street fighter in this neighbourhood; it's just big ape chest thumping and swagger. They won't act in contempt of their own courts. They will probably leave a token presence after a display of alpha yapping and muscle flexing."

A roaring engine from the other side of town announced the arrival of another Humvee – this one was hand-painted bright pink with native symbols stencilled all over it. It joined the group and Timmy and the Warriors piled out, all armed with the heaviest automatics the Nehwe could muster. He offered Mike the seized Kalashnikov.

"No, no," Mike told him. "We're not fighting. Spread your guys about but nobody open fire or act hostile. Calm down the construction guys; they're crapping themselves. We're not being attacked. The strongest guy in the land, any land I suppose, just wants to get our attention."

Jon and Fi watched without any apparent concern. Jackson and Rex chatted together then came close to Mike.

"If they use force we should all surrender straight away," Jackson told him.

"It's cool," Mike said. "We are not going to fight."

The airborne fleet arrived. Two of the Chinooks hovered over the centre of the town at about fifty feet. Their rotors threw up dust from the downdraught. The twin rotors spinning in opposite directions created vortices that produced mini tornados of twirling dust and made a deafening noise. A few roof tiles blew off the buildings closest to them. The gunships circled the town, adding to the great cacophony and generating the impression of an overwhelmingly powerful force making a mighty angry roar.

The third Chinook set down about three hundred yards into the desert. The rear ramp descended. For a moment, nothing happened and then two figures in full US battle gear walked down onto the ground. With assault rifles across their chests, they walked towards the town. When they were clear, the Chinook took off again and hovered.

As the two soldiers approached, they briefly raised their arms to show no immediate hostile intent. One of them spoke into a radio at his shoulder. Moments later all of the helicopters reacquired their formation and flew noisily back into the desert, slowly fading into the milky distance.

Mike walked to meet the two soldiers. He was quickly joined by Jackson, Rex, Jon and Fi. Rex was preparing his AR15 but Jackson punched him in the arm and told him to just let it rest on its strap.

The two US soldiers stopped, assessed the small greeting committee and decided that Mike was the leader.

"Sir," said the older, taller soldier, "my name is Major Cy

Langham. This here is Sergeant Dane Swartz." He spoke with a vaguely Tex-Mex accent though looked white.

"We are to stay here to stake the American claim," said Swartz. "We have no intention of violence or harm. We have everything we need with us and hope to deal with this, er, unusual situation peacefully and in accordance with any further orders we may eventually receive."

Mike bade them welcome. He gave them a flat across the street from Jon and Fi. They declined to disarm and Mike didn't press the issue. The two British soldiers introduced themselves and they all shook hands. They all walked off together to get the Americans settled in.

"Get them to make a shopping list," Mike called after them. "Tell them it's safe to wear normal clothing; they'll bake if they keep that lot on."

George walked over to Mike. "I'll go inform Mambi and the council."

"I think they'll already know unless they're deaf," Mike told him.

"I'll take your pick-up," said George and wandered off.

Mike spoke with the construction workers' gang boss. It was agreed that they take a couple of weeks off, fully paid, while everybody waited to see what happened next. Mike explained that it all depended on talks between the US, UK and UN.

He called Mambi on the Wolf phone and explained he'd be staying in town for the moment. He occupied one of the new flats above the Town Manager's office. There were two new flats there now; George used the other one when he stayed in town. He called Jan Adams on the devil phone and updated her on events.

As all the new residents settled in and those who'd rushed to the defence withdrew, he sat and enjoyed a vape and a warm, weak beer from the can. Then he settled down onto the handmade bed and slept.

He'd only dozed off for a short while when he was awoken by raucous laughter and shouting. He went to the window and saw Jon and Fi with Cy and Dane.

The Americans didn't have their assault rifles with them and had shed much of their body armour. The four soldiers looked like any group of healthy military personnel messing about and just noisily bonding. Mike smiled and returned to bed.

Since the incident with the Serbs, Mike had fewer and less extreme bad dreams. He supposed that in some way it had provided him with partial closure. John was in his dreams but in a pleasant way – they were playing football. He woke as usual to the early desert light. This morning there was no anger and more than just contentment. Today, for the first time in a long time, he felt happy.

He went to his computer. Since a thicker, heavier-duty electricity cable had been fed from the road to a small new substation, the town had normal levels of electric power. The larger water inlet feeding four raised tower tanks was well under way. The town was coming along well.

He e-mailed his ex-wife, Mel, to ensure she was well. He asked for pictures of John and some other family photos to be e-mailed to him. He also assured her that money would keep finding its way to her.

She'd replied by the time he had showered and eaten. Mel informed him that he and Gutusipe Daindi were all over the news. She sent some pictures and said she'd keep them coming until he had everything. She told him she was coping with her new life and that the old life with him and John had been perfect. She knew that they could no longer work as a couple and wished him well. She signed off, 'Fight for what is right – it's what you've always done'. It brought a small tear to his eye.

Then he realised that if this matter was big news then he should seek to exploit that. First he phoned Mambi to get agreement. Next he e-mailed every news outlet he could think of and introduced himself and Mambi; he used a joint Nehwe council mail address. The replies started to pour in almost immediately. He didn't bother to look at them; it was time for his morning stroll around the town.

As he wandered down the main street, Wolf arrived in his pick-up followed by Timmy in the pink Humvee. Wolf parked outside the Town Manager's office and he walked over to her. She got out and hugged him. She smelled of flowers that he couldn't name, just nice. He kissed her on the top of her head.

Timmy came over and they slapped hands. They were all chatting when four very fit-looking people ran around a corner towards them.

The two pairs of soldiers looked as if they were transitioning from exercise to competition. The three chatting friends returned their wave and laughed.

"I'm determined that this will not fall away into any fighting," Mike said.

"Me too," said Timmy. "You need to know this; I've done some sums."

Wolf giggled. "Go on then, Einstein, what have you worked out?"

Timmy ruffled Wolf's hair and laughed at her annoyed look. "Well," he said, "given the size of this land and what we've found so far, it's massive. If we just dug down twenty feet everywhere and took what was easy to grab, the silver here I estimate to be worth ten billion dollars at current prices."

"Wow," Mike exclaimed.

"More than that," Timmy continued, "if we were to deep mine or even managed open cast, we could easily produce something approaching a hundred billion or more."

Wolf joined in, "It's even more than that – it is likely that further down may be gold or even uranium, though that's less likely."

Timmy said, "The point is, this land could easily hold several hundreds of billions or more – tell him, Wolf."

She laughed. "I've had some deeper soil analysed. It is rich in rare earth metals. More valuable than gold or diamonds. Several hundred billion might be a serious underestimate. We could be talking trillions."

Mike thought for a moment. "Oh, shit. No wonder everybody is so interested. I think it's very important we keep the eyes of the world on us. If the big guys get stroppy we're gonna get squashed."

Chapter Sixteen

The few days after the revelation of riches quiescent in the ground had been quiet. Joe and Jimmy had moved permanently into town. They took one of the completed side street houses on the desert side. Joe brought a couple of M16 rifles with him and Jimmy a pump action shotgun. Mike was growing a little uncomfortable with the number of weapons coming into town.

He spent most days talking by phone to various news people. He did his best to explain the situation but mainly referred them to Mambi. He declined requests to make Zoom calls to any of them.

On the morning of the third day he was surprised to see the pink Humvee parked outside the Town Manager's office. He noticed it from his window as he drank some coffee.

He also saw the four soldiers on their morning run. They slowed at sight of the Humvee. Fi jogged over to it and put her hand to the front grill.

"Cold," she called out to the others. They continued to run.

Mike knew that they would run about four miles into the desert and back, a thing he considered to be an act of insanity but that's tough guys for you. He was pleased they were getting along. He also knew that if their respective governments instructed them to become enemies they would do that in a heartbeat.

He was still idly watching the street ten minutes later. He saw Timmy walk around a corner from the direction of the soldiers' flats, get into the Humvee and drive off towards the other side of town. As Timmy drove away, Joe and Jimmy slid out from some other part-complete buildings and walked off towards their house.

Mike decided to make this a lazy morning. He was now expecting a call. Sure enough, a few hours later, as he sat reading a book, the Wolf phone rang.

"Good morning," Mike greeted the caller.

"It was nothing dangerous," said a sheepish-sounding Wolf.

"Timmy saw me watching?"

"No, Joe did." Wolf was silent for a moment. "We have done nothing that will harm them. We haven't booby trapped the flats or poisoned their food or anything like that."

"What have you done then?"

Wolf was silent for another moment. "Timmy disabled their assault rifles. He left the handguns alone but the rifles won't fire. That's all, I promise."

Mike sighed. "Oh Wolf. I know you all meant well, but, but, well… these guys are very good; they'll notice."

"Timmy says they won't. He knows what he's doing. He replaced the firing pins with very soft metal identical-looking things. It will all look the same and not be obvious unless they try to fire the guns."

"Let's hope so," Mike said. "It's not actually a bad idea but, just but, you know what I'm going to say."

Wolf sounded almost relieved. "I know. I'll confess to Mambi and George. I'm sorry Mike, we would have let you know but Timmy was afraid you'd stop him. The Warriors all agreed that it was for the best."

Mike rubbed his face. "Yeah, Wolf, but if we're going to try to become a group who answer to ourselves we must have a proper decision-making protocol. We just have to or we become just as bad as some lawless gang. We just have to do things properly or there will be more blood."

"Nobody disagrees with that, Mike." Wolf sounded contrite. "It's done now. I promise, really promise that in future we will get the OK from the council for what we do. After Mambi beats me up I'll come and see you, so will Timmy. He's sorry as well."

By now the soldiers would have almost completed their run. Mike knew that after doing that they spent a long while doing all sorts of strength building and suppleness exercises before running back to the flats.

He was just cooking up some porridge when he heard them pounding down the street. He then heard a dull thump and raucous laughter.

From the window he saw Fi in a fighting position. Dane was about ten feet from her doubled over and clutching his face. He spat bloodily onto the dirt. The other two were practically falling into each other laughing. Mike opened the window.

"Mike," Cy called up to him, still laughing, "no problem, buddy. The guy copped a sneaky feel and got more than he bargained for."

Dane looked up and was also laughing, blood coating his teeth and trickling from his mouth. He loudly apologised to Fi. She showed her acceptance by dropping her fists and running on. The others followed her.

Mike's suspicious attitude extended to everything. He asked himself what that was really about. That little fight could have happened anywhere, why here? Not the best spot to cop a sneaky feel, not after a hot sweaty run and workout. No, that was staged. Besides, Dane didn't strike him as the sort of dick who'd do that anyway.

He finished his porridge and went outside. He stood outside the Town Manager's office just looking. Nothing was obvious.

He crossed the street to the partly constructed buildings there. This part of town was intended as a commercial centre and had cowboy town-style covered raised walkways in front of the intended stores.

On the side of one of the support posts he saw a light brown matchbox-sized device. It was held by small spikes into the wood; it would have just been pushed into position. He pulled it off to examine it.

It was a small camera, probably movement activated. A small and expensive version of the kind of wildlife-watching camera commonly available. Interesting that the two groups were clearly working together at the moment.

He took the camera back to his flat. He texted Mambi to inform her and then searched for an envelope. On the envelope he wrote the word 'no' and placed the camera in it. He then walked down to where the soldiers were staying. He knew he was being watched from each flat as he pinned the envelope to a post.

"Just no," he called out loudly and then walked back.

A while later there was a knocking at his door. The access to his new flat was via open stairs at the side of the building. He opened the door and Dane was standing on the small landing atop the flight of stairs.

Dane was smiling repentantly at him. "I guess I took a shot in the mouth for no reason, then."

"Come in and talk, Dane. What do you want?"

Dane accepted a coffee but sipped at it gingerly as he avoided the inside split on his lower lip. "We just wondered what the Indian was here for last night. The camera was to check if he came back."

"There are no Indians here," Mike spoke irritably and slowly. "Mainly Americans and a spit of Brits. The man you're talking about is American and Nehwe, a former marine who served in Afghanistan so show some fucking respect."

"Ner what?" said a startled Dane; he hadn't expected the robust angry response.

"Nehwe," Mike repeated. "The Nehwe Shoshone are the original occupants of this land. They became American later, not through choice. We want to settle this thing through the courts but if you guys act against us, me and my Warriors will escort you all off this land. We have to be clear about who is here by right and who is just a guest. Timmy was visiting me last night; he got a bit drunk and slept it off here, OK?"

Dane just nodded. He apologised for any offence he'd caused and left. As he reached the street his professional eye noted that two people were watching him from upper-storey windows. Jimmy waved at him when it was clear he'd been seen.

Mike phoned Mambi and updated her. Half an hour later there was more knocking at his door. He opened a draw, took out his push knife and fitted it to the rear of his belt.

Standing at his door this time was Jon and Cy. Cy handed him a disposable cup filled with warm, vanilla-flavoured coffee.

"Wow," Mike said as he took a sip of the delicious beverage, "has someone opened a Starbuck's nearby without me knowing?"

Cy explained it was part of the rations they'd brought with them and now a peace offering. Mike invited them in.

Cy spoke first. "We're sorry if we overstepped the mark. We didn't mean to spy on you, just looking to our own security."

Mike nodded. "I'm OK if we just write off this little bit of foolishness. Nobody's hurt, except Dane of course but that was funny to watch." The two soldiers laughed.

Jon clapped his hands together. "Problem was, is, we are getting along as military professionals and hope we don't have to act against each other. Yeah, we've bonded a bit; it caused us to act as one group. It's a known effect in situations like this. None of us are normal dig in and pound the enemy soldiers. We all end up in some odd spots. This is one of the better ones, believe me."

Cy nodded enthusiastically. "Strictly speaking, me and Dane are not even soldiers in the usual sense. We're a team that works to the FBI, Homeland Security, whoever has government permission to task us. We do a similar job to Jon and Fi. Got a farm full of messianic nutcases to storm, that's us. Need a single bod to infiltrate a nest of weirdo terrorists, that's us as well."

Jon chuckled. "Nobody knew what to do with you, that's why we ended up here. We will play a straight bat, Mike, but we act for our governments. We have no personal issues with you."

Mike assured them that he understood. They left after a bit more small talk. Then he phoned Mambi to update her further.

"You will have more visitors soon," she told him. "Be nice. They are crossing the ridge now. They're friendlies, no weapons. I've told Hunter to let them pass; it's his turn up on the ridge at the moment."

Mike went outside to see what turned up. He saw two large box vans, one black the other green, trundling into town towards him. As they came closer he could see that the black one was marked 'BBC' and the other 'FOX news'. Fox was leading and as soon as it arrived, a peroxide blonde, brown eyebrows, slim woman slithered out.

"Hey, Mike? Mike Key, hero. Talk to me," she said with far too much bonhomie, make-up, hard ambitious eyes and a really annoying high-pitched American nasal screech.

"Fox news. Nah, you fuck off. I'll speak to the BBC – you can watch if you want but interfere and I'll have you chucked off this land."

The BBC arrived a few seconds later. The woman who introduced herself to him was a little familiar. Probably he'd seen her on TV. She was younger than he would have expected for this task but very confident. He missed her name and didn't bother to ask it again. As the camera crew supported her, he noticed that Fox's crew filmed from one side as well.

"Best enter into an agreement with that lot not to nick your work," he said to the BBC lady. He also noticed that Jon wandered over and stood watching. A few moments later Cy joined Jon and they watched together.

Ms BBC gave him the 'you can trust me' smile. "What are your feelings about the demonstrators on their way here?"

"What demonstrators?" he said. Then the Wolf phone rang.

"Hello?" he asked as the news crews continued to film.

"Hi, it's Mambi. My bad, the news crews were followed by a bunch of trucks, all stars and bars and maga hats. I'm sending Timmy to join Hunter and George is calling the other two now. Jackson and Rex are already on their way."

"You got followed," he said to BBC.

As if to underscore the point, Joe and Jimmy roared round the corner on the two motorbikes. They didn't slow as they passed the group and raced off towards the ridge.

"We were worried we might be," simpered BBC and just smiled again.

Two phones rang in unison and both Jon and Cy answered the calls. They just looked at each other then spoke together momentarily and nodded.

"We both have orders to support your guys," called Cy. "We need wheels."

Mike threw them the key fob for his pick-up, telling them it was parked at the back of the new flats. "It's all go here," he said to BBC.

She asked a few pointless questions. "How do you feel now? What's it like being the land owner? Do you enjoy being king?" and other rubbish.

His pick-up spun round the corner with Fi at the wheel. Jon and the Americans were in the open back. The Americans were in full battle dress and had their assault rifles with them. They accelerated hard towards the ridge.

"Tell you what," he said to BBC, "give me a lift up there and you get some good film." He called over to Fox, "You follow if you like; if you stay here don't break anything." He climbed into the BBC van.

Fox followed the BBC to the point on the ridge overlooking the flat between that and the highway. All of the Warriors were deployed behind cover at various points. Jackson and Rex stood in the open, though close to cover, watching below. The soldiers all stood to one side, also close to cover. Mike joined the two cops, ex-cops.

Further down the road to the flat land, Mike could see a sign on a pole but it was turned towards the crowd below. The BBC parked their van somewhere safe and joined him, filming all along.

The crowd below probably looked huge when it was on the highway. Now they'd brought their several Dukes of Hazzard motors into the vast desert, sixty or so guys didn't look quite so intimidating. Various flags, stars and stripes, stars and bars, some odd red and blue flags that made no apparent sense and a strange flag that looked like three sevens inverted into a symbol. More disturbingly, many were armed with rifles, handguns and many in a varied collection of military-style clothing including some body armour.

"Who are they?" Mike asked.

"Dunno really," Jackson answered. "Last saw this type in 2021, at the capitol and around there. Dunno what they want but they're upset about something."

"They don't seem very confident about coming up here."

Jackson laughed. "They've looked for another way past but the next pass is over fifty miles further down and that just leads into the far desert. The sign down there says that anybody passing beyond it will be shot. A couple of them have tested the water but Hunter put a red dot on them and they went back."

Mike looked along the ridge and saw Hunter. He was higher up and in possession of a monster-looking rifle, fifty cal he later called it. It rested on a bipod and sported a large telescopic sight with a red laser target finder.

"Timmy said the man was a sniper in a previous life, army I think," Jackson informed him.

"What will you do, Mike?" asked Ms BBC.

"Nothing. If they don't come up here then nothing will happen. I don't think they will cos we hold a pretty defensible position here.

They're in the desert with no services for at least a hundred miles. They'll cook, sweat and thirst then go away."

Fox declared they would speak with the patriots below and drove their van down to them.

"Patriots? Fucking dick Klan shitheads," whispered Jackson.

Mike nodded at him. "They're terrified we might take away people they can subtly bully and feel superior to. Just proud boys struggling with their sexual orientation." Jackson laughed.

Mambi and Wolf arrived in George's old clapped out truck. Everyone on the ridge grinned at the old heap smoking its way to their aid. Wolf had her M16 with her and went to join Timmy. She hugged Joe and Jimmy as she passed them.

Mambi told Mike that once this was over they'd leave two people on this part of the ridge for the next week or so. Probably one scouting the desert as well but since Jackson and Rex did that anyway that should be enough.

The demonstrators stayed for about six hours or so. They chanted and shouted various meaningless threats and insults. None of it made any sense. Then, as one, they entered their vehicles and drove in convoy towards the highway.

"I'll inform the highway patrol and sort out some guard here," Mambi told Mike. They kissed and Mike invited the BBC to take him back to town.

They interviewed him in the main street. He explained his position and told them that this was the homeland of the Nehwe No'ipinKoi Shoshone and explained that unusual native group. He told them he wasn't challenging the USA but they had to accept that for reasons explained in court, this land was autonomous. He invited Britain to oversee this in accordance with their historic treaty with the Nehwe No'ipinKoi Shoshone.

Without warning, Ms BBC asked, "Did you murder David Milenkovic?"

Mike was quiet for a moment. "Milenkovic was a war criminal, that is he was a criminal who used a war as cover to commit some horrible crimes. He invaded this autonomous territory and died in the attempt. I did not murder him because he was not murdered. He died when this town was defended. I have nothing more to say on that."

Ms BBC winked at him and asked if they could film the town. He told them they could film as much as they wanted; Gutusipe Daindi had nothing to hide. When they were finished they could leave in their own time; nobody would bother them. He gave her the number of the Wolf phone in case of problems. He also gave her Adams' phone number if she wanted a carefully crafted platitude to quote.

Mike was just putting his feet up in his flat. He had phone conversations with Wolf, Mambi and George. Everybody was up to date and content.

Jimmy called on him and left him a chilled bottle of wine. He explained that he'd grabbed some from the settlement after the demonstration and he remembered to get one for Mike as well. They sat and shared a couple of glasses and chatted before Jimmy went back to Joe.

Not long after, there was knocking at his door. Dane Swartz was there and said he needed to talk. Mike invited him in and gave him a glass of wine.

"Oh boy," said Dane happily. "Cy is gonna be so pissed when he finds out I got some chilled wine."

"What brings you here, Dane?"

Dane looked at him. "Cy thought that seeing as I annoyed you last time, I should come again. He reckons if I annoy you again, no problem, and if I don't that's a bonus."

"Go on."

Dane sipped some more wine. "Well, first of all, as an American I, we, apologise for the dicks you saw today."

Mike chortled. "That's OK. Everybody has fools like that. They're just afraid. Who they are is focused on being innately better than some other people. It's not good but that's how it is. They're pretty dumb and easily stirred up if their delusional view of the world is challenged. That's not why you are here."

"No, we want our firing pins back. Somebody did a good job; we didn't notice until we prepared for battle. We'd cleaned the rifles as well and still didn't spot it before. Failed a test fire."

Mike laughed. "No problem. It was unauthorised and the guy who did it meant well. He wasn't out to harm you, just to limit your ability to do harm. I'll get them back to you."

"Timmy?" Dane asked.

"Oh, come on," Mike said. "You know I can't say. We've dealt with the indiscipline; it won't happen again."

Dane laughed as well. "Yeah, Timmy. OK, no problem. Let's call that quits. I knew we were right to try the camera." They both laughed.

"We are sorry. And thanks for your comments about the demonstration and thanks for backing up my guys – we appreciate it," Mike told him.

"Fucking redneck dirtbags still pissed that they can't keep slaves. Fuck 'em," snapped Dane.

Mike laughed again. "Not quite that simple in my view but I know what you mean. Redneck just means descendent of confederate soldiers. Many, most of them, are OK."

Dane shook his head. "All redneck trash. Southerners OK, rednecks scum."

Mike sang the first line of the song 'The Night They Drove Old Dixie Down'. "That song was written by a guy who was a Jewish half Mohawk Canadian. He saw what I see. The trouble with what I'm gonna say is that I sound like an apologist for slavery. I'm not. I don't for one second belittle the horror of slavery. But, it's more than that, it's not just losing the right to own other human beings that led to the dicks we saw today."

"Now you go on; I've got to hear you justify that," said Dane.

Mike sucked his teeth. "Well, you have a German name – are you or your ancestors Nazi scum?"

Dane smiled but had a bit of a 'be careful' look in his eye. "No. No way. My great-grandfather came to America after the first war; he could see Germany getting worse."

Mike nodded. "That's because the victors, the allies, imposed severe penalties to get back the cost of the war. Making Germany pay led to the rise of the Nazi party."

Dane held out his glass for the offered last dregs of the wine.

"Same after your civil war," Mike continued. "The south was asset stripped. Not just the slave owners, who should have been put on trial but were not, everybody in the south was punished; they were made to pay as their manufacturing was destroyed and their land burnt. They were made to pay reparations this way. Most of them just saw themselves as ordinary working people and as always manipulated by the rich bods. It led to the rise of the Klan and the dicks we saw today. Just saying. Try to understand your enemy and then you stand a chance of making him not your enemy. Oh, educate him and don't let him put up monuments to the generals who got him defeated."

Dane just nodded and mumbled that he understood the point. "You can't ignore the anger of the victims though."

"No, but you can look to limit the vengeance to justice. Israel still hunts down old Nazis but doesn't demand anything of Germany itself except fair play. It's true that those who still feel the ongoing disadvantage of slavery should have that addressed; I don't know how. But I do know that you can't do that by punishing everybody just because they lived on the losing side. Two wrongs don't make a right and it will just build up into conflict with both sides feeling that they are the victim. You can't compare levels of unfairness; you just have to find fairness somehow. Mandela did it."

"Dunno," commented Dane.

Mike shrugged. "All I'm saying is that just as the real effects of slavery have never been addressed, leading to disadvantage now, same with the rednecks. You can still punish the guilty but if you drive a whole people into disadvantage, well, they're going to react a few generations later. Easy to believe any old rubbish if you already feel downtrodden, come on in fake news and crazy conspiracies."

"You one interesting guy, Mike," Dane told him. "Gentle guy, tough guy, fighter, peacemaker. Even if we end up with orders to stop this town, I will still respect you. I want you to know that."

Mike nodded. "I don't think you will get those orders. If you do, know that I still like you and Cy even if we come into conflict."

Dane smiled. "I hope you are right. I'm actually wishing you well. Probably Stockholm syndrome." They both laughed and Dane left.

Just before he went to bed, the devil phone rang. Adams told him to be at the United Nations building in New York at 9am in five days.

"Things are moving forward," she ended without further explanation.

Chapter Seventeen

The council decided that Mike should not be alone on this trip. Given the injuries that came with the last jaunt he should have some serious protection with him this time. Jackson and Rex would accompany him and he was told to take their advice even if he disagreed. Jackson's skilled risk assessment research was comprehensive.

Blake was in prison and would be for the next fifteen to twenty-five years. While he spent his time avoiding overfriendly cellmates, there didn't appear to be anybody likely to seek payback on his behalf.

The surviving Serbs were back in the Balkans doing goodness knows what. There was no intelligence to suggest they were planning revenge.

The people Mike had referred to as the 'maga twats' might make some noise. It was unlikely they'd look for a stand-up fight in New York.

Adams was still not trustworthy in the normal sense but knew where her golden, or silver, calf was grazing. She could be discounted as a threat purely because she'd follow her own self-interest. The only real risk was the city of New York itself. The greatest perils were crime, unfriendliness, casual nutcases and uncivil cab drivers.

Jackson told him, "I had to use up a lot of favours to get all of this info – I hope it's worth it."

Mike replied, "Oh, and booking top rooms in one of the most expensive hotels, was that an essential part of my protection as well?"

Rex laughed and said, "It was either that or Trump Tower. We have our tolerance limits, you know."

The 'room' was in fact a tastefully decorated and furnished yet subtly opulent suite with three bedrooms.

Mike sighed as they walked in. "Really," he said, "a few thousand a night for sure. Really?"

"Twelve," said Rex then shut up as his dad glared at him.

Jackson tapped Mike's arm. "Listen, Mike. You know the effect of separate rooms if things go wrong; you've still got the bruises. If we are to protect you then we are using this room. Yeah, it's expensive. Yeah, it's flash. It also gets used by politicians and business giants. The windows and doors are bulletproof; we have a direct line to hotel security and the local cops. We can protect you here; it is a safe space, OK?"

Mike nodded. "It's probably bugged as well." He walked over to a bunch of flowers in a vase and spoke loudly into them, "The last president was a nutter; the current president is very odd; and I think the vice president is a secret royalist."

Jackson and Rex laughed. Rex picked up the phone and ordered a full-scale multi-course meal to be brought to the room.

The following morning Jackson and Rex escorted Mike to the front of the hotel. There were already two cabs waiting outside. They were ignored and Rex walked a little way down the street and hailed the third taxi that passed him. He was clearly counting them.

"Is this really necessary?" asked Mike.

Jackson pulled him towards the cab. "If it's not then we just look silly. If it is then maybe we just saved your life. Get in."

"I'm so grateful," Mike said mockingly as he was pushed into the cab. "I'll get your wages doubled. Joke."

Rex poked him in the arm. "Too late, man, you said it. It's happening. Dunno how you'll explain it to the council."

"Where to, jokers?" asked the clearly life-weary driver.

"The United Nations' building, please," said Mike.

"Turtle Bay," said Jackson, talking over him. He turned to Mike. "Just say Turtle Bay, everyone will know where you mean."

"Rich guy land, filthy Manhattan, money-spinning arseholes," called the driver almost ecstatically.

The driver dropped them in front of a large but not especially imposing towering and elongated office block.

"The land of milk 'em and baloney. Twenty-three dollars, guys," declared the driver.

There were New York cops and UN security standing around. When they entered they were searched, no weapons found, and allowed to enter the large foyer. It had the ambience of an only moderately successful international corporation. The foyer was bare and functional, adorned only by a small statue of somebody Mike didn't recognise near the door. They walked over to the reception desk.

A young black man wearing a blue and white 'staff' suit greeted them. "How can I help you, gentlemen?"

Mike gave him his name. "I'm supposed to meet my lawyer here; her name is Jan Adams."

"One moment," the receptionist said, picking up a phone. "Ms Adams?" Pause. "They're here."

Adams appeared from a corridor. "Come with me – you need briefing before you meet the big cheeses."

She took them to a nearby small meeting room. She objected to the presence of Jackson and Rex but deferred when Mike told her they would stay.

Adams explained that the Americans had started quite belligerently. They talked about military force to seize the lands and threatened Britain with force if they interfered or tried to take any jurisdiction.

"Oh dear," said Mike. "Brits won't take kindly to being openly threatened."

"They didn't," Adams told him. "They deployed their own military to blockade US bases in Britain and advised the US to adopt a more traditionally diplomatic position."

She went on to explain that wiser heads soon prevailed. The Brits decided that the 'special relationship' was damaged a bit but then reflected that it wasn't up to much anyway. They removed their blockades, expecting better US behaviour in the future.

The US dismissed the bullish general causing the trouble, a leftover from a previous administration. They then invited the British ambassador to dinner in order to paper over the cracks.

Both sides agreed that in light of the court decisions, they had a problem. Both countries felt they had a legal obligation to defend their own position even if it meant using force. They also agreed that conflict would not be productive.

"We need your common support for reasons of international legitimacy but you realise we'd win a war between us, don't you?" paraphrases the US position.

"We need your support for reasons of our economy and we know you are stronger, but you do realise that in a war between us we'd destroy most of your major infrastructure before we lost, don't you?" paraphrases the British response.

Eventually they agreed to put the matter before the Security Council at the UN. That soon proved to be a mistake. Russia vetoed every decision and started to make noises about Alaska. France left the Russians to do all the vetoing but made a few noises about Louisiana and even managed an irrelevant reference to Canada. The Chinese remained quiet, just enjoying the show.

That's when the UN Secretary General stepped in. After much cajoling, flattering and quiet threats of UN sanctions, the Security Council ordered that the matter be put to a special court convened in the UN. Both the US and the UK agreed to abide by the decision of that court made up of several judges from disinterested nations from all continents except Australasia.

The Aussies and New Zealanders were excluded because the UN felt that they might be inclined to naturally support Britain. The Brits worried that they might be naturally inclined to automatically make life difficult for Britain.

Both the US and the UK secretly resolved to ignore the court if they didn't get a cut of the wealth and, in the case of the Americans, retain some kind of control of the land.

Adams returned to the hearing which had already been running for two days. Jackson and Rex had disappeared to somewhere. Alone and not entirely on top of the situation, Mike spent several hours reading out-of-date magazines available in the small room. At one point a UN staff member brought him a trolley of hot drinks, water and snacks. He continued to read and learn the important skill of hosting an upmarket society dinner.

At about four o'clock, Adams returned and announced, "You're on."

He followed her along a few confusing corridors and entered a full modern courtroom. He was shown to what was clearly a witness stand where he was invited to sit. He chose to stand; he was familiar with appearing in English courts where the speaker stands not sits. He wanted to at least place himself in a not entirely unaccustomed position.

"Mr Michael Key?" asked a middle-aged woman of Arab appearance who seemed to lead a bench of about ten others of all ethnicities. Mike assumed they were the judges.

"Michael Key Nehwe," he said.

"Michael Key?" said lead judge again.

"Michael Key Nehwe," Mike repeated.

"Is that the same as Michael Key, the owner of the Ash Lands?" the woman said, not in the least put out by his response.

"I was Christened Michael Key; under the US federal view of land ownership I am registered as the title owner. The most important people in this case, the Nehwe No'ipinKoi Shoshone, the historical occupants and guardians of the land and a people to whom I am related and claim their name, have been ignored."

He noticed that some members of the judicial panel nodded. He also noted that the American observer, a tall, thin, grey-haired, thoughtful-looking man, raised his head in interest and the British observer smiled.

"How would you like us to address you?" asked the woman.

"I wanted to make the point I just made – I answer to just Key or Mike. Since nobody has bothered to even speak to the Nehwe, I consider myself their representative. I am here to make a few points relevant to your deliberations. It may take some time and I apologise if I bore you but it's important. I am here to support a people who are very very important to me, of whom I am part and who have reached a position where they, I, will challenge their legally imposed marginalisation and slow genocide."

The woman smiled. "Listening to long speeches is what we do. You will not bore us and we will listen carefully. Please take the oath."

Mike swore on a bible that he would speak the truth as he saw it and tell no lies.

The woman then spoke again. "We will listen to your statement tomorrow; this international special court will now adjourn for the day and sit again at ten in the morning. The court thanks you, Michael Key Nehwe. Mr Key, please return in the morning."

With that, everybody stood while the judges left and then it was over for the day. Adams joined him to return to the foyer.

"Wow," she said, "I think I'll just let you run. I'll only interject if there is any legal problem brought up. Just wow, Mike." She walked off as Jackson and Rex came up to him.

Jackson grinned. "We've been meeting some people. Cop to cop talk. We now both have temporary permits to carry concealed weapons in New York so now we're armed. We have to leave them with security when we come in here but that's OK."

The two national observers sauntered up behind him. They were chatting happily and there was no indication of animosity.

"You got balls, my friend. Can't agree with you but good to see you fight your corner," the American said, slapping him on the back.

"Gone native, Mr Key?" laughed the British observer as the two men walked on.

"Check my back for recording or tracking devices just put there," Mike said to his bodyguards.

"And you call us paranoid," laughed Rex, checking him.

The following morning Rex again did his third cab thing when they left the hotel.

"Why'd you do it that way?" asked Mike as they slowly ground their way through New York nearly gridlocked rush hour traffic.

"He likes Sherlock Holmes," laughed Jackson. "The addled drug-addicted great detective suggested that, he says."

"It worked for him," defended Rex.

"He wasn't real," said Mike.

"It still worked, though, didn't it?" Rex insisted. Jackson laughed and Mike just sat back and watched the traffic.

They arrived just after nine-thirty and Adams was already in the reception area. They retired to the same small room and obtained some drinks and snacks. Then they headed for the courtroom.

The lady in charge explained that their earlier deliberation had led them to the same conclusion as both Supreme Courts. She then invited the British representative to address the court.

The Brit stood and spoke briefly. "Madam, I am instructed by Her Majesty's Government that our case is complete. We stand by the national court's initial findings and will accept the decision of this court. We have no further case to put and now stand down."

She thanked him and asked him to sit. She then invited the American to make representation. He clearly had something to add and strode to the witness stand where he sat to speak.

He loosened his tie, a standard debating trick to show resolve. He coughed. "Madam, the USA wishes to begin by expressing our resentment at yesterday's use, by Mr Key, of the word genocide. We refute that entirely and ask you to consider it an example of a tendency to hyperbolise by Mr Key. This of course questions his reliability as a witness."

"He's good. Listen to each point and counter it when you're on," Adams whispered to Mike. The chief judge glanced at Adams and she shut up.

"The simple and easily verified fact is this," continued the American, "the United States pays in excess of one billion dollars each year towards the education, health and cultural heritage of the Indian nations. The Department of the Interior via its Indian Affairs team ensures the continuation and validity of the nations through reserved spaces, genetic identification of true bloods and recognition of individual leaders.

"We do not recognise the invented tribe Nehwe and nor do we recognise the native origins of Mr Key. We do recognise the Shoshone but no group, such as the invented Nehwe, can become recognised just by claiming to be a new group. We do not challenge Mr Key's genuinely held views but deny we must act in accordance with them. We have no hostility towards Mr Key or the small unregistered Shoshone group unlawfully occupying his land.

"We invite this court to refer the matter of trespass to the highest court in Nevada. We further invite this court to declare that the territory in question is within the jurisdiction of the US federal authority who will undertake to work with Mr Key. For the sake of simple fairness we are prepared to come to a financial settlement with our British friends, without surrendering the land, to satisfy their genuine though mistaken belief that they hold a fiduciary interest in the land. Thank you."

The court thanked him for his short and succinct presentation of the American view. The woman in charge then invited Mike to take the witness stand.

He walked slowly to the stand. He again chose not to sit. He wore no tie to loosen and spent a few seconds surveying the court judges, the two national representatives and a few other observers and staff.

The chief judge reminded him of the oath he'd taken the previous day.

"Yes," he replied. "Yes, I know, madam. I want to start by saying that I am a little cross at the suggestion I am not reliable. I hope that when I have finished you will agree with me that the treatment of the Nehwe No'ipinKoi Shoshone, named and recognised in the valid 1780 treaty between them and Britain, does amount to genocide by either negligent accident or deliberate act."

He spent a second or two glaring at the American but the court called his attention back to them.

"May I, madam?" Adams asked from her seat. She was allowed to sit next to Mike and received permission to pass him notes if it was necessary but not to lead his evidence.

"This department, who are they?" Mike questioned. "They talk of Indians. Really? Indians? Are we still doing that? They are native, this group we're talking about are Shoshone, Nehwe No'ipinKoi Shoshone. They say that no such group exists but we know they were there before 1780 and probably a lot longer." He wiped his brow and pointed at the American representative. "Who do they think they are? They issue certificates to say who is and is not a legitimate member of any native group. What? Juden carry identification papers? Redskin equal yellow star? Who do they think they are?

"And this one billion dollars they so graciously spend each year. It is the money from the tribes themselves; they are forced to have it held in trust by the federal overlords, by federal law. Some of it gets given back and is called a grant. Nehwe No'ipinKoi Shoshone don't see much of it. A bit of health screening, not treatment cos they have to pay for that themselves. A few H bombs set off on the land and now they have all kinds of medical problems, not to mention reduced genetic diversity through murder, massacre in the nineteenth century, child theft now, yes child theft and the federal authorities do nothing because, well, it's just Indians, isn't it?"

Adams handed him a note. He read it and just stood there. He glared at Adams.

"Mr Key?" said the chief judge.

"My apologies, madam. I was going to describe how a couple of decades ago many Nehwe No'ipinKoi Shoshone children were taken by criminals, and a lot of women were taken too. The Federal authorities decided it was outside their jurisdiction, something they now deny. Suddenly this undeveloped land rich in unsuspected resources is magically federal jurisdiction.

"This note informs me that one of the kids taken was the daughter of a good friend of mine." His voice was rising. A tear ran slowly down his face. A short pause then, "Just who do they think they are? They steal the land, they steal the soul and do fuck all when monsters steal the children. They leave these people to quietly die off." He wiped his mouth and his voice rose into a shout as he pointed at the American. "You just want the money – you don't care who dies as long as you get it. Who the fuck do you think you are?"

The court adjourned for an early lunch; the chief judge advised Mike to spend the time getting control of himself.

During the break he advised Adams to stay out of his way. She could have told him this thing before but she waited until it had maximum emotional effect. Rex and Jackson stayed close to him, more to protect other people than protect him.

When the court resumed, the chief judge addressed him. "Mr Key, the court is both impressed by your passion for this matter and concerned at the potential for you to lose control. Please continue your statement."

Slowly and in a flat, emotionless voice, Mike described the condition of the Nehwe No'ipinKoi Shoshone. The borderline deprivation, the loss of almost a whole generation, the effects of irradiated genes, the diabetes and the lack of a voice. He described the group who invaded the land; he even described Greg's murder and the fight where he killed Milenkovic. He described the stand-off with the alt right and the hard work going into rebuilding. He kept control.

The chief judge looked at him for what seemed a long while. "Thank you for your candour, Mr Michael Key Nehwe. This court is not able to make judgement on the fatal incident in the town. We note that afterwards the federal authority stated that the matter was purely within Nehwe jurisdiction. Whether that indicates a divergence of view between the FBI and the Department of the Interior may be relevant in our deliberations. Please note, and may your lawyer also note, that the evidence you gave us today is privileged by international treaty and nothing you have said can be used in any national court within any other jurisdiction."

The court adjourned for two weeks. It was their intention to give their judgement at that time.

"In my judgment that judgement will be the key," Adams said, standing at a safe distance in the foyer. Jackson placed himself strategically between them.

"Not now," said Mike. "I'm in no mood for your clever little word plays at the moment. See you in two weeks."

Mike, Jackson and Rex returned to the hotel. They were still wondering whether it was best to leave and return in two weeks or stay for the judgement.

They were all surprised when they saw Mambi, Wolf and Timmy waiting in the reception area.

"Why did you not tell me about your daughter?" Mike whispered as he hugged Mambi.

"Her name is Silver," she told him. "I'm sorry. I didn't want you worrying about me; you are dragged into our fight now and that's enough of a burden for you. I told the bitch not to tell you. Jackson called to tell me what she told you."

Jackson put his hand on Mambi's shoulder as he passed. Rex looked as if he might say something but then left.

"It's not a burden," Mike said. "Her father?"

"Dead. Diabetes, stress and a broken heart swimming in whiskey." She hugged him tighter. "I know that if there is another life then he thanks you from it; he thanks you for delivering justice on the bastard."

She explained that the council had authorised another two weeks on the room. They'd sent Joe and Jimmy out to dig enough silver to pay for it which made everybody laugh.

The suite was big enough. Mambi would share with Mike; Wolf and Timmy would share; and Rex would move in with his dad. In their room, the hotel replaced the double bed with two singles.

The two weeks were spent as a vacation/holiday. They did all the tourist spots. Mike and Mambi shared pictures of their lost children and wept together. Wolf informed Rex that the Nehwe girl he'd been living with was pregnant. He looked intimidated and Jackson looked delighted.

"That's why I'm here," declared Timmy. Then he chanted quietly and tapped Rex on the head. Then he chanted some more and also tapped Jackson on the head, much to everyone's amusement.

Mambi hugged them both. "That means you are both now adopted sons of the Nehwe No'ipinKoi Shoshone. Welcome."

"Hey, we're the first black Shoshone," declared Rex jubilantly.

Mambi punched him in the arm. "My great-grandaddy would dispute that," she laughed.

Wolf hugged both men. Mike and Timmy shook their hands. It obliged a visit to the swankiest restaurant they could find nearby using Google. Rex earned a slap around the head from Jackson when he asked if they still got paid.

"What was with the head tapping?" Mike asked Timmy during the evening.

"Just couldn't resist it," he half-drunkenly answered. "I just made that bit up."

On the day of the judgement only Mike and his bodyguards went to the UN; the others waited in the hotel. As they approached

Turtle Bay they saw a large crowd separated from a smaller crowd by lots of police.

"Oh dear," mumbled Mike.

The larger crowd seemed to be made up of various protest and pressure groups. There were a couple of BLM flags, a few Biden flags, lots of UN flags, a few red flags and many other unidentifiable groups, some of whom looked like sixties hippies time warped in from Woodstock.

The smaller group were more easily identified. The police had already removed anybody openly armed; this was UN territory and they let NYPD enforce UN rules which forbid general arming. This left just the usual mix of discordant and clashing quasimilitary clothing. A few shabby maga hats still managed to make an appearance along with the stars and bars.

Rex was entertaining himself by flipping the finger at the smaller group. Mike told him not to but he didn't seem chastised. As they left the cab, the N word could clearly be heard from somebody in that group.

Mike looked and saw it was just one young man repeatedly shouting the abusive term. Rex marched straight towards him with Mike following trying to bring him back. Many in the larger group shouted encouragement to them. A huge New York cop, a black man, blocked their path.

"Sir," he said, pointing to the UN building. Both Mike and Rex apologised to him and went back towards the building. The cop turned to look at the offensive young man who quickly fled into the crowd.

The bodyguards surrendered their weapons. Once inside they were met by Adams.

"I was going to phone you, Mike," she said. "You were so cross, so I didn't, but now you're here, I apologise. The note, I mean. It was a sound tactic, though. Your intensity really worked for us."

"I suppose so but it didn't do much to make me like you," Mike replied.

Mike and Adams entered the courtroom and waited in silence. The British and American representatives entered shortly after. The Brit nodded at Mike.

The American went over to Mike. "Mr Key, please know that I was impressed by your performance last time. I regret that you cannot succeed but on one level I'd be happy if you do. Isn't that odd?"

"No," said Mike. "It just means that you recognise the wrong but follow your instructions anyway. I wonder if history can give us any other examples of that."

"A bit harsh," the American said as he returned to his seat.

Everybody stood as the judges entered the room. The same woman sat as chief judge and would deliver the court's decision. The clerk ensured that all interested bodies were present and then invited the chief judge to begin.

She cleared her throat and began. "It is never easy for an international court to decide on a member nation's limits of sovereignty. Such a thing encompasses not just history and law but must also take account of the reality on the ground, so to speak. In coming to our decision we have had regard to all these things. Our decision is unanimous and there is no dissenting judgement."

The clerk stood. "All present please be silent. This court will now deliver its verdict on the matter at hand. All member nations of this United Nations' assembly are required by treaty to accept the verdict."

The chief judge drank a sip from a glass of water. "The 1780 treaty signed by Sebastian Ash on behalf of the British Crown and Dakayivani, also known as David Leadbeater, on behalf of the No'ipinKoi Shoshone is valid in international law. The Nehwe No'ipinKoi Shoshone are a valid cultural and ethnic group and are recognised by this court as descendants of the signatories; they live on the land as of right.

"At the time of the treaty, the United States had no valid claim over the land, indeed it did not exist since it was at that time a series of British colonies in revolt. The US did not seize it at the end of the war for independence when, by the Treaty of Paris 1783, the US came into recognised existence. Therefore, the land remained as described in the treaty. In view of this, the 1861 declaration of US territory can have no effect on the land now known as Gutusipe Daindi. Consequently, the 1864 move to statehood and the Nevada Constitution of the same year cannot have effect in law on or in Gutusipe Daindi. In reaching this conclusion the court also made orbiter reference to the fact that at the time the now state of Nevada contained ten thousand recognised people, which means white people entitled to vote, whereas law at the time required sixty thousand such people to be resident.

"The extent and border of Gutusipe Daindi are laid out in the maps provided by the US Department of the Interior and designated as reserved land. This cannot be since the land was never lawfully subject to US jurisdiction regardless of US defacto control at the time.

"The land so described comes by default to be the independent state of Gutusipe Daindi and controlled in law by the Nehwe No'ipinKoi Shoshone and the lawful heir to Sebastian Ash, Mr Michael Key." Here she paused to take breath and allow the full implications to sink into the minds of those present.

"Fucking hell," Adams whispered to Mike.

"Fuckin' hell," the American mumbled with his head in his hands.

"Fucking hell," the British representative said in a very posh and refined accent.

The American stood.

"The court recognises the American representative," the chief judge said.

"Madam," he said slowly, "this matter must be referred immediately to the Security Council. The effect of the decision can only be armed conflict between the two nation states and the Shoshone group on the land. A three-way conflict in which there can be no moral winners."

The British representative stood and supported the move.

She smiled at them both. "Please be seated. You may make representation at the end if you wish. The judgement continues. This court understands the reality of the new situation. The land lies entirely within the territory of the United States. It cannot function without US cooperation and in practice nobody can prevent US occupation although that would be unlawful. This court in consultation with the UN Secretary General proposes the following solution:

"The land known as Gutusipe Daindi shall be recognised as extraterritorial to the United States. This means that it becomes an autonomous native enclave free to make its own laws within an undertaking of compatibility with US legal principles, state and federal.

"That Gutusipe Daindi pay a yet to be agreed sales tax, or other agreed compensation, to the federal and state authorities in relation to the extraction of minerals from the land.

"The US undertakes to protect Gutusipe Daindi against external threats and provide emergency assistance if and when required and suffer utility services, cable, water, electricity etc. to enter into the land.

"The United Kingdom to be paid an annual fee based on the value of minerals extracted. The UK further undertakes to support US protection of Gutusipe Daindi on the understanding that UK military so acting do so on the sufferance of the US within US territory or Gutusipe Daindi itself.

"Gutusipe Daindi is no longer required to pay into the fund held by the Department of the Interior and is free to make its own arrangements for health care and education.

"That Mr Michael Key be provided with an indefinite right to remain in the US so that he can perform his duties within Gutusipe Daindi without constantly renewing a visa whenever he steps outside the lands.

"That it is the council of the Nehwe who decide who is a member of their group and not some outside body. The Department of the Interior no longer has any influence within Gutusipe Daindi.

"Finally, on a personal note and not forming part of the recommendations, the Department of the Interior might want to consider abandoning the term 'Indian Affairs' unless it is actually dealing with India."

The court invited the national representative to make representation. Neither of them moved. The chief judge handed a note to the clerk who handed it to Mike. The court then rose and the judges left.

Mike opened the note and laughed. He showed it to Adams. The note just said 'fucking hell'.

The six flew back to Las Vegas and went straight to an airport bar. While the others waited, Rex headed to a car dealer with whom he'd previously arranged to buy a new car.

He returned in a new, large, white, all-terrain vehicle.

"Blimey, we must be paying him too much," Mike said.

"No, that's definitely not true," Jackson replied to general quiet laughter.

Mambi had spoken to George and discovered that there was an ongoing protest at the ridge track leading to the settlement and the town.

She advised, "We can avoid it by entering the desert about fifty miles further down and swinging round in a curve to come in the other way." She sat up front with Rex to navigate. There were two rows of rear seats and they all fitted comfortably.

As they passed the point on the highway where normally they'd turn off towards the ridge, they saw a couple of news vans, a few cars and two food trucks. They drove straight past them. A few people standing around eating or drinking stared at them as they passed.

Fifty or so miles further on, Mambi told Rex to turn off. He turned right into the desert and just followed instructions. He drove about forty miles into emptiness and then started to track a wide curve. A few hours later the far side of Gutusipe Daindi town and the ridge arm alongside it came into view.

As they drew closer, they saw Cy and Dane standing on the edge of the town's far side. They were fully armed and wearing helmets and body armour but otherwise bare chested to allow cooling. Cy watched through binoculars as they approached. Rex stopped about sixty feet from them; they would not know this vehicle and the occupants needed to identify themselves.

As Mike got out and walked towards them, Dane raised his rifle and looked through a small telescopic sight fitted onto it. The rifle immediately fell to a safe position. Dane waved.

"Rear guard?" Mike said to them.

"Welcome home, Mike," Cy replied. "We heard about the court and the UN. When we finished laughing we asked for orders. The orders were to protect this place and call for backup if we needed it."

"Where's everybody else?"

"A couple are guarding the other side of the ridge. I think it's a couple of the older guys from the council, they're in radio contact. Everybody else is on the far ridge much of the time. That includes the Brits who told us they had orders to protect George. Do we have to call you sir now that you're in charge of a small country?" Cy laughed at him.

Wolf and Timmy were dropped off in the town. They wanted to check the town, arm up and support the rear guard. The others drove on up to the ridge.

Once there, they saw that things were well in hand. George and the two Brits greeted them. Hunter sat up on the higher ridge. Joe and Jimmy ran errands for refreshments and took turns to relieve Hunter. The BBC van was back in position and Ms BBC was talking to camera.

At the foot of the ridge about one hundred fully equipped US troops held a line preventing entry to the ridge track. Behind them were two obvious transport and supply vehicles.

"That's one of the interesting effects of your little scuffle with the UN. US troops can't normally be deployed on US soil, that's for the National Guard in each state. Now though, this is not strictly speaking US soil anymore so the troops can be sent here," Jon informed Mike.

The other side of the troops, the protest group was more or less the same ensemble as before. A mixed bag of disaffected ultra conservative no changers. The warning sign had been removed and lay about twenty feet away. The protesters were mainly quiet but occasionally broke into a surprisingly harmonious rendition of 'This Land is Our Land'.

"Isn't that a church song?" Mike said to George as they walked together towards the troops.

"Either that or Girl Guides," George replied, clearly amused.

Jon and Fi followed closely behind. They had orders to protect George and that's what they would do.

George introduced Mike to Major Fitzgerald, the commanding officer.

Mike shook his hand. "I'm sorry you and your guys are stuck out here. As soon as we can organise we'll employ security so you can go do something that's more interesting for you."

"It's not a problem, sir," the major told him. "It's a pleasure to meet the man who turned up, wasted a piece of filth who needed wasting and then shouted so loud that the most powerful nation in the world gave him his own country."

Mike laughed. "It's a bit more complicated than that. What's more, if the States wasn't fundamentally a decent land I'd be strung up by now and you wouldn't be here. Those tossers over there would be running the place."

Major Fitzgerald smiled. "They won't stay too much longer. Most of the real pecker fumblers, you know, big guns maketh the man shit, they only lasted about a day. This lot have been here a couple of days but are growing bored now. Yeah, they'll go soon, maybe a day or so. They won't fire on or rush at us cos they know what will happen if they do. I assure you that we have this; the place is secure."

Mike thanked him. "When this is over, if you need to hang on to let your guys chill, that's fine. You can go down to the town maybe; we don't have many resources yet but you can get shade and rest down there if you need to."

Ms BBC had spotted him and rushed over. "Mike, how do you feel? You defeated the USA." The camera crew filmed.

Mike shook his head. "No, I didn't defeat anybody. The USA has chosen to follow the rule of law, as a civilised country should. Don't talk in terms of victory or defeat. That kind of idiocy leads to hissy fits by the likes of the wankers down there; fuck off now, please."

He decided it was probably not the finest oration ever heard from a leader. He smirked as he wondered how much of it would be aired or turned into bleeps.

George decided he'd stay for a while longer. Mike jumped back into Rex's flash new car and they headed for the settlement.

Mambi tapped him on the shoulder. "I've been getting an update – a lot has happened."

The update was massive. The state department had been in touch with the council to discuss the new status of Gutusipe Daindi. Tax values would be agreed and the other court recommendations adhered to. The British Foreign Office had made contact and declared itself content with whatever annual sum the council decide for them. Then, they said, they don't want it all sent to them but half should be diverted to a fund as a British contribution to education and health care for the Nehwe.

Mike laughed. "Yeah, that's very British. Use your money to look like aid from them. I expect that's where the Department for the Interior learned the trick."

Both countries had another request. They would both like to use parts of Gutusipe Daindi for their military to undertake desert training. The council had no objection and the details of that would be thrashed out later.

"Don't underestimate the size of the task ahead," Mambi told him. "We now have to think like a country and organise appropriately."

"Yeah," said Mike, leaning back, "so much for my enjoyment of a nice piece of inherited real estate. Where's my foot stool and beer for a nice quiet evening?"

Mambi leaned over. She kissed him and whispered, "Your evenings are not going to be quiet and inactive, trust me."

Chapter Eighteen

The aroma of tobacco and stale beer wafted from the old stone tavern in the mountainside village. The night air was cold, filled with the smell of firewood smoke and wet pine. Snow crowned the nearby mountains. At this time of year the Balkan region was slowly and reluctantly shedding its winter vista for the promise of a fecund spring.

In the rear room of the tavern, twenty or so fit and strong-looking early middle-aged men sat on a varied selection of antique-looking chairs. They all faced front and listened to one older man dressed in the same worn uniform as themselves with faded patches and threadbare elbows.

"Friends," he spoke in Serbian, "our end grows closer each day." The crowd murmured objection. "Our blessed land struggles as it is forced unwillingly to abandon our sacred past and prostitutes itself to the highest bidder. Reluctantly or not, our land now sinks into decadence and decay and may never return to our once proud perfection. The future is not for real men." More mumbles of dissent from the room. "Weak and subservient catamites now occupy the government and the army. But real men do not die quietly. Real men do not bow and submit while they still possess breath to fight." Loud agreement from the crowd.

"Chetnik," shouted one of the audience.

"Chetnik, Chetnik, Chetnik," responded the crowd until the man speaking raised his hand to quell them.

"We continue to the end; we fight asymmetric war that we know we can never win but they shall know that they have dealt with men." Some cheering from the crowd. "Bring me the bastard."

Previously concealed by a curtain behind the speaker, two men pulled a weak and probably drugged young man to him. From a nearby table, the speaker picked up a humane cattle destroyer, little more than a metal spike in a tube operated by a powerful spring. He pulled hard on the other end to compress the spring and prepare the bolt gun as the spike withdrew into the tube.

"Here we make a statement through this American spy, this child sent to do a treacherous man's job." He put one hand behind the young man's neck and pulled him close. He kissed the victim on the top of his head and then placed the bolt gun against the skull just beyond the highest point of the forehead.

"Chetnik," he said as he pressed a lever with his thumb. The spring released with a loud plunk. The spiked bolt extended with great force and shattered through the bone into the brain.

"Ung… ung er," the young man mumbled. Blood appeared around the rim of the pipe pressed against his head. He convulsed a little while still standing and his eyes rolled upwards. His legs buckled and he sank to the floor.

"Chetnik, Chetnik," roared the spectators.

The speaker threw the bolt gun back onto the table. "My brothers, my love for you all is everlasting. This must be our last general meeting in our own land, but we still long for the old world ripped from us by the bastard mercenaries of the west. One day, perhaps, we may dominate again." The crowd roared approval. "Until that time the command will retreat to Moscow where our cousins wait to offer us all sanctuary. From there we will deploy and instruct the teams we send worldwide to avenge and remind the world of our resolve. We deploy several teams to many European countries to locate and kill many traitors and murderers who came to our land. We send teams to Australia for the same purpose and also the United States. After a couple of decades they feel safe. They will all learn that we fight until the end and there is no end while we live." More approval from the crowd. "Rest assured, just as we seek and destroy traitors and murderers in America we also send a very special team, a team to avenge the murder of our beloved Colonel Milenkovic." Roars of support. "We destroy his murderers and wipe out the cursed infection of the cockroaches who helped them. Chetnik. Chetnik."

"Chetnik," returned the crowd. "Chetnik."

More drink was brought in by waiters. Young women were handed out to the guests by other burlier waiters and food tables set up. The body of the dead young man was dragged out.

A small group of musicians filed in and began to play traditional tunes.

The speaker worked his way through the room. After many masculine hugs and boozy manly kisses he exited the front where a car was waiting. The sounds of carousal filtered from the tavern.

The young driver assured him that all of the money was in the back.

"And those who worked in the chain of transactions to produce this cash?" the speaker asked.

"Eliminated," said the driver.

"Moscow then, my son."

They drove to Austria where they changed cars and drove on into Germany. They changed cars again and drove to Poland. They changed cars yet again and drove through Lithuania and Latvia to Estonia.

Once there, they bribed a fishing boat crew to take them back down the Baltic to Kaliningrad, from where they boarded a plane to Moscow. It was a very long journey in total.

Chapter Nineteen

The last ten months had been a hectic time of change. The town of Gutusipe Daindi was far from complete but still coming along nicely.

The Town Manager's office now housed Mike, George and Mambi. Mambi managed income and expenditure. George carried on much as before and Mike managed building, security and land use as well as liaising with outside bodies. Mike and Mambi now occupied a house in one of the side streets. Adams was retained at a substantial cost; her political and legal contacts were now invaluable and, in spite of her questionable character, she was a good lawyer.

The permanent demonstration hadn't lasted for more than two weeks. After the last unstable but feisty fomenter of discord had left, the two pairs of national soldiers went as well. Most people had grown to like them and gave them a good send-off. The federal troops had enjoyed a day basking in the desert sun before they left. The Nehwe provided an excellent barbecue and oceans of beer.

Shortly after that, the UN said they'd like to keep a long-term presence in the town to head off any problems. The council, which had declined to move to the town and still used the old building, agreed.

The US formed a new department, the Office for Extraterritorial Liaison, and appointed one Stuart O'Rourke as its lead and only employee. It transpired that he was the same man Mike remembered as the American representative at the United Nations courtroom.

Mike spoke to him by phone, the new line into town supported lots of landlines so he used one in his office.

O'Rourke began by congratulating him on his success at the UN.

"I'd expected you to be a bit browned off," Mike began.

"No, not really," O'Rourke told him. "It's not personal for me. I dance to the tune of my paymaster, that's the USA. Funnily enough, Uncle Sam's not much annoyed with you either. That said, they intend to make sure that your situation remains unique."

Mike told him he was pleased about that. "What about the UK?" he asked.

O'Rourke gave a short, throaty laugh. "They're OK with it all really. They don't really care but see it as a way to garner influence with the US. They're probably right. We need them to keep supporting our intention to keep you guys unique and ensure they support us on other issues. Whoever thought we'd have to start considering the possibility of a fight with them. Everybody is glad that's over."

Mike laughed this time. "Well, the world throws up some unexpected situations. I don't suppose they'd try to burn down the White House again."

"The way that things were not so long ago I thought we might do that for ourselves," O'Rourke sounded only half jokey. "That might even come round again; I'm trying not to think about it."

"You are being very open," said Mike. "I appreciate that. Listen, feel free to visit whenever you want; you don't even need to call ahead. We need a good relationship with you, with the US."

O'Rourke made a guttural sound of agreement. "Herm herm. Mike, your situation has thrown us a bit of a curve ball. The foreign nations testing the water over land they used to have but is now ours, well they'll just be told where to get off. No, the problem is the other tribes. Many of them are now starting to fuss about similar deals. The Hawaiians are the most insistent. We can't have that. The first nations, notice I've learned not to say Indian, have to understand that you and your land are unique. We're gonna make a big deal over the 1780 treaty and the native Anglo mix of the Nehwe. We've got to make you unique so that we can make the situation unique. See, the last thing we want is trouble with you; we have to make you successful so that we can keep the other tribes content. The other Shoshone groups will be a problem; that's why we now recognise the Nehwe as an independent discrete group with unique ethnicity. Does that make sense?"

Mike thought for second. "Yeah, it does. I will avoid commenting on it; I'm sure you can guess my views there. Still, I didn't come here to start a new range war; I'm just trying to have a quiet and restful life."

"You should have stayed in England then, Mike," O'Rourke laughed. "You got all the problems of a small country and a major mining concern – good luck, buddy."

Opposite the Town Manager's office, Mike had one of the intended shops turned into a UN office. He informed the UN when it was complete and they said that they'd send some military observers to occupy it.

Mike reminded the UN that there was no war but they said military observers were standard and they would not look to interfere, just observe in the hope that all parties complied with the special court's ruling.

While the Nehwe awaited the threatened observers, Mike busied himself first with ensuring that enough new flats and houses were ready for anybody to move in from the settlement.

Second, he worked to authorise a mining company to survey and exploit the land. The council were going to impose some strict guidelines so he needed a business that was more than just a grab and profit concern.

The council rejected a Chinese group. Then they rejected an American group. Then they rejected a European consortium.

In the end the Americans and British formed a new joint company where everybody involved held profit rights in various proportions. The Nehwe held sixty-five per cent no tax, the Americans twenty-five and the British ten per cent. Voting rights in meetings were held equally between all three with a quorum of at least two people from each of the benefiting groups. The council finally authorised that but imposed strict conditions on where, when and how work occurred. They also decided that the currency in Nehwe land was the US dollar, no point in overcomplicating things.

It would be policed by Jackson and Rex. Rex and his new family had a nice house in a side street and Jackson was next door to them.

There was one sad end of a relationship. The girl that Hunter had brought to the lands wanted to move to a city. Hunter spent a long time considering his options. He discussed his situation with the Warriors, with Mambi, with some council members. Ultimately, he decided he wanted to remain in Gutusipe Daindi. The parting was in no way acrimonious but still left a thin veil of sadness over Hunter and those who loved him.

Then the weddings started. As a land without a legal process to do such things, Adams was set to work to create one and obtain legal recognition for it in other jurisdictions.

It was really Joe and Jimmy who started it off. They decided they wanted to be married and live in town. Then Timmy and Wolf joined the clamour to marry. Then Mambi and Mike decided they'd join in as well. Finally, not to be outdone, Rex and Joanne, his girlfriend and mother of his son Abraham, put in their request.

That's how this small community managed to throw up a quadruple wedding that attracted worldwide attention. A heart-warming people story, apparently.

"Why does Joanne not have a Shoshone name?" Mike asked George at the reception.

"Her mother was among the taken. She was saved by some quick-thinking older guys who hid her on the ridge along with some others.

Somehow the name Joanne just stuck and it was felt that nobody had the right to change it. Her father was killed fighting during the raid," was George's heart-breaking reply.

Jackson got a little drunk and had to spend the ceremony sitting hiccupping and trying not to cry. He was comforted by a couple of the older women who he had befriended.

The only problem was naming Wolf's father for the Nehwe records. Wolf herself solved that problem with a quick word to the council. Just before the wedding she was declared adopted daughter of Mike, the Land Chief of the Nehwe No'ipinKoi Shoshone and son of the founders of the Nehwe.

"What the hell is a land chief?" he whispered to George.

"Dunno, they just made it up."

"We really need to sort out some laws for ourselves to decide who's who," Mike replied.

A few days later, Wolf called Mike out of the office. He walked out into the main street and she pointed towards the ridge. Driving at a sensible speed into town was the Pink Humvee being driven by Timmy. Just behind it was a white armoured Humvee with UN insignia on the sides and the UN flag flying from the roof.

Both vehicles pulled up and Timmy jumped out. "You won't believe this," he called over to Mike.

The doors on the UN car opened and out climbed Jon, Fi, Cy and Dane. They were all dressed in military uniforms and all carried assault rifles, Jon and Fi with the short British bullpup rifle that makes British troops stand out a bit. They all wore blue berets with UN emblems rather than hard helmets but boasted national flag patches on their upper arms.

"What the hell, how did that happen?" exclaimed Mike as they all shook hands.

Cy laughed at him. "I have the honour of command of this rag tag bunch of observers. When the UN asked each country to supply people we all volunteered."

Jon clapped him on the back. "We answer to the UN and our own governments, of course. As long as our own people agree we are all currently answerable to the UN."

Mike looked pleased. "Your old flats are still available; you weren't exactly gone for long. The saloon is nearly finished – we best stock it with some more booze. Best you liaise with Rex and Jackson – they police the lands. I'm in my office most of the time and you know my house if you need me after that. Oh, boomer guy, forget magic tech again, make sure you all have my cell number."

George came up to join them. "I'll tell Mambi to get some extra beer in," he growled and wandered off.

For the next few weeks things just continued as normal and the rebuild pushed on. The soil had proved itself richer in rare earths than previously thought. Disappointingly, no gold had been found, not even by some deep drilling tests. It did show that the silver continued to at least two hundred feet.

Early one morning Mike answered the phone in his office.

"Hello, Mike?" said Stuart O'Rourke.

"Hi Stu," Mike answered. "What can I do for you?"

"Just a quick heads up, Mike. We have stopped eight small teams from the old Serbian crews, Milenkovic's crowd, trying to enter at various airports. We don't know if we got them all."

"What do they want, are they planning something?" Mike asked.

"The guys we have in custody are tough and they won't tell us much. We think they were after some old enemies from the old war, Serbs who helped us who now live here. The Serbian government disavows any knowledge and we believe them, or at least we act as if we do. That's politics, above my pay grade."

"Will they come here?" Mike rubbed his face and sounded concerned.

"Hard to say, Mike. We've informed the UN and their four guys, our two and the Brit's two, and they are authorised to engage them if they do. We have some support on standby if it's needed. I just thought you should know."

"Thanks, Stu," said Mike. "I really appreciate it."

Mike sat for a moment then picked up the phone and started to dial Jackson. Before he'd finished, the door opened and in walked Jon with Cy and Jackson with Rex.

They all discussed the threat and decided to just carry on but remain alert. The Warriors and the council were informed. Mambi called and told him that Timmy and Wolf had been searching social media without any result. Hunter had taken to camping on the ridge with his fifty cal and Joe and Jimmy had taken AR15s from the armoury. George had driven to town and topped up the ammunition store.

Mike went home and donned his revolver and push knife. Then he walked down to see how the new town medical centre was coming along. He had in mind that he'd like to incorporate an education centre as well in the not too distant future. He made a mental memo to find some educationalists; this town needed a school.

Almost a week passed without anything of note. Everybody remained alert but it settled into the kind of casual alertness common in soldiers in wartime or police almost anytime and anywhere.

Mike was chatting with the mining supervisor in the main street. He was a man of about sixty, overweight with a face that reflected many decades of hard work and stress. His dusty overalls and dirty yellow hard hat somehow out of place in the growing new old town.

While Mike signed some papers to authorise some dirt removal for processing, the large supervisor removed his incongruous headgear. As he did so a boom sounded from the ridge. It didn't sound like a normal gunshot, which in reality sounds more like popcorn cracking. It was more than that but at the same time less than an explosion.

Less than a second later and preceded by a high-pitched undulating whine, the supervisor's head just exploded. A red-grey misty bubble of bone, blood, snot and brains burst in all directions, splattering Mike and the surrounding area for about a yard. The man just folded down from standing into a piled heap.

There followed a couple of seconds of silence and inaction. Then the four soldiers and Timmy burst out of the UN office all fully armed, Timmy with a stubby machine pistol.

"Mike, down down, now," screamed Dane.

Mike spun to face them, his hair, face and chest heavily dappled with the organic gunk of the murdered supervisor. He dropped to the floor as instructed. At the same time there was another boom, again the strange sound and a thump as dirt kicked up about eight feet beyond Mike.

"Roll to the buildings; get alongside the walkway," was Dane's new instruction and Mike complied.

"Are you hurt?" called Jon.

"No, what's happening?" Mike called back.

"That's a fifty cal; it's coming from the side ridge – stay behind cover. Mike, get to your office when you can. You're the target," shouted Timmy.

"Hunter?" asked Mike.

"We know, go to ground and leave this to us," Jon shouted at him.

The five dashed close to the building line down a side street oriented towards the side ridge. About halfway along, Timmy disappeared into a building. The other four took up covered positions at the street's end.

Joe and Jimmy came out of another building, both armed. They spoke quickly with Cy and then ran up to Mike.

"Mike, don't argue now, just do as we say," ordered Joe. "We take you to your office and then we will take up positions in the main street."

Mike meekly complied with their shoving and pulling as they bundled him into the Town Manager's office. Then they darted off to acquire protective positions along the main street.

Timmy reappeared from the building he'd run into. He carried with him a monstrously huge gun. It had several barrels that looked as if they rotated, like a Gatling gun. It was so heavy that it was supported by a strap across Timmy's shoulder. There was an unfeasibly large ammunition box attached below it and a side lever the operator could use to direct it.

Wolf appeared from nowhere and moved with him. They reached Cy and Dane, talked for a moment and then spoke across the street to Jon and Fi.

They gave it a second and then Fi simply walked out into the open desert that separated town from ridge. She just stood in the open making rude gestures at the ridge. There was a boom and then the whining approach of death.

As Fi dived and rolled to one side, the projectile kicked up dirt a few feet behind her. All the other soldiers pointed to the same spot on the ridge. Timmy stepped out and opened fire with his heavy artillery. At a rate of at least two thousand rounds a minute, the huge gun splattered at the source of the last boom, throwing up rocks and soil all around it.

The force from the return caused Timmy to lean into the massive recoil as if he were walking against a fierce wind as a shower of brass casings arced into the air and clattered to the ground. At the same time, all four soldiers sprinted the four hundred yards to the base of the ridge. Falling into a professional advance and covering each other as they went, they slowly crept higher towards the still unseen enemy.

As Timmy expended all of his ammunition, he dropped back to join Wolf near the building line. The multi barrels of the giant weapon whirred loudly as they spun uselessly.

Mike was recovering his composure in the office. He was still deciding what to do when the Wolf phone rang.

"Mike," said Mambi, "you OK?"

"Yeah, a bit shaken but getting there. They killed the mine supervisor, the fucking shits. The soldiers are trying to reach the shooter."

"I've spoken to the guys at the mine. They haven't seen anything odd," she said. That was not surprising – the mine was about thirty miles from the town and in a remote spot. They were drilling a test well to see what turned up.

"I'll call O'Rourke," he replied. He was dabbing at his face with a tissue when he heard another exchange of fire from the side ridge. He called O'Rourke.

"Hi, Mike. I've heard what's happening; we've had a drone watching you. The soldiers called us as well; we have support on the way. Just sit tight and stay safe. There is some serious talent on the ground, just let them do their thing."

Mike sounded offended. "A drone? Fucking cheek. Sorry, I understand. Still shaken up, that's all. I thank you for your help."

O'Rourke chuckled. "It's all cool, Mike. Just stay safe. We'll speak later."

There were several shots from further along the main street. Mike drew his revolver and went to the door. Racing down the road was a large, heavy off-roader; he could see three men in it. They were firing automatic weapons from the windows at the building line. He could see Joe and Jimmy returning fire from two different locations.

Timmy and Wolf appeared from the side street. Timmy peppered it with his machine pistol and Wolf rattled at it with her M16.

Mike lay on the floor and tapped away with his revolver. It probably made no difference but to him it at least felt he was not hiding and was part of this. Another vehicle could be heard racing into town from the other direction.

It seemed the big off-roader may have been armoured. Nonetheless, the total volume of fire smashing into it was enormous.

The vehicle made a hasty about turn and headed back towards the desert, the engine labouring loudly under hard acceleration.

Suddenly all opposing fire ceased and just one automatic weapon could be heard. Passing the office at speed and in pursuit rushed the armoured Humvee used by Jackson and Rex. Rex was driving and

Jackson standing up through a roof aperture blitzing away with the Kalashnikov.

The chase continued into the desert. Joe and Jimmy sprinted off for their motorcycles. Timmy and Wolf dashed over to Mike.

Wolf held both of his hands. "Mike, go get cleaned up. The soldiers found two bastards on the ridge. One is dead and the other's wounded."

"Hunter?" Mike asked. "The soldiers?"

"The soldiers are all OK," Wolf told him.

"Hunter?" he insisted.

Wolf looked at Timmy. Her eyes were filling with tears. Timmy hugged her.

"He was on one of his wandering guard rounds on the ridge." Timmy wiped his mouth and the darkness in his eyes revealed the potential for violence that dwelled within. "They must have taken him from behind. He's badly hurt. They failed to break his neck, though they tried. He's got a couple of stab wounds to his back and they cut his throat. It somehow missed his carotid but opened his trachea. He's getting battlefield medic aid now."

As if to punctuate his words, there was a whooshing sound and an explosion from the desert.

"Get me out there," Mike demanded.

Timmy told him to follow and they ran down another side street to collect the pink Humvee. They climbed in and Timmy gunned it into the desert.

As they drove, Mike saw that helicopters were now in the incident. There was a Chinook landed at the ridge base and an Apache hovered above the ridge top.

"That's a medic ship," said Timmy. "They'll take Hunter and the two attackers as well."

"I wanted the wounded one," Mike growled.

Just a couple of miles into the desert they came to the result of the explosion they'd heard. The attacking vehicle was on its side and the engine compartment shattered. The driver was hanging half out, the car resting on him and obviously dead. Another man lay about eight feet away and was badly injured with blood seeping from his head and chest. A third man sat on the floor nearby being guarded by Jackson. Rex was surveying the wreckage.

Joe and Jimmy roared up, decided there was nothing for them to do and raced off again back to town.

"Drone strike," said Timmy. "They like you if they went that far, wow."

"They like the money we're producing. They like looking like the good guys helping the poor helpless Nehwe," Mike told him.

Mike drew his revolver and walked up to the wounded man. Standing over the prostrate man, he reloaded his gun. He then shot the man in the face, waited a few seconds and then shot him twice in the chest.

"In life we call this picking on the wrong victim," Mike said in a gentle voice to the now clearly dead man.

"Fuck," said Timmy.

"Fuck, Mike," called Rex. "Just fuck, man. No more. Payback done, yeah?"

"Take him to the bus," Mike told Jackson, pointing at the sitting captive. "Get him patched up if he needs it."

On the journey back to the office, Timmy kept glancing at Mike.

"What?" said Mike, laughing a little.

"What the fuck, Mike. That was about as cold as I've ever seen. He was gonna die anyway, why?"

"Theatre," said Mike. "That other shit now knows what I'm prepared to do. When I talk to him, in his head he'll keep seeing me cold bloodedly offing his mate. He will know I'm serious."

Timmy just whistled once and kept driving as he slowly shook his head.

"Anyway, where the hell did you get that Big Bertha monster gun you had?" Mike asked.

"Friends in the marines, thought we might need an edge at some point."

Mike laughed again.

Chapter Twenty

The next day began with an ancient ceremony intended to honour great warriors. Those who by their courage on the battlefield had protected and saved the people.

In the old wooden hall of the settlement Timmy began the ceremony of the Eagle's Claw. All present considered it the equivalent to an award of the Victoria Cross or the Congressional Medal of Honor, or Honour if spelt correctly.

He spoke in both Shoshone and English and a designated member of the council walked up to Fi and fell to his knees before her. He held up his hands to offer a solid silver model of an eagle's claw. Traditionally, it would have been a real claw but things change over time and they could now afford this.

Fi accepted the claw and all present whooped and applauded, the other three soldiers most of all.

"With this we honour your courage; with this we commit ourselves to fight for and defend you. With this we thank you and will inform our children of you. Thank you," intoned Timmy. "I think you're the first woman to receive this."

Fi looked at him. "Yeah, well maybe you should look again at your diversity policies."

She maintained a serious though confused look as most present found that highly amusing.

There wasn't much of an after ceremony party. Most people were still worried about Hunter. Also, Mike needed to return to the town and try to handle the fallout of the battle.

Once back in his office, Mike decided to leave the captive for a short while, give him time to worry and weaken in resolve. He made sure that there was always a guard and that food and water were given to him. He also persuaded the council to forward a significant sum of money to the family of the murdered mining supervisor.

O'Rourke called him in the office. "We need to talk, Mike. You can't hold a prisoner."

"Yes I can," Mike told him. "We are extraterritorial, remember. We can do anything we want. We won't kill him or harm him much and you can have him after we're done with him."

"What are you going to do?"

"Just talk," Mike said. "Really, just talk. There're things we need to know, things he will tell us. When he's told us then you can talk to him."

O'Rourke sighed. "Mike, you can't beat information out of him; you are an area under UN supervision. You can't use torture or even hold him without putting him into a proper legal system. He has to come into full US jurisdiction."

Mike laughed at him. "Er, Guantanamo Bay, Stu? Heard of it? Waterboarding and small cramped cages. You are not in a strong moral position, my friend."

"Oh, Mike. Please pal, just hand him over."

"Two more days," Mike insisted. "Two more days and he's yours. I won't mess him up. What I'm going to do is very subtle, very non-invasive. No drugs, no blood, no drowning, no electricity. I will just get my information and hand him over. He's OK, we had a medic check him and he's strong."

"The thing in the desert, Mike?" O'Rourke asked him.

"That's different," Mike said. "I shot and killed an attacker. I don't need to defend that; it's a Nehwe matter, nothing to do with outsiders. Speak to my bitch of a lawyer if you want more. I did what I needed to do, that's it."

O'Rourke sounded reconciled with the situation. "Two days, Mike. Two days and then we come get him."

Mike made himself a coffee and then sat to call Mambi while he sucked on his vaping pipe. She and Jimmy were at the military hospital where Hunter had been taken.

"Still unconscious," she told him. "He'd managed to hold his throat together with his hand but still suffered oxygen deprivation. He lost a lot of blood. I'll let you know if there's any change. One more thing, Mike."

"Go on," he invited.

"I love you, Mike. Don't start to enjoy the killing – that's not who you are. What you did, it's OK but try not to be that person if you can."

"I know," Mike spoke tenderly. "I had a reason, part of a plan. I'm sorry but I intend to win this thing, even if it hurts me to do so; I love you too." He hung up the phone.

He left the office and walked to his flat. As he walked, he phoned Wolf.

"Hi ya dirty fatso," she said, her voice gentle and clearly concerned for him.

"I'm going to sleep for a few hours, then I'm going to interrogate our man. Please don't let anybody disturb me and wake me in three hours. Sorry to use you as an alarm clock."

"I'm coming with you," she told him, her tone allowing no objection. "I'll call in three hours; stay controlled, Mike. Don't release the monster inside." She made a kissing sound and rang off.

While he slept the dreams returned but somehow different again. The shattered, tortured children, the raped and murdered women, joined now by unknown uniformed soldiers ripped to death in various nasty ways. They formed a guard of honour as he walked along the line hand in hand with John. Mel stood among them, smiling at him. As John left his grip and went to his mother, Wolf, George, Mambi and Hunter waited for him at the end.

"The heart of a warrior should be tempered by the soul of an angel," Mambi whispered to him.

"Dirty old man," laughed Wolf.

"Stay dangerous," said Hunter.

Jon and Fi appeared behind him.

"Fight for the right not to fight," Fi said to him in the voice of Dane.

The rapping at the door woke him. He felt a slight anger but nothing overpowering.

"Come on, Mike. Wake up, you lazy arsehole," called Wolf.

He stumbled to the door to greet her and Timmy. They drank coffee and then waited while Mike washed his face and changed his shirt. Then they all set off towards the side ridge.

At the entrance of the tunnel that led to the bus sat Rex, cradling his AR15.

"Hi Mike," he said. "You want me to come down or stay here or go, or what?"

Mike touched his arm. "Stay here please, Rex. Just ignore any screaming. In the unlikely event he comes out on his own, kill him."

"Your wish is my command, possibly one that's accompanied by a life sentence," Rex said lightly.

Wolf hugged Rex and then the three of them entered the tunnel with Mike leading.

The folding door to the buried bus was not secured and Mike just pulled it open. There was a light on inside.

"Would have been better if he'd been in the dark but it's too late now," said Mike.

Wolf punched him lightly in the back. "Yeah, well Rex is a nice guy and doesn't have your evil streak." That made Timmy chuckle.

"Fucking kill me," said the captive. He was a large and muscular older man. His feet were chained and two sets of loose linked handcuffs held his wrists to the eye bolt in the concrete block. "I have nothing to say; fuck you, you arsehole and fuck your people."

Wolf and Timmy sat. Mike disarmed and handed his weapons to Wolf then walked up to the captive.

"What's your name?" he asked.

"I'm the horse that fucked your mother, call me Horse, you weak fucker."

"I'm gonna hurt you, Horse. You are going to answer my questions and then I'm giving you to the Americans who will take you to Guantanamo Bay or somewhere like it, whatever they use nowadays. You have an interesting future. You can stop me hurting you by just answering a few easy questions."

"Fuck you," the captive spat at him but missed.

"You served under Colonel Milenkovic; you went rogue with him, correct?"

"David Milenkovic is one of the greatest men to have ever lived. I love his soul and in my heart serve him forever. Chetnik, Chetnik."

Mike sighed. "The questions I have are in no way connected to what happened in the Balkans. I'm interested in what happened here. By answering them you will not harm your people or the memory of the fine soldier you so revere. Please just answer my questions."

"Fuck you," snarled the captive but didn't sound convinced by it himself.

Mike took a handcuff key from his pocket. He released the man's right hand and twisted the hand and wrist around into a straight arm lock. Pulling the arm behind the man's back, Mike placed his left hand onto the inner elbow. By pushing at this point he caused the arm to lay across the captive's back. He then placed his own left arm on the inside of the lower bent arm and reached across to hold the top of the same arm.

Mike whispered to him almost lovingly, "This used to be called a hammer lock and bar. It's a standard hold but I'm going to show you a little trick that most of us learned."

He reached up with his right hand until his fingers found the joint where the arm meets the shoulder. He pushed his fingers into the joint.

The captive immediately screamed and writhed. Mike kept pushing for a few seconds and then stopped.

Mike continued to whisper gently, "Incredible, isn't it? So much pain but no physical harm and no marks, well maybe a little bruise. Takes no real effort on my part and I can keep it up until your screams deafen me. It activates a nerve cluster, or so I'm told." He pushed his fingers in again.

The captive screamed and shouted abuse and screamed some more. Mike again stopped pushing.

"They say that torture is useless as an interrogation tool. It's not true, you know. Sure, it's useless to get a confession, the subject will eventually admit anything he's told to. But in some circumstances it works. If your subject knows that you can check the information he gives and then visit again if it's wrong, well then it can work. Pain and the certainty of more pain will produce truth." Mike pushed in his fingers again and the screams were more defeatist, more accepting, more honest.

"I will answer some of your questions," puffed the captive. "Know that there are some things I'd rather face an agonising death than tell you, but as long as it doesn't hurt my people, I will talk."

Mike handcuffed him to the block again, gave him some water and told him he had a few minutes to recover. Mike then left the bus and walked back up the tunnel; Wolf and Timmy followed him.

Once outside, Timmy spoke. "What was that, Mike? I've been around but I've never seen that. What did you call it?"

"Hammer lock and bar, followed by an illegal move," Mike told him.

"Shit, you didn't," exclaimed Rex, laughing.

"You know this, too," snapped Timmy.

Rex said, "It's a cop thing. International, obviously."

"Show me," Timmy said to Mike. "It's great."

"And you worry about me," Mike said to Wolf.

She just smiled. "He's a marine. Not subtle. Blood and guts and lots of cuts." Everybody laughed a little.

The three of them returned to what Mike asked Timmy to stop referring to as the torture chamber. This time he placed a chair in front of the prisoner and sat to talk with him.

Mike handed him more water. "Truth, please. If you refuse any answer I will have to consider whether I can do without it. If I can't we're back to screaming again. I don't want to if I can avoid it."

The captive looked at him with an evil eye. "Weak, you are weak. Here's some truth for you, if I get the chance I will kill you all, you will take a long time to die. I will fuck her as well."

Mike waved Timmy back as he started to advance. "She is the biological daughter of your beloved Milenkovic."

"Now I'm his daughter, you piece of shit," interjected Wolf, pointing at Mike but looking at the captive.

Mike went to her and hugged her. "Don't volunteer information; we are here to get it not give it, only give if it benefits us," he whispered and kissed her on the forehead. Then he returned to the captive.

"Name?" asked Mike.

"I'd rather die."

"Interesting. I'll come back to that if I need to. Were you with Milenkovic when he stole the children from this place?"

The captive was quiet for a few seconds. "A long time ago. When we first got here, retreating from the NATO forces overrunning us. We needed to start business and these people were easy. Nobody cares about them. The US authorities didn't even investigate. It was easy."

Mike heard the quiet shoosh of a knife being drawn from a leather sheath. He spun to see Timmy advancing, Ka-Bar in hand.

"No, Timmy, no. You go, I understand but if you can't keep your cool you need to go," Mike snapped at him.

Timmy stood hunched, trapped between the need to attack and the need to walk away. Wolf put her hand on his shoulder. He replaced his knife and walked out.

"You should have let him; he's not weak," the smiling captive told him.

"Where did you take the children?" asked Mike.

"Fuck knows where they ended up. We sold them to a dealer. Good rates as well."

Mike wiped his face. "How do I find him?"

"He's a rancher. Good man, tough and strong."

"How do I find him?" Mike whispered.

"I don't know. He's somewhere in Arizona, I think."

"Name?" Mike demanded.

"Not sure. Davey called him Kes. Yeah, Cowboss Kes, that's all I know."

"Why did you come back here?"

"Silver, and the girl. Davey was going to give her to the son of our leader. She would not have been hurt. The last time was just to kill you."

Mike laughed. "Well, that worked out well for you."

The captive laughed as well. "We will always be coming for you. You are dead, English. Just a matter of time."

Mike stared at him. "Anything else you can tell me about Cowboss Kes or the children and women, do it now. The Americans will give you back to me anytime I ask. Tell me now and maybe we don't call you back here."

"I don't know anything else, really I don't. I was just a soldier and did what Davey told us to do. Loyal Chetnik, loyal to death."

Mike nodded. He took the captive from the concrete block and handcuffed his hands behind his back. He told Wolf to walk ahead and warn Rex they were coming out. He then pushed the captive ahead of him through the tunnel.

"I'm taking him to the cell in the Town Manager's office," he told Rex who walked with him towards the town. A very surly Timmy walked a little way behind them, being soothed by Wolf.

As they walked, Mike tapped out a call on his phone. "Jon, hi. Favour please. Can you and Fi meet us in the main street with full medical gear, battlefield wounds and nasty holes and things?"

The two soldiers were waiting as they arrived in the main street, a large medical bergan on the floor in front of them.

Mike pulled the captive to one side. He drew his revolver, pushed it into the back of the man's right knee joint and fired. The kneecapping caused the man to scream in pained anguish and fall to the floor writhing. Jon and Fi walked over and administered aid to him.

"Good enough?" Mike said to Timmy.

"It will have to do," Timmy replied and walked off. Wolf went with him.

Once the captive had been patched up he was taken to the holding cell in the office.

"He's been given some morphine so will be out of it for a while," Jon told Mike. "Call us immediately if there's excessive bleeding. He should be OK but will need restorative surgery. Check him every hour."

Mike phoned O'Rourke.

The following morning O'Rourke arrived in a large van with four FBI agents dressed in combat gear.

Mike greeted them. "Hi, Stu. He's all yours. I've got all I'm gonna get from him, you can start drowning and crushing him. Good luck, he's one tough cookie."

O'Rourke checked the captive. "You said no blood and he'd be in one piece."

Mike smiled. "Happened afterwards. It was either this or one of my guys would have killed him. He hasn't made many friends here, poor social skills."

The prisoner was searched by the FBI contingent and taken to the back of the van. He walked with great difficulty, the injured leg stiff with the tightly bound dressings placed on it. Once in, they shut the rear doors and O'Rourke returned to the van, getting into the driving seat to Mike's surprise.

"Mike, you will hear from the UN. They will insist you sign this place up to their Human Rights agreement. Too late for limping dick in the back, though," O'Rourke laughed as he drove off.

Sure enough, within a day, Adams made contact and informed him the UN wanted Gutusipe Daindi to sign up to their Convention on Human Rights. Mike agreed but advised her the document must be sent to the council for ratification.

"I'm not dictator. I'm not even in charge. The council is the government here," he told her.

The day after that he called a general meeting in his office. The remaining Warriors, the soldiers, the two ex-cops, Wolf and George were all present. Jimmy was absent this day because he was still with Hunter.

"I need to explain something," he told them. "I will need the council's OK but I'm going ahead anyway; I can't see them objecting. I'm gonna try and go after some of the taken. I'm looking to attempt a rescue mission. On US soil or anywhere else for that matter."

There was an initial silence while that sunk in.

"I'm in," said Joe.

"Yep," said Timmy.

"Mike, thanks for the invite but you know we can't," said Cy.

Mike nodded. "I know that. Still wanted you to be here; you are friends and we want to be open." Cy nodded at him.

Mike stood. "Thing is, this is different. The fight on the ridge, it needed soldiers and that's who did the job. For this, we need people used to operating around complex communities. We'll use everyone if we need to hit anywhere or anyone, but for the initial work it has to be cops."

Jackson and Rex nodded. Timmy didn't look convinced but nodded as well. Mike looked to the two cops.

"Yeah, we're in," offered Jackson.

Rex nodded. "My dad says we're in so we are. You coming with us?"

Mike nodded as well. "I plan to. I'm just trying to locate somewhere the prisoner told us about. When we've researched it and worked on a plan, we go."

Later, Mambi phoned to update him on Hunter. "He's awake," she told him. "They will keep him heavily sedated for a few more days but looks like he'll make it."

Mike told her he was ecstatic at the news and everybody else would be as well. He told her of the plan.

"Go, Mike. Do it. Let's get back anybody we can."

"You know there are no guarantees?" he said.

"No, but at least we're fighting back – go do it, Mike."

Chapter Twenty-One

The insistent morning light of the desert continued to wake Mike but he had developed the knack of slowly dozing to wakefulness. It had been an intense few weeks since the attack. Hunter was still in hospital but well on the way to recovery. Everyone visited him regularly and he was keen to come home.

As Mike lay dozing, he realised that Mambi stretched out next to him had also awoken.

"Morning, hot stuff," he said as he kissed her.

"Morning, stink pot," she replied, pushing him off. "What today?"

"Just the meeting. The council say it's in the office not the council hall; if it goes wrong I take the fall. It's sensible."

"Best have a decent last breakfast then," she said, rolling off the comfortable large bed.

He waited for a while trying to recall any dreams but decided he hadn't had any. He got up and followed her.

The office was full. The former cops, Timmy, Wolf, Mambi, Joe and Jimmy, even the UN soldiers. A couple of elderly council members sat at the back and a few other older faces who'd come just to listen. George was with Hunter this day.

"Pray silence for the pronouncements of our revered land chief, whatever that is," called out Timmy.

"Shut up," said Mike as a few people giggled.

"Everybody, thanks for coming," Mike began. "Cy, Jon, Fi and Dane, you should leave. You don't want to become part of this."

"Why did I get mentioned last?" demanded Dane in mock outrage to more ripples of laughter.

"We're already gone, Mike," Cy told him. "Just go on as if we're not here cos we're not. If you imagine you see us it's just wishful thinking." More laughter.

"Right," said Mike, "this is the situation. We think we have located the guy called Cowboss Kes. He has a huge ranch in Arizona, nor far from the California border. We are only going to talk to him. By 'we' I mean me, Jackson and Rex. Stuart O'Rourke will be calling me later. He knows we're up to something and he will try to persuade me to act through his office. Opinions please."

"Fuck him," said Timmy. Wolf put her hand on his arm.

"Just get what you can from the Cowboss, Mike," spoke Jimmy. "Hurt him if you have to. We've been street searching for years and got nowhere. You three have the skills to achieve something, get something from him." Several people murmured agreement.

One of the council members stood and raised his hand. Mike pointed his hand at the old man and invited him to speak.

"If it rescues just one single child, the council supports whatever you do. Speak to the man O'Rourke, tell him you are investigating the theft. He will not want the publicity of refusing you. Tell him where you are going and tell him that if he stops you, you will call a news interview. He will help."

Mike nodded. "We are a people who value the wisdom of experience," he said.

The meeting continued for a while but nothing more of significance happened. Overall, the consensus was with the council suggestion. As people left, the old man who had spoken came up to Mike and put his hands on his shoulders. He said nothing, just smiled and nodded his head before he walked out.

Several hours later, Mike had just about given up on the expected call from O'Rourke. The phone on his desk rang as he was leaving the office.

"You took your time," Mike said without preamble.

"It's me. Rex. I know you were expecting O'Rourke. He won't be calling cos he just landed in a very expensive-looking passenger 'copter. It's just out in the desert and the main man is walking towards your office now."

Mike smiled. "Thanks, Rex. Can you please make sure the pilot and crew have food and water and give them anything they might need."

He was close to finishing the coffee he was making when there was a not very assertive rapping on the office front door.

"Jeez, Stu," called Mike, "just walk in. You gone all shy and retiring all of a sudden?"

O'Rourke entered carrying a small briefcase and Mike handed him a cup. They sat at the desk to talk.

"I'm assuming that Cy informed you of our meeting; I'd asked him to," said Mike.

O'Rourke put down his cup. "Yep, course he did. I had a lot of people to talk to after that. Have you signed up to the UN convention yet?"

"Scattergun subject approach?" Mike said. "I don't see the connection but yes, we did sign up. Apparently they want us to comply with their views on human rights and not cause pain to murdering lowlifes."

O'Rourke laughed. "It's for the best, Mike. The connection is with your plan to visit a US citizen on US soil. It has created some concerns."

Jackson and Rex entered the office. Jackson went over to the coffee pod machine to make them both a drink.

"Stu said he wanted us to be here," Rex explained.

"Go on, Stu. We are not going to hurt anyone and we just intend to talk to a man. I mean talk, not like it was here for the other guy," said Mike.

"I know," O'Rourke responded. "That's why I spoke to some people, people as far up as the White House. Really high up." He opened up his briefcase and extracted a few sheets of paper.

"Have we got to sign a contract?" asked an amused-sounding Mike.

O'Rourke placed the papers on the desk. "I have authority to legitimise what you are doing and at the same time keep it within acceptable parameters. We know that you have two former capitol police officers here. If one of them signs he will become a US Marshall under special attachment to the Office for Extraterritorial Liaison and based in Gutusipe Daindi."

"Under your control?" asked Mike.

"Hmm, supervision, not control. He can be tasked by Nehwe for inquiries within US jurisdiction. All he needs to do is advise me and ensure the task remains within US law. I can veto but I can't order him to act on anything. If I do he can resign his post at any time. If he ensures that everything happens as it should, involves relevant US agencies when necessary and submits reports to me after each action, the US will just let you get on with your investigation."

"If we locate any Nehwe women?" Mike enquired.

"Then take them back home, Mike. If crimes have been committed, let us know. They are your people, I wish you nothing but luck," O'Rourke told him.

Mike looked thoughtful. "Why is the US now willing to do this for us?"

O'Rourke laughed. "Politics, Mike. You guys have become a bit of a heroic band in some quarters. Bit of a pariah in some other quarters, mind. The people who see you as good guys are the same groups who normally vote for the party currently in power. Just politics, Mike. Offer a politician some votes and he'll give you his grandma and his daughter, that's just the way it is."

After some discussion it was agreed that Jackson would take on the role of Marshall. He was delighted when he realised he'd get paid the going rate as well. It was agreed that other Nehwe could act alongside him in US areas but when doing so were under his command. Only he would be armed and any required backup would be requested from US agencies.

O'Rourke stayed to socialise for a while. A couple of hours later Rex escorted the unsteady G-man back to his flash aircraft.

Jackson stayed in the office. "You all ready to accept my command, then?" he asked lightly.

"On paper, in theory, er only." Mike looked at him with raised eyebrows and a questioning look.

"Thought so," Jackson laughed.

Three days after the meeting, Mike and Rex were with Marshall Jackson in a cheap but clean Arizona motel room. They were sitting on the beds talking and drinking coffee.

"What we know from O'Rourke is this," Mike said, "Cowboss Kes, real name Claymore Kessing, is the owner of a large ranch that studs horses, grows a significant amount of crops and keeps cattle. Known to Homeland Security as a very right but not really far right non-political NRA enthusiast, more pioneer gunman than resentful rebel. No criminal record and not considered a terrorist threat. Long suspected of using cheap imported labour. Milenkovic is known to have visited here, possibly supplying the labour. We talk to him."

"I have informed O'Rourke that we are here and I've informed local police. We have no warrant but can get one if we need to," Jackson told them.

Mike had no firearms but kept his push knife on his belt. Rex had no firearms but kept a taser and a pepper spray in his jacket.

Jackson had decided that as the only one in lawful possession of a firearm, he needed to have some decent firepower available. On a shoulder strap under his jacket he kept Timmy's stubby machine pistol. He carried a small bag in which were three Glocks to hand out if necessary.

The ranch was easy to find from the map coordinates that Mike had obtained. A little gift, a sneaky bit of further under-the-counter information from O'Rourke.

The main house was set a long way off road. It was clearly not a poor house and Jackson, recalling his childhood TV, suggested it looked like a wealthy Ponderosa.

They approached it in Rex's big all-terrain vehicle. He'd enjoyed the long drive from the lands and was looking forward to putting more miles on his expensive toy. Rex parked right in front of the big, stylised, Old West log ranch house and they all got out.

They spent a few moments assessing the place. It was quiet and it seemed as if nobody was about.

"I'm uncomfortable," Mike informed the others. "We've walked in blind with little information, no recon, and I feel nervous, like we're in a trap."

"Welcome to our world," Jackson said and Rex laughed.

"It's always like this but I think we're OK," Rex told him. "Must be the same policing in England, constant blind entry and just deal with whatever turns up?"

Mike nodded. "Mind you, Brits aren't normally armed heavily enough to survive the apocalypse, can be pretty nerve-wracking though."

The large double front doors of 'the Ponderosa' opened and Cowboss Kes walked onto the porch.

"How might I be of service to you, gentlemen?" asked Kes. He rested his right hand on the silver revolver at his hip. With his other hand he tipped the front of his Stetson. He was the embodiment of 1950's cowboy movies presented in wealthy gaudy clothing. If country and western music could become human, this is what it would look like.

Jackson stepped forwards. "I'm Marshall X," he said, extending his hand and showing his badge.

"X?" asked the Cowboss. "X, my man, do you abandon your given surname?"

"Yeah, X. My daddy didn't like his not so kindly given surname and was a progressive sixties guy, so X we became. Problem for you?" asked Jackson with just a hint of belligerence.

Cowboss Kes gave a beaming smile. "No, no, sir. No problem. I respect any man who fights against those who would hold him down; you are a free man because your recent ancestors had the balls to fight for it. You are welcome to my home. What can I do for you?"

"Sir," said Mike, "our situation is a bit unusual, if I might explain why we are here and then ask you some questions we would be grateful?"

"I could say no, get off my land," Kes offered, still smiling.

Jackson smiled just as amiably. "I could get a warrant on a phone call and have local cops and feds all over this place in five minutes."

"We're not here to harm you or your world; we just need some answers and then we're gone," Mike interrupted.

"I know who you are," said Kes. "Come on in; we'll talk."

As they walked through the large hallway towards a well-appointed lounge, Jackson hung back warily, looking around him.

"No traps," Kes informed him.

"Too quiet, nobody else around," Jackson explained.

From inside the lounge Kes explained, "I knew you were coming and sent everybody away for the day. I have my own sources of information."

"Why?" asked Mike.

"Well, you guys have a reputation. The way you defended your town was big news, well done by the way."

"But you stayed here to meet us?" Mike continued to press him.

Kes was pouring drinks for everybody and sighed. "Look, I reason it this way. I don't need to fight you, if I do it's nothing but a problem for me. If I win then the next set of visitors will be a tad less neighbourly, yes? If I lose then the feds come and join the autopsy and question my sources of wealth. No, from my point of view I talk, I'm happy to talk."

"Milenkovic?" said Mike.

"Piece of shit trafficker, I just needed him to provide financially viable labour. Kept him and his goons in drink and whores, made sure he didn't abuse the workforce. When the work was done I made sure the workers just melted into some town or other, their choice."

Mike spent a couple of seconds controlling his anger. "A long time ago, kids and some women were stolen from the Nehwe people – did they come here?"

Kes shook his head. "That was twenty-five years ago, my friend."

"I'm no friend of yours, do you know what happened to them?"

Kes kept his face impassive. "My daddy was in charge back then; I did as he told me. He wouldn't let the Serbs bring the kids onto this ranch. I think he took them to some camp they had in Utah – I will give you the address. I'm sorry you suffered."

Mike put down his drink without even taking a sip. "The reason we three are here and not others of our people is very simple. We have no personal experience of that time. If some of our other people came here you'd be in a fire fight by now."

Kes smiled. "Well, I sure do appreciate that kindness. Tell me what you need and if I can supply it I will. My 'sources' that I mentioned, they tell me that if I don't cooperate with you I lose their influence, can't afford that."

Mike stared at him. "I want the location of the Serb camp, any details of any other Serb camps that you know of and a list of other people traffickers that you might use. I want anything and everything that might help us track the stolen people."

Kes made a deep throaty sound of assent. "Dunno about any other Serbs but the rest I can do. I'll write it all down for you. My politician buddies tell me I got to stop using Mex labour for a while, that'll push up the price of peanuts. They also say they can't take on the feds you got on your side, I take my hat off to you."

As they left with the list, Rex whispered to Mike, "Can't I just shoot him anyway?"

"No," said Mike. "You don't have a gun for a start and I think your dad will be a bit pissed if you do."

Mike was chuckling to himself as they got in the car.

"What's funny?" asked Jackson.

"When you filled out employment forms, when you joined us, I thought that X was just a way of minimising exposure to the feds. But now I know that his name really is Rex X. Rexex, it's funny."

"Shut the fuck up, Mike," Rex told him. Jackson just nodded his agreement about that.

When they finally persuaded Mike to stop using paper maps, the sat nav found the place in Utah without difficulty. It was obvious that the Cowboss had been there at some time because he told them about the cross of Lorraine marker post. They stopped just inside the narrow track and Mike called O'Rourke.

"Hi, Mike. Hear you've been to see Claymore Kessing yesterday. Productive, I hope."

"Stu, he's got politicians on his payroll. He's got eyes inside the federal services and uses illegal labour," Mike told him.

O'Rourke gave a world-weary laugh. "Yeah, Mike. They're not on his payroll; they are his investors. It's mainly just state politicians and a fed or two, and possibly maybe a congressman or so. It's a fucked up world, you already know that."

Mike was quiet for a second. "Stu, I need to know. You?"

"No, Mike," O'Rourke replied. "Not me, not ever. The man and his contacts know when to stand off. I promise you, not me. Couldn't afford to invest anyway, big money and big people on that side. If anything, it's to our advantage. They will agree to almost anything we, you, do. They know that you can't be used by them and they also know you've got the equivalent of a small army backing you up, not to mention the media interest. No, Mike, they will let this run, I promise you."

"OK, we're at Milenkovic's old camp. We're going to check it out. Jackson has informed the local cops and they might send somebody to watch over us. Just updating you."

They drove as far as the sliding entrance gate, which was open, when Rex said, "There's a car coming behind us."

They all got out and Jackson readied his machine pistol. He put it down when the car was clearly marked 'Sheriff' and came to a halt behind their vehicle.

Two female uniformed deputies got out – both were about thirty; one was black and the other had clear native features.

"No way," mumbled Rex.

"No, no way," she said in confirmation. "I'm Paiute, a group called the Mono Paiute, there's a few of us in this county. For some reason a lot of us join the police here."

After a general shaking of hands, they all started to explore the abandoned camp. Rex seemed to lose focus as he pulled both officers into social chat and happy joviality.

"Er, Mr Rex," called Mike. "Yes, that Mr Rex, the one with the wife and baby. Remember why we are here, please."

Jackson glared at Rex and the two women laughed.

"It's cool," said the black officer. "He's just a young guy guided by the advice from inside his pants; it ain't that rare you know."

"We're having a serious talk later, son," said Jackson to everyone's amusement.

Nothing was found at the camp. The bonfire pile yielded nothing and the team that had abandoned the place had done a good job of track covering.

Before departure they all shook hands again and the deputies asked for Jackson's badge, just so that they could include details on their report.

"Marshall X," said the black deputy. "That's cool, my friend."

The native deputy turned to Rex. "Goodbye, pretty son of X, keep it zippered." They drove away being waved off by the trio.

"What now?" asked Jackson.

Mike pulled out the list. "The thing the Cowboss gave us, he underscored one name and put an asterisk next to it. I think we go speak to him. Is it far to Texas?"

Chapter Twenty-Two

Mike soon discovered that Texas was quite a long way. With shared driving they made it in three days. It could probably have been done in two but they factored in plenty of food and small exercise periods. The route took them very close to the border and at one point past the Alamo.

Mike tunelessly sang the opening lines of 'The Ballad of the Alamo' before the other two told him to stop, for pity's sake stop. They expressed surprise when he told them that when he was young the country and western singer Marty Robbins was fairly popular in England.

It was agreed that they needed to rest, freshen up and plan before doing anything. They booked a suite in a reasonably good hotel well south of San Antonio. Mike e-mailed the list to Mambi and O'Rourke. After food and rest and phone calls to Mambi, Wolf, George, Joanne and O'Rourke, they slept.

The planning meeting took place in the morning. Jackson visited the local police to research the target; Rex and Mike made local enquiries with store owners and such like to find out what they could. Then they all met up at the hotel again.

Mike started the briefing. "The name we have from the Cowboss is Miguel Smith. The list suggests he runs a transport depot near the border. We have located his place of business and need a way to get close to him. Our old-style plod around town didn't produce anything. Jackson."

Jackson sat on a stool about two sizes too small for him. "The local cops don't have a very high opinion of Smith, not his real name but they don't know what that is. He has six arrests and just one conviction, that's for threatening a police officer. He served nine months in county for it; I don't know the details of what he did but nine months is quite heavy for that. The things he's got away with include murder and rape. Witnesses have disappeared, jurors have changed their minds, all the usual tough guy ganged up baloney."

"Any pics?" asked Mike.

"Yep," said Jackson handing out copies of the mugshot. "About five years out of date."

"Looks white with Spanish features," opined Rex.

Jackson nodded. "Yeah, not quite as white as in this photo, they told me. Olive skinned. Likes to wear a goatee, local cop told me he still had that a few days ago when he saw him in the street."

"Easily noticed scar along his chin," Mike said.

Jackson chuckled. "A little gift from the cop that he threatened." The other two laughed softly as well.

"Can we trust the local cops?" Mike asked.

"I think so, they really don't like him. O'Rourke reckons so as well," Jackson replied. "Day after tomorrow we recon, local cops will help with that. Rex, my wayward son, your fine good looks and fit bod will be leading the way on that."

The border settlement could be called either a large village or a small town. It sat just a few hundred yards north of a heavy metal fence separating the US and Mexico. The fence itself ran in both directions as far as the eye could see. The south side was just open desert and deadly heat.

The only thing near it was a compressed earth track that seemed to stretch along the length of the barrier on the American side. Further north to the town itself, two buildings, about fifty yards apart, faced the border.

The first was a small, flat-roofed white building with a sign saying 'Border Patrol', the other was a sandy-coloured warehouse-type structure with a sign declaring 'Smith Transport' and set close to the road side of a huge, gated, empty compound. The metalled road itself ran along the town and parallel to the track.

Rex entered the town from the north at breakneck speed. Far behind him was a Sheriff's cruiser, clearly intent on catching up, lots of waa waa woop noises and flashing red and blue lights.

As Rex reached the south side of town, he turned hard to the right, tyres screeching. He accelerated hard for a moment and then came to a squealing halt just outside the firm of Smith Transport.

The pursuing police car was out of sight for the time being. Rex leapt out with a small bag and raced through the open gate and into the compound. He placed the bag by a door and sprinted back to the car. He put his hands on his head and stood next to the vehicle.

Seconds later the cruiser tore around the corner and braked hard to a halt behind him. The two white male deputies initially stayed in the car.

"Turn away from us and step away from the car, keep your hands on your head," the public address system ordered. Rex complied.

The officers then left the car. One of them trained a shotgun on him and the other, pistol drawn, approached him. The shotgun cop occasionally repositioned to keep his partner out of the firing line. Rex was searched and then his hands were cuffed behind his back.

"Why you running, boy?" the cop said in a strong Texan accent. The other started to search the car.

"Sir, I wasn't running. Yeah, I was driving fast and badly but I didn't see you behind me until the last second, then I stopped."

"Where you going, then?"

"Here, sir. I'm looking for driving work and thought I'd just try out here."

The cop didn't look convinced. "Where you from?"

"New York, sir. Trying to leave the bad places, trying to get my shit together and live a good life. Trying to leave the bad behind," Rex told him.

"Nothing," the search cop declared.

The other cop smiled. "Good, I'm pleased. I like to see a boy trying to make a go of it. You so polite I'm gonna give you the benefit of the doubt. Maybe you didn't see me. I'm gonna write you up for your dangerous driving. After I've checked for warrants, I'll let you go."

They took details from Rex's driving permit; one of them returned to the cruiser to make the checks and the other wrote up the ticket.

While this was happening, Rex noticed a man he recognised as Smith. He strolled out of the warehouse and stood near the door, by the bag, watching casually as he smoked a cigarette.

The officer gave Rex the ticket, just tapped him with it and threw it in the car, then he removed the handcuffs. "You drive safely now, boy. If you staying 'round here, just behave and we'll never have a problem."

"Yes, sir, yes I will, thank you, sir," said Rex.

As the cop walked back to the car, he stopped briefly. He touched two fingers to his own eyes and pointed at Smith. "Watching you, bro." Once back in the cruiser, he turned it around and drove slowly back into town.

Rex walked towards Smith, rubbing his wrists. As he got close, Smith picked up the bag.

"Sir," said Rex, "I'm just looking to see if you have any work available. May I please have my bag back?"

Smith looked into the bag and saw one Glock. "Call me Miguel, come on in and have a coffee."

A couple of hours later, Rex took a slow, careful drive back to the hotel, a journey of about twenty miles. He doubled around a few times and twice pulled into other hotels and went inside for a little while, all just to check if he was followed. He was sure he was not.

He parked up at the real hotel and went to the foyer. He was met by Mike and Jackson and to his surprise the two cops. By way of more surprise, one of them quickly took the knee in front of him before standing and talking.

"I'm just here to say sorry, man. I know we agreed but it was ugly and I feel bad. Just wanted to apologise," he said.

Rex touched him on the shoulder. "You just did, friend. It's OK, we agreed it, so no apology is necessary. You did a disturbingly good quietly racist cop, though."

"Yeah, well I've known one or two," he replied.

Rex shook his hand. "Thank you for today. You didn't need to do it and we've now got a way in. We are grateful."

The cop grinned. "No need, the sooner somebody takes that piece of shit down, the better. You've got my cell, call me if you need anything."

After the officers left, the three men went to the room. Rex insisted on a shower first so Mike and Jackson watched TV while they waited.

"Just wanted to clean my dirtied soul, that warehouse was creepy," Rex said when he returned.

"Well, report spy Rex, what are we facing?" Mike asked.

Rex settled down to talk. "At least one Glock, he didn't give it back."

Jackson laughed. "That's OK, I had Timmy make me one of those soft useless firing pins and show me how to fit it. That Glock won't fire."

Rex continued, "He's planning to collect more Mex and south Am workers next week. He calls it the clean trip, clean cos nobody gets much abused, it's just illegal labour. He thinks I'm gonna drive one of his trucks.

"He showed me round; he's got part of the place set up for slaves, man. Chains on the wall, neck braces, the works. Was the most I could do not to put him down, there and then. It didn't look as though it had been used recently. He's focusing on drugs at the present moment.

"There's a feeling there, though. Can't describe it really, just a feeling. You know how you sense a violent crime scene before you walk in, a bit like that but lingering, creepy. His trucks come in three days. Until then he's alone, spends a couple of hours there each day.

"Don't know where he lives. One other thing, he said he was alone and I didn't see anybody else, but again got a sense. I think there was somebody else there. Just lurking, you know?"

Rex went on to outline the geography of the place. A small wooden shed office in a front corner, an internal wall isolating the far end with its chains and sense of evil. A couple of entrances and a large weapons locker wide open and empty.

"In the morning?" suggested Mike.

"Day after," said Jackson. "Give us time to prepare, rest, arm up and whatever."

Mike nodded. "OK, inform O'Rourke, Jackson. Rex, let your new buddy know as well but give him a wrong time, say a few hours out, just in case. Tonight we enjoy a good meal. Tomorrow we go over our plan of attack and the day after we leave early, really early, to get this done."

During the meal in the hotel restaurant, the Wolf phone rang. Mike answered it and just listened before thanking the caller.

"You and me just got promoted," he said to Rex. "That was O'Rourke. On the day we go out and for one day only you and me have been appointed official federal deputies to US Marshall Jackson X, here. We can tool up, seems nobody likes our Mr Smith."

Jackson laughed. "You two best stop drinking then. I don't like my employees abusing alcohol."

The morning of the second day started early. They were out of the hotel by four and drove to a police car pound about halfway to the target. O'Rourke was truly coming good for them; at the pound they met up with an off-roader marked as 'Border Patrol'.

The officer driving remained silent but drove them to the border patrol office next to Smith Transport. He parked in front of the isolated border post and without a word just went in, leaving them in the car.

"Well at least we didn't have to tip him," said Mike. "Let's go."

They went the long way around the border patrol office and to the side of the warehouse compound. Rex had a small set of wire cutters but they found an existing hole in the chain link and entered through that.

About halfway down the side of the building they found a rotted wooden window. It was easy to prise it open and they all climbed in. The place was unexpectedly light inside because the roof was clear corrugated plastic.

They looked about and the place was just as described by Rex. They all agreed it did indeed have an indefinably creepy feel. The office was locked and they didn't force it open. The three men just settled down and waited.

Half an hour later they heard the border patrol vehicle leave. About three hours after that they heard a vehicle at the compound gates. The gates were unlocked and then it moved up to the warehouse's main double doors. The doors opened and a little while later a large red transit-type van drove into the warehouse.

Smith left the van and walked over to close the doors. The three intruders stayed just inside the prison section. They watched as Smith went to the rear of the van and opened the doors. He pulled from the van a woman of about thirty. She had shoulder-length black hair, a mix of mainly native with slight European features and wore a not entirely clean off-white smock; her feet were bare.

Jackson gasped as it became clear that she also wore a studded dog collar. Smith moved her by means of a leash attached to it. He took her to the side of the office and she seemed familiar with his requirement for her to walk into the gap between it and the main warehouse. Once she was in her storage place, Smith unlocked and entered the main office.

Mike and Rex both pulled Glocks from inside their jackets. Jackson held the stubby machine pistol. They all walked quietly up to the office. The original plan was to question him about the taken. Things had changed a bit now and the girl introduced a new dynamic.

As they reached the office, Smith walked out and stood looking at them, startled and unclear of the situation.

"Stay still," said Mike, pointing his Glock at the man's face. "Do as we say when we say. One wrong or sudden move, one refusal and I will remove your face, understand?" Smith nodded as Jackson handcuffed him behind his back; the man glared wickedly at Rex. They brought a stool from the office and sat him on it.

Rex went to the back of the office shed. "You can come out, miss. We work for the feds; we are deputies – you can come out. You are safe."

"What is the girl's name?" Mike demanded from Smith. The man just looked at him with defiance and insolence. "I ask one more time and then I hurt you – what is her name?"

"Fuck off," said Smith.

Mike produced his push knife and made a cut of about two inches long and shallow along Smith's left collar bone. The man jolted and made a small pained sound.

"Tell me or each new cut will be longer and deeper than the last. What is her name?"

"She answers to bitch," Smith told him.

"I'm not saying that," called Rex. "You hear that evil fuck, miss? We know that's not your name. We are here to help you. Please come out. We can keep you safe." She slowly came out from behind the office.

The woman flinched as Smith started to call out to her. He was silenced when Jackson slapped him across the face. Mike dragged him to the van. The rear compartment was bare and self-contained. There was only one way in or out and no access to the front cab. Mike searched him and seized a small revolver, a lock knife and a large wad of bills.

"I think you know who we are, any noise or attempt to escape and I will kill you here and now, *comprende?*" Mike said, speaking gently as he pushed him in. Smith nodded.

Rex called his new cop friend who raced to the warehouse. While they were waiting they rifled through the office for any other information. Jackson took a few documents and a laptop. They also found the lost Glock in the office and Jackson put it in his jacket pocket. It would need to be reactivated.

Miguel Smith was taken to a police station in San Antonio. The trio booked into a hotel nearby. The detective assigned to this was very unhappy about the treatment dished out at the warehouse. O'Rourke made contact and told him this was now a joint federal and local matter and the FBI would take it over but based at this police station and would work with him.

Mike informed Mambi of the find; he stressed that they didn't really know who the woman was yet. It happened that Rex was a bit of a computer nerd on the side and he was able to access the data on the laptop. Jackson made copies of the documents he'd seized before handing them over; Rex did the same with the laptop hard disk.

While Smith's appointed lawyer made a terrible fuss over his treatment, the recovered woman was given medical treatment and psychiatric assistance. It didn't take much imagination to realise what her life was like and the horrible details were for the FBI to establish and deal with.

After a week the three were invited to the police station. They learned that the court had granted the FBI permission to hold Smith until his trial. They let Mike meet briefly with him. They directed Jackson and Rex to the hospital where the woman was being treated.

"I hope the cut's healed up well," Mike told him and meant it.

"Fuck you," sneered Smith.

Mike laughed at him. "Full of contrition, I see. No, fuck you. We're gonna find every shit that hurt those kids back then, you know what I'm talking about. We will be on your arse forever until we know everything."

"Dunno what you mean," said Smith but his voice suggested he felt insecure.

Mike stared at him. "I think you do. We have names, places, dates. We have cash details between you and the Serbs." Mike saw him wince at that. "We killed most of the Serbs; the only reason you're still alive is because we're on US soil. One day you will talk to us; we are never going to stop looking."

As Smith's lawyer dissolved into apoplectic objection, Mike left the room.

Next he was taken to a nearby hospital. The team helping the woman had formed the opinion that it might be of some benefit if the rescuers spoke with her, under supervision.

When he arrived, the girl was with a doctor and sitting with Jackson and Rex in a comfortable consulting room.

"Hi, Mike," Jackson greeted him. "Our lady here has come a long way; she's keen to meet you."

"Hello," Mike said to her. She still looked shell-shocked but content in her present surroundings. She had various small dressings for wounds on her wrists, neck and legs.

She nodded at him. She just stared for what seemed a long time. "Thank you," she whispered in a hoarse voice.

"Do you feel able to talk to me, would it be possible for you to answer some questions?"

She smiled, revealing good but not well-cared-for teeth. "Maybe, I hope so. It's hard to talk. I can try."

"How long?" Mike asked.

"Forever. I remember some things when I was small. I remember the monsters; I remember crying." A tear ran down her face.

Mike glanced at the doctor who nodded.

"I remember a song; I've sung it to myself for years." She sang a song in a native language; it was rhythmic and somehow soothing.

Mike dialled on the Wolf phone. After a while he said, "George, please don't ask questions, just listen please."

The woman met Mike's request to sing it again. He held the phone to her and when she'd finished put it back to his ear.

"Mike," George sounded choked, "Mike, that's a Shoshone lullaby; it's common in most Shoshone groups but the inflection, the specific way it is sung, Mike, that's a Nehwe No'ipinKoi song."

Mike could hear George was on the verge of tears. He asked the old man to keep it to himself for the time being.

"Do you know your name?" Mike asked gently.

"I have a memory of being cuddled, the arms of a warm, safe mother, I remember that," she said. She took a tissue from the doctor to wipe her tears. "I remember a name like Aishi, something more, that's all."

"*Aishi-waahni?*" Mike said.

"Maybe," she said very quietly.

Mike got her permission to photograph her on his phone. The doctor then called a halt to the meeting.

"Come back soon," she said to them all. Then she hugged Rex and left with the doctor.

"What?" asked Jackson when they were alone.

"*Aishi-waahni* is the Shoshone word for fox or silver. Silver, I think she might be Mambi's daughter," Mike told him.

"Holy shit," Rex exclaimed. "Get Mambi. Listen, I know you both already know this. Since Abraham was born it changed me." Both of the other men smiled and nodded. "What I mean is, if he was taken and I saw a picture twenty-five years later, I might recognise him and I might not. But put him in front of me, well it's like a psychic link or something; I would know him when I met him, anywhere, anytime. Get Mama Mambi."

Two days later Mambi and George arrived; they booked into the same hotel as the others. Mambi was hopeful from the picture she'd been sent but reserved her belief, the pain of being wrong would be too great. George remained constantly attentive to her, even when she got cross with him about it.

They visited the hospital but did not see the rescued woman. Blood samples were taken from Mambi and George. The medical team discussed the challenges of reintegration if the result proved positive.

Mike and Jackson visited the police station but were told that Smith was now held in county.

"Can we go visit him there?" Jackson asked the lead detective.

"I doubt that," the detective laughed. "The FBI are worried about what you might do and his lawyer is still screaming about you." He pointed at Mike. "My professional respects, man."

Another two days later they were all called to the hospital. They met with a doctor, a middle-aged, well-dressed white woman who gave her name as Regan Whitman.

"Reagan, as in the former president?" Mike asked by way of clarification.

"No," she laughed. "Like the devil possessed girl in *The Exorcist.* My parents were great fans, a bit disturbingly. Probably why I ended up in psychiatry." There was some soft but uncomfortable restrained laughter from everyone.

"You asked us to come here," said Jackson.

"Yes," she said, looking at Mambi. "We have completed the DNA analysis. We have no doubt – she is the daughter of Mambi Nehwe. There is no possible error."

Mambi wobbled on her legs and was grabbed by Mike and George. A couple of nurses were brought in to care for her and all of the others were asked to leave. It was explained that the process of reunion was delicate and took careful planning.

Mambi stayed at the hospital for the next week. O'Rourke visited Mike and the others in the hotel to discuss a way forward from here.

"I want this to now be an FBI operation," he told them as they sat in the bar.

"Too late for that," said an angry George. "The feds did nothing in the past. We grew stronger and now we will do it. Nehwe will fight if you try to stop us."

"Whoa," Mike said as Jackson put a hand on George's arm. "Just, no, we are not going to fight the feds or anybody else if we don't have to."

O'Rourke looked kindly at the old man. "I understand the feeling. It was wrong in the past when nothing was done. We are prepared to work with your team to move forward. We are content for you to make enquiries on the same basis as before. Frankly, we are stunned at the result."

"Move forward?" scoffed Mike. "We are not 'moving forward'; we are looking for the lost in a sensible and controlled manner. We will not stop; we look to you for help but will continue whether or not we get it."

O'Rourke sighed deeply. "I have something bad to tell you."

"Go on, Stu," said Mike.

"That warehouse, we found fifteen bodies buried at the back, the part with the chains and things. They ranged in age from small children to adults."

"Who are they?" asked George.

"Not sure yet, they are with the coroner and I have an FBI team looking to identify them. I'm sorry," said O'Rourke.

"We have two objectives," Mike told him. "First, we find as many of the taken as we can. Second we put all of the child-snatcher bastards before justice, as many as we can. Your justice or ours, doesn't matter."

"I know, Mike," was all O'Rourke said.

Mike looked around. "Show of hands please. Who's with me? We continue; it never ever stops. Nehwe No'ipinKoi Shoshone here declare that we search until we find or we ourselves die. There is no end." He raised his hand.

George, Jackson and Rex all raised their hand immediately. O'Rourke looked at them and slowly raised his as well.

"Looks like I'm your guy," he said, sighing.

Once back in Gutusipe Daindi, Mike and George informed the council of the undertaking they made. The council expressed concern that the mission team had taken it on themselves to commit Nehwe to an ongoing action. Both men gave their apologies and asked for understanding.

The council stated that of course they understood. There was no suggestion of censure, merely a comment on correct conduct. The council ratified the undertaking and thanked the team for their achievement. It was agreed to provide any and all funding for as long as necessary. They asked for regular updates through George.

Mambi and her daughter had not travelled back with the others; they remained at the hospital. The rescued woman was happiest with the name Aishi and so that was used in preference to either Silver or the longer version in Shoshone.

O'Rourke visited and asked for a permanent FBI office to be set up in Gutusipe Daindi. The council vetoed that but agreed the Office for Extraterritorial Liaison could base itself in the town if it so wished.

A few techies moved into the town for a couple of days. They configured the upper story of the existing UN station for the comms and computer systems that would be required. The new high-tech office was occupied by Stuart O'Rourke himself.

Wolf, Mike and O'Rourke met in the Town Manager's office, sharing an Irish coffee. Mike suggested it was to celebrate Stu's Irish heritage and it was unanimously agreed that was as good an excuse as any.

"I have things to tell you, things about the warehouse in Texas," said O'Rourke.

Wolf raised a hand to stop him. "We want to hear that, but first things first. You shouldn't be here alone. You have no enemies here but you need friends as well; I don't mean just people you're friendly with, like us. I mean proper friends, people you turn to for sanity. It's not good to be alone."

"I have my wife and grown-up daughters. I can call them whenever I like – I'm OK."

"We'll make a house available to you," Mike said. "Your wife could join you here. Nehwe will meet the additional costs of keeping your present home as well. We need you happy here, Stu."

O'Rourke smiled at them both. "Good people. Yeah, good people. I'll talk to my wife about that. Right now I have to speak about the result of the finds at the warehouse."

"I know, go on, Stu," Mike said.

He coughed. "As you know, we found fifteen sets of human remains. Three adults and twelve children of various ages. It proved impossible to establish any cause of death. Our forensic teams found it hard to recover DNA but eventually managed it. Two of the children are Nehwe, based on the DNA from Mambi and George. We'd like to bring in a team to sample more people here to try and identify relatives."

"What about the others?" asked Wolf.

"Mainly Mexican and South American, one African and one Anglo, that's all we know so far." O'Rourke shook his head. "The FBI will look for whatever they can, relatives for the others and things."

"Part of me wishes I'd offed that shithead," said Mike. The other two nodded.

"How goes your ongoing investigation?" O'Rourke asked.

Mike exhaled loudly. "Slow, Stu, painfully slow. We're trying to avoid just working our way through Kes's list. We may have to do that but our best bet is to talk with Smith again. George and Timmy are making up a full list of all of the missing. Nehwe were so demoralised at that point it was never done."

"Give us Smith," Wolf said to O'Rourke.

He just shook his head. "If it was up to me I would have brought him with me. He's convicted now, twenty-five to life in federal. We would need a warrant to get him and any decent lawyer could stop that by arguing it's just a speculative information-gathering exercise. I don't think we can get at him."

"No such thing as can't get to, nobody is beyond reach," Mike told him. "Harder though if we stay legal and I suppose we will."

"Don't see why," complained Wolf.

Mike smiled at her. "Stu, I've set Jan Adams to work. Since we are not strictly speaking part of the States, we will look to see if we can make an extradition request for him. Doesn't matter how long it takes, we are nothing if not patient."

O'Rourke laughed. "You guys are great, no wonder he's shit scared of you. He'll do all he can to avoid that."

Two days after this meeting George rushed into town to find Mike. "Mambi and her girl are coming home," he blurted out excitedly.

Mambi had stated she would at first use the home in the settlement. Aishi might remember that and so it would help. They'd move into the town later if they could. She apologised to Mike but asked him to continue using his flat; things would change when they could.

There was only one contentious point. The authorities would only release Aishi if constant professional assistance could be obtained. Recovery was a very long-term thing.

The council declared no financial limit. Consequently, Regan Whitman, the psychiatrist at the hospital, was made a salary offer that no sane person could ever refuse. They would all arrive in a few more days.

George insisted that the council make money available in the FBI search for relatives of the non-Nehwe victims. The council agreed and O'Rourke was informed.

They later made a council declaration, effectively a Nehwe law. Any and all non-Nehwe victims found by Mike's continued investigation would automatically come under Nehwe protection.

Mike informed O'Rourke.

"There really is no end to this, is there Mike?" he said.

Mike grinned. "That's what we all signed up for. Still with us?"

"Give me another of those coffees and you've got me for life."